PLOUGH OVER
THE BONES

DAVID GARNETT

MACMILLAN

© David Garnett 1973

SBN 333 15393 6

First published 1973 by
MACMILLAN LONDON LTD
London and Basingstoke
Associated companies in New York
Dublin Melbourne Johannesburg & Madras

Printed in Great Britain by
JOHN SHERRATT AND SON LTD
the St Ann's Press, Park Road, Altrincham

PLOUGH OVER THE BONES

CHAPTER ONE

The Maurice Farman biplane cleared the ridge that was crowned by the village of Dorlotte, passing a hundred metres to the right of the church steeple, and to the left, a street of grey limestone houses that ran irregularly up along the crest of the hill with their outhouses and gardens stretching behind them and with orchards of plum-trees making a screen to the north. The road to Ste Menehould turned a sharp corner in the centre of the village, was then hidden by houses and trees, and reappeared beyond the village as a narrow riband of white dust between the fields, which levelled out until they ran up against a wall of forest to the north. The fields were of all sorts: pasture near to the village, then the grey-gold stubble of wheat and barley already harvested, the green of the sugar-beet, the ash-grey and yellow withered haulms of potatoes not yet dug, a field or two of cow cabbage. The men in the Farman had no eyes for these details. He in the front seat shouted and pointed to his companion who, for an instant, saw, or thought he saw, greenish clumps spreading from the road across the fields by the edge of the forest.

Before he could lift his binoculars, or bring them to bear, there was an explosion and the Farman fell sideways into a small field of clover below. A few seconds later it caught fire.

A man who had been swinging his scythe in a corner of the field stood motionless, aghast, but a boy of fifteen who had been pitching the green meat into a cart drawn by two bullocks, raced up to the plane, still holding his pitchfork. In the wreckage there were two men. The man in front had fallen forward and, supported by wires, was poised in the very heart of the fire. He did not move.

The other man seemed to be trying to wriggle his way out of the nacelle, away from the flames. The boy did not hesitate, but dived into an opening between the crumpled canvas wings, stuck one of the prongs of his fork under the shoulder strap of the man's coat and jerked at him. At the third pull the man cleared a wire that was holding him and fell the last two metres. The boy dived forward, almost into the flames, and dragged him away. The man with the scythe had run up.

'Get away quick, Georges,' he exclaimed.

'Lend a hand, Joseph,' said the boy.

Between them they hoisted the airman to his feet and supported him as far as the cart.

'The other one is done for. He's being grilled like a sausage,' said the boy.

As he spoke there was a series of explosions; the belt of cartridges of the machine-gun in the aeroplane went off. These reports were followed immediately by a fusillade coming from the direction of the forest. The man, Joseph, let go of the airman and began to run. The boy, Georges, kept hold and shouted:

'Hey, Joseph! I can't manage him by myself.'

Joseph continued his flight and Georges was left alone with his prize.

The airman was alive, but he was half-stunned and he behaved like a drunk man. His ankle was dislocated and his collar-bone broken, one tine of the pitchfork had torn his ear which was bleeding. However, he had escaped serious burns thanks to his boots, gauntlets and leather flying helmet and goggles. But it was his lips under his singed moustache and the scorched tip of his nose which hurt and of which he became aware first of all.

Georges had dropped him on a pile of clover. The cartridges

had all exploded, but now the boy could hear occasional shots being fired from the village while a continuous firing came from the forest and bullets occasionally whizzed past overhead.

The airman sat up. Occasionally he cursed.

'The Boches are here,' said Georges.

'I must get away, or they'll take me prisoner,' said the airman. He tried to stand up, gave a cry of pain and sat down abruptly. 'I must hide,' he said. He looked at Georges for the first time and thought that he had seldom seen an uglier boy. He was short, strongly built, with long arms and bandy legs and he had a dirty yellow face with freckles. His mouth was big and his eyes were neither green nor brown, but like oil-stained khaki. He came nearer to the airman and breathed garlic into his face.

'What's your name, Mister?' he asked suddenly.

'Maurice de L'Espinasse, Lieutenant.'

'Georges Roux.' The boy held out his hand and Lieutenant de L'Espinasse touched it without enthusiasm.

'Get into the cart,' said the boy.

He helped the airman up and shoved and then covered him with clover. Then with a quiet: 'Come up. Get on with you,' addressed to the oxen, and after he had laid the long goad gently across their backs, they started off and with a creaking of wheels and bumping over ruts, went out of the meadow into a chalky lane which wound uphill towards the church. As the ox-cart creaked slowly along, the village was swept by a perfect storm of bullets and Lieutenant de L'Espinasse, who could not see what was happening, or where he was being taken, had the impression that he was being carried into the heart of a battlefield. As the village had been abandoned by the French Army during its headlong retreat, he could not understand the reason for the enemy fire. He longed to look out, to tell the boy who had so nearly skewered him with his damned pitchfork to turn the cart round and make for somewhere else. Occasionally he heard Georges speaking firmly but gently to one of the oxen.

'Hey, Blackbird, pull your share, dirty cow.'

This momentarily reassured him, until the next lot of bullets came whistling round the cart.

For two days before that morning, the enemy had been hourly expected. Retreating French troops had streamed through the village and more than half of the inhabitants of Dorlotte-en-Jarrets had fled, headed by M. le Maire, who was a sick man, M. l'Adjoint, the schoolmaster, the schoolmistress and the postmaster, so that there was no representative of either the central, or the local Government of the Republic left, except the roadman – the *cantonnier*, M. Michael Fournier. With them had gone all the faster forms of transport: horses drawing gigs, dogcarts, a waggonette, the old two-horse diligence and all the bicycles. No one in the summer of 1914 at Dorlotte had made the great experiment of buying a motor car.

Those who remained in the village were dismayed at the number of additional burdens which had been thrust upon them.

'I've got to look after the schoolteacher's rabbits,' grumbled Madame Lorcey. 'There are four hutches and I shall have to spend half the morning collecting enough green stuff for them.'

'Madame Doriot told me to look after her fowls. Calm as you please – and when I asked about the eggs, she told me: "Lay them down in preservative. There are plenty of jars." Can you beat that for meanness?' said Madame Blanchard who 'obliged' Madame Doriot by going in for two days a week to do for her and M. le Maire.

'I said to her: "What about the Germans? Perhaps they will fancy making themselves an omelette!" She was ever so cross. She said: "Mind you get a signed paper for every egg those devils requisition. My husband says we shall need evidence in order to claim for war damage, and the sooner we start collecting it the better." '

'M. le Maire should have stayed at his post. He had no right to run off to Paris just when he is wanted. What did we elect him for? He ought to be here to collect his own evidence and there'll be more smashed than a few eggs,' said old Rouault who had stopped to listen to the two women.

In the afternoon of the day before the enemy arrived, the road was packed with teams of guns, ammunition waggons and masses of retreating infantry. Many of the inhabitants locked up their houses before going to work in the fields: some of the older women locked themselves in and stayed at home.

Before dark Captain Tinayre of the Chasseurs halted his men and picked out twenty from his company, put them under the command of a Corsican sergeant, Zafferelli, and told them they were to stay in the village as a rearguard and hold up the German advance for as long as possible.

Zafferelli walked round the village and picked out the cemetery at the top of the hill as the strongest defensible position.

Then he ordered Madame Muller at the inn to cook a supper with roast chicken for his men and posted a sentry to prevent stragglers going in and eating it up. Three hours later, when they had eaten and drunk their fill, he and his men pushed their way in the darkness to the cemetery through the crowds of exhausted marching men. Zafferelli was not surprised when he got there, to discover that fifteen out of the twenty men had disappeared.

'I fed the bastards too soon. But they would have run anyway,' he confided to the five remaining.

By midnight the throng of tired men had thinned out, and by three in the morning only an odd man or two came limping along the road. Zafferelli posted two men as sentries to watch for any sign of the enemy. Then he told the other three to get some sleep and lay down beside a grave in the cemetery himself and in a minute was asleep. The night was calm and curiously silent. Only a mutter of gunfire and a few flickerings on the horizon to the west, showed that they were still fighting somewhere near Chalons.

There was a gentle wind which kept fog from forming. Only a few patches of white vapour rose from the stream bordered by a row of poplars which wound between the ridge and the forest north of the village.

During the early morning, at first light, three soldiers came into the village. One of them, Corporal Simon, was a tall fellow with a long thin face and pale lips between which yellow fangs protruded when he smiled. Every step he took was painful. In order to reassure his companions that he could reach the village he had abandoned his greatcoat and his pack and carried his rifle slung and walked with the help of a stick he had pulled out of a fence. With him, holding his arm, was a Pole who had been a gamekeeper, called Skribenski, and a very tired Spaniard, Pablo Ortiz, who had joined the French Army to avoid extradition.

'We'll make a stand here, we shall have a good view of them. They have no cover,' said Simon when they had got to the *marie*. Oritz had a lump of cheese and some apples which he shared with his companions. Each of them took a long drink of water from the fountain. Then they chose positions and made themselves comfortable. They fell asleep. It seemed that in no time at all they were woken up by the sound of an aeroplane and next moment an explosion, followed by a silence. Then, when Simon had got to his feet and was looking out, came the ripple of exploding cartridges, answered by a fusillade from the direction of the forest.

'Here they come,' he said.

The fountain was a large stone saucer, surmounting a stone pedestal, above which rose a nubile figure from whose right nipple a narrow brass faucet shot a stream of water into the saucer-shaped pool below. Her left breast was veiled in sandstone drapery.

Simon put Skribenski under the fountain on the left where he had a perfect view of the road and Ortiz on the right from where he commanded a view of Conduchet's farmyard where it was obvious that the enemy, finding the road defended, would take cover. He himself, with help from his companions, climbed over the wall of the mayor's garden and took up a position in the attic of the coach-house from which he had a view covering both the road, the farmyard, and the lane from which the enemy might attempt to encircle the village.

Zafferelli woke before the three by the fountain. All five of his rearguard command had disappeared . . . He was not surprised or dismayed.

Just before the aeroplane came over and fell, he detected a movement of something coming out of the forest along the road. Presently he could make out three mounted men – no doubt enemy scouts. He adjusted the sights of his rifle carefully and fired. A horse plunged and fell and after three more shots he got the rider who was standing with his back to him, tugging at the reins. The other horsemen disappeared from sight riding into a field on the east side. The aeroplane came over and fell into a field. There was a lot of random firing from the forest after what he guessed were cartridges exploding. Smoke rose from where the plane had fallen. Then unexpectedly three shots came from the east of the village.

'I have been unfair to those bastards,' Zafferelli reflected, but he thought no more, because the road in front was suddenly full of the enemy. He could hardly miss. The others were firing regularly. The village of Dorlotte was being defended by four resolute men.

A Bavarian major who had never been in action, saw his men being picked off and ordered them off the road. From behind a convenient haystack he consulted with his Captain. They sneaked up to Conduchet's farm and, in the farmyard, came under fire again.

Old Clementine Rouillac who had never got married, as she 'wasn't quite right' – which had not prevented her from

13

having two imbecile children – carrying a bucket, walked down to the fountain. Skribenski was lying under the stone saucer and firing whenever a German appeared on the road. Ortiz was picking off any man who showed in Conduchet's farmyard.

Mademoiselle Rouillac surveyed the scene angrily and stepping past the muzzle of Skribenski's rifle, stood her bucket in the basin under the faucet and looked down towards the farm. Seeing the head of a German appear over the farm wall, she shook her fist at him. Then when her bucket was full, she lifted it down and marched off up the street. Skribenski turned his head and waved to her. Next moment he was shot dead. A German had been watching through field glasses and the movement had been detected.

The Germans concentrated their fire on the fountain and Ortiz lay flat while bullets drilled their way into the limestone blocks of the wall behind and to each side of him. They had not spotted Simon in his attic who was firing through, or rather from behind, a sack of oats. He was down to his last packet of cartridges and only fired when he felt certain of getting his man. Ortiz lifted his head and fired several shots as the Germans came out of the gateway and charged up the lane towards him. Then, losing his nerve, he jumped up and ran. A bullet caught him in the calf of the leg and he fell. But before the enemy reached him, he had crawled under the entrance gate of the garden and none of them bothered to look for him when they had reached that point.

Seeing them coming, Corporal Simon took careful aim at the major leading his men, and shot him through the chest. Then he dropped to the ground. A bullet caught him in the ribs as he turned and scrambled through the *marie* and hid under the currant bushes in Marcelle Duvernois's garden on the other side of the road. Every breath gave him agony. The bullet had touched a lung.

During this fight, Zafferelli in the cemetery had been picking off every German who dared come up the road. Altogether he killed thirteen and wounded thirty-nine men.

'Give the fellows longer to get away,' was how he justified his last stand to himself. The Germans, fanning out, surrounded the cemetery and Zafferelli, who had not seen anyone to shoot at for a few minutes, was suddenly presented with a target at fifteen yards. He shot the young lieutenant who had come up that moment through the chest and blew the bridge of the nose off a private who darted out to try and rescue his officer. It was his last shot. A Bavarian forester who had been given a leg-up over the cemetery wall, tiptoed up from behind and bayonetted him through the kidney and then to make sure stuck him again between the shoulders. The defence of Dorlotte was over, but it had cost the Bavarians twenty-three killed and ninety-three wounded. The men were frightened and angry and the higher ranking officers were furious. The battalions on each of their flanks had moved forward without casualties with a minimum of resistance and were some kilometres ahead. They now had to borrow ambulances from them and were in no shape to take their allotted place in the advance. A colonel said: 'Franc-tireurs, I suppose. They gave us a lot of trouble in 1870 I'm told. Make an example of the place. Take hostages.'

While the last stand was being made, Germaine Conduchet ran out of her father's farm two minutes before the Germans swarmed into it. She ran up the main street, met some women, including two girls of her own age – her best friends – Marie and Aline Muller, and joined by five other women either unmarried or without children, ran off to the woods near Belmont, meeting nobody on the way. Aline began looking for girolles and ceps, but the other girls thought she was heartless. However, when they got hungry they were glad to eat them. In the early afternoon a light west wind brought the smell of burning to them.

The pair of oxen plodded slowly uphill, Georges loitering beside them and an occasional bullet whistling overhead.

They were safe when they reached the church as it faced the *mairie*, a solid stone façade with its pair of couchant stone lions one on each side of the steps leading to the entrance. Georges laid the goad gently along the backs of the beasts and the oxen halted.

'Slip out quick, Lieutenant. There's nobody looking.'

De L'Espinasse did his best to obey. Georges brushed the shreds of clover off him and led him quickly into the church. There was a woman kneeling. Georges went up to her and said in patois: 'Eh, La Fouine. You better see naught this morning.'

The woman raised a ravaged face and looked at both of them out of almond brown eyes. She had been weeping and there were streaks of dirt down her cheeks. Then she nodded her head and bent it again in prayer.

Georges walked into the vestry, opened a deal cupboard in which a black soutane and choirboys' surplices were hanging. He pulled down the soutane.

'Get into that. Then I'll hide you up in the belfry.'

'No,' said de L'Espinasse. It was the first word he had spoken since he had got into the cart. 'No, I can't climb up there with my bad leg. Besides, they'll send a look-out up there.'

'Into the crypt then,' said Georges. While he was ushering him in, he suddenly exclaimed: 'Golly, there's a job I've forgotten.' He almost shoved the officer down the steps, slammed the door, locked it.

'Mind, La Fouine. You saw naught and you heard naught,' he said roughly to the praying woman.

She raised her head, nodded, and he ran out of the church. 'What does that blessed boy take me for – a fool?' La Fouine muttered to herself angrily. 'Getting too big for his boots,' she added five minutes later.

Georges ran all the way from the church to his home: a cottage that lay in a slight hollow a few yards from the main road, but sheltered from it by an orchard of old apple-trees and plums. He did not take a direct route, for the German army was charging up the road. Resistance was over. However he got there. His aunt had fled from the village the day before and his mother was, as he had left her two hours earlier, lying dead drunk on her bed.

Georges darted into the cottage, scarcely glanced at his mother, but snatched his father's old double-barrelled gun from where it hung over the fireplace and then going to the toolshed, took a fork and ran with them both to the rubbish heap. There he dug a hole and, taking a chance, fetched a tin of grease and an old sack. He smeared the lock and hammers and plugged each barrel with a wad of grease. Then he wrapped the gun in the sack, put it in the shallow grave and spread some of the rotting vegetables and bits and pieces from the rubbish heap on top. A couple of Germans with rifles at the ready were pushing into the garden. Taking the fork with him, Georges slipped unseen through the hedge. He waited for a little while, listening while the Germans shouted at his mother. Then he slipped in among the stalks of the artichokes and lay there. Presently he was joined by a companion – a big and handsome tom cat. By this time, and because he was hiding, Georges was feeling very frightened, and the abuse and ravings of his mother as the German soldiers pulled her out of bed and dumped her in the garden, shouting at her: 'Heraus, heraus' did not restore his courage. Puss rubbed his cheeks and purred and Georges clasped the cat in his arms and burst into sobs. Suddenly he realised he was crying noisily and swallowed down and bit his lip and lay still. Then he remembered that he had put the key of the crypt in his pocket and realised that if anything went wrong with him, Lieutenant de L'Espinasse might die in there of hunger and his courage came back, knowing that he had another job to do.

But it could wait . . .

The village and the fields around it had suddenly become full of German soldiers in their coalscuttle helmets and grey-green uniforms. They filled the street, they swarmed into the three houses where drink was sold and helped themselves to bottles of *prune*: spirit distilled from plums. There was plenty of it, as everyone in the village made it. It is best matured for several years, so there is always a stock of bottles maturing in every house with a few plum-trees in its garden. It was what they felt they needed – soon many were very drunk indeed. Presently a squad of soldiers with rifles and fixed bayonets went from house to house, bursting open the doors and shouting;

'Heraus, heraus!'

If the inhabitants were slow to understand and to obey, they caught hold of the women and pulled them into the street; if a man, they gestured and made as though to prod with the bayonet.

'Heraus, heraus,' was being shouted at one door after another. Outside the crowd of women and children was sorted from the men and larger boys.

Pierre Lanfrey had slept late. He had taken his daughter Brigitte to Bar-le-Duc where his sister was a nun and had persuaded the Mother Superior to let her stay in the convent for a few days. Then he had walked back against the tide of soldiers and refugees and did not get home till two o'clock in the morning. He had slept all through the noise of rifle fire and his wife did not wake him up until she heard the German soldiers shouting: 'Heraus!' in the houses down the street. Pierre had just got out of bed when a German threw open the door and stood in the doorway, shouting. Then, as Jeanne did not seem to understand, he caught hold of her to pull her out.

Pierre Lanfrey stepped forward. He was wearing a nightshirt and the steel hook that had replaced his right hand protruded from the empty sleeve.

'Wass wollen Sie?' he asked.

The soldier, still gripping Jeanne by the wrist, turned to him, startled at the German words.

18

'Heraus!' he shouted.

'Wir kommen so schnell wie möglich,' said Pierre and tapped the soldier's arm with his steel hook.

The soldier let go of Jeanne and Pierre, pushing aside the bayonet, gently shoved him over the threshold and shut the door. Pierre dressed rapidly, and Jeanne was doing up the laces of his boots when two soldiers returned.

'Wir sind fertig,' said Pierre.

The street was full of villagers : the women and children on one side, the men in a more orderly and sparser line on the other. Both groups were guarded by soldiers with fixed bayonets.

'March,' shouted a German corporal and the men moved off uphill.

'They are taking us to the cemetery. It doesn't look too promising,' said old Conduchet, the richest of the farmers present, winking at Pierre and trying to keep his spirits up with a joke.

There were no more jokes cracked after they had reached the cemetery and were being shepherded into it, for there, lying on his face in a pool of blood was the body of a French soldier : Zafferelli. The men stepped aside and the guards motioned for them to line up against the wall. Pierre Lanfrey stopped by the corpse and began to take off his overcoat. A guard shouted at him and made as though to prod him with his bayonet.

Pierre looked at him and said : 'Die Kinder . . . nicht sehen.'

The corporal, who had come up, nodded and the guard stood back while Pierre covered Zafferelli's body with his coat, leaving only the two legs sticking out. Old Rouault hobbled up, took off his jacket and covered the legs and then went back to his place against the wall in his shirt. So when the large body of women and children began crowding into the cemetery, there was no corpse and no pool of blood facing them.

The villagers waited. The corporal in charge took a pipe out of his pocket, settled down with his back to a gravestone and began smoking.

The men began talking in low voices. Some of them had believed that they had been taken to the cemetery to be shot and buried in a mass grave. But if so it was clear that the execution was not going to take place immediately.

Presently two soldiers came up with Madame Cange carrying her baby and with her two little children tagging along after her. The Germans had missed her cottage during the round-up. Julie Cange was the young, vigorous and rather unattractive wife of a Parisian baker from whom she had separated. She had a bad reputation among the pious older women in the village, who avoided speaking to her. The baby at any rate was illegitimate. But directly she entered the cemetery, she cried out: 'They are burning all the houses.' All the women crowded round her, eager to ask questions. Amid the cries of horror and disbelief, Julie could be heard saying:

'The first thing I knew was when a soldier with a sack came into the room and was just going to light one of their black biscuits when he saw me. He chased me out – no time to get my bag with my money, or even my jacket. Just had to grab the baby . . .'

'Yes, they throw a sort of black biscuit into the houses and the flames shoot up. They are burning everything, the barns, even the rabbit hutches . . .' she continued excitedly.

'But it's not possible . . .' However, a smell of burning drifted over the wall and, soon afterwards, they could all see smoke and black particles rising into the air and then hear the crackling of the burning houses. Arguments broke out and everyone began to jabber.

Jacques Turpin went up to the Corporal and could be heard saying:

'I protest . . . The laws of war. The Geneva convention . . . Civilian populations . . .'

The German corporal went on smoking and Turpin shook

20

his fist in his face, and began to scream at him and dance with rage.

'Barbarian . . . Pig!'

Pierre went up and took Jacques by the sleeve. 'You'll only make it worse. They stuck a bayonet in Rousillon's leg for less than what you are doing.'

'We'll make the pigs pay. When our troops get into Germany our Senegalese will cook them and eat them.'

'Shut up Jacques. We are in the enemy's hands. If you make a fuss it will go badly for the women. Keep calm.'

The air was full of smoke and above the crackling of the burning village, they could hear German soldiers shouting at each other. The morning wore on. Suddenly an officer rode up and while he dismounted the corporal thrust his pipe among the flowers on a tombstone and sprang to attention.

'Name? . . . Name? . . . Name . . . I'll take this fellow Jacob Fournier . . . shoemaker . . . and this one: Adolphe Legrand.'

'That's wrong,' said the man he was pointing to. The officer glared at him.

'Silence,' roared the corporal.

'You've got my name wrong. It's Leblond, not Legrand.' But the officer and the corporal had moved further along the line. When he came opposite Pierre Lanfrey, the officer said:

'I'll take . . .' then catching sight of the steel hook said quickly: 'No, not him . . . he's only got one arm. He'll be no good to them.'

'This fellow has been protesting,' said the corporal pointing to Jacques Turpin.

'Put him on the list. He can protest in prison,' said the officer. Six men were chosen as hostages for the good behaviour of the rest of the population. They were marched out of the cemetery and were not seen again.

Before the officer left, Marcelle Duvernois stepped up to him and said: 'The children are hungry. They have had nothing to eat.'

The officer smiled, embarrassed. Marcelle pointed to a little girl and opened her own mouth, gesturing with her hand, so as to be sure the young officer understood. He nodded, said he would see about it, got on his horse and rode away. The afternoon wore on. No food came and some of the children began to cry and could not be soothed. The corporal had resumed his pipe and was reading a book he had taken out of his pocket. About four o'clock he pulled out his watch, stood up, called to the guards and without explanation marched with them out of the cemetery. After a little while the villagers, now walking in family groups, left the cemetery in order to return to their homes, but they had no homes. As they stepped out of the cemetery with its high walls, they saw the flames that rose far and near and the clouds of smoke that blew across in front of them, obscuring everything familiar. The houses and barns were burning, some smouldering slowly, others enveloped in flame. It was impossible for them to go to their homes; it was impossible even to go far down the street without choking and being half-blinded with smoke.

The groups of men, women and children waited, most of them in silence. One or two of the men conferred together in subdued voices.

'Take everyone around to windward of the village. Then we shall be able to see if there are any buildings left and find some place where the women and children can shelter.' The wind was north-east so they set off in a body down the Ste Menehould road, and then cut across by the lane leading to Conduchet's farm. The house and farm buildings were standing and were crowded with Germans. The last of the wounded men were being carried out on stretchers to a waiting ambulance, and the villagers drew aside and went out into the fields, making a wide circle round the buildings. Then, those of them in the front saw that the *lavoir*, hidden in the poplar trees that bordered the little stream, was still standing. They made their way there. It was peaceful and unchanged: the open roofed shed covering the long cemented floor sloping down to the narrow oblong pool through which the stream ran. All the women had knelt there, sousing the week's wash in the cold water, beating out the dirt and rinsing each garment again and again in the running water. The *lavoir* was where the women met and talked of all the village doings, the place where they were free of masculine repression. Now that familiar spot offered them shelter when their homes beyond were hidden in smoke, punctuated here and there by bursts of flame that blazed up fiercely and then disappeared.

It was not a silent scene for there were frequent crashes as walls tumbled, floors fell in, or tiles cascaded down into the yards or the street. From the *lavoir* there were no Germans to be seen.

Many of the villagers were fascinated by the spectacle. It was hard for those who lived on the further side of the village to identify their homes. When there was a sudden blaze of flame a girl would ask: 'Is it our house or that of the Thomas's?' – and her mother wringing her hands mechanically would reply:

'One can't tell. Don't look any more.' But in spite of such words they waited watching, until one of the men, grown surly, growled:

'Haven't you anything better to do than to stand there gaping? We want to eat before it's dark.'

Georges was hungry and he knew that the fellow in the crypt would be hungry too. The whole village was blazing and there were a great many Germans about, though from the sounds they made most of them were drunk. He gave the tom cat a hug which surprised the animal though he did not resent it. Then he crept out of the far side of the artichoke patch, nipped across the lane into the Leblonds' back garden and then kept well away from the burning houses until he came to the baker's. The shop was a roaring furnace and the bakehouse at the back was alight but there was a sack with loaves three days old in the yard. Georges dragged it off and hid it, but first took two loaves. At the *charcuterie* next door he was able to abstract a big sausage hanging in the store in the back yard. He did it almost at the risk of his life, for the wind changed and a gust of flame blew back and he ran with his hair and jacket singeing, unable to draw a breath. The *marie* was burning fiercely behind the façade of stone which protected the church across the road.

There were two Germans standing in the nave. La Fouine was there in attendance. She turned her head and saw him. Georges waited. Then the Germans dropped on their knees to pray and he darted forward and dived down and unlocked the crypt. Lieutenant de L'Espinasse said in a loud voice:

'My God, but you've been a long time. And what's the smell of burning?'

Georges put his finger on his lips. The airman took the food but gave no thanks. 'Why haven't you brought a bottle of wine?' He was thirsty.

'Bottles don't grow on the trees like apples,' said Georges. Then, when the Germans had left the church, he went to the vestry and brought de L'Espinasse the chalice filled with holy water. He might have brought it full of Vino Sacro, but La Fouine would not have liked it and he could not risk offending her. He left the key of the crypt with de L'Espinasse, warning him not to come out whatever happened. The village was full of German soldiers. He was to unlock the door to anyone who said: 'The Virgin is here to help you.' Georges thought it would be a good joke if he got La Fouine to look after the airman. A fine virgin!

The sun had sunk low. The flames of the burning village had sunk, but the heat was terrific. There were three drunk Germans laughing and holding on to the railings round the *mairie* garden, from which came a shout and a scream. Then another German soldier came into sight dragging something – a man. The three helped pull him out into the road and took turns at kicking him and, at each kick, the man on the ground

24

let out a scream. The man who had found him picked up his rifle which had been leaning against the fence and hit the man once or twice with the butt of it. But the figure on the ground still wriggled and rolled about and screamed. The four men who had been kicking and beating him staggered back and considered what to do next. It was tiring work and they were exhausted. Then the man with the rifle seemed to have an idea and talked to the other three. Very unsteadily, they bent down, picked up the man on the ground and carried him across the street to a house where the flames had died down and threw him on to a bed of glowing embers.

There was a stifled shriek, stifled because the man could not draw another breath, and the flames leapt up. The three men recoiled from the heat and two of them wiped their foreheads. Then, without waiting to watch the results of their devotion to duty, they turned their backs and staggered back to the railings where the youngest of them was sick. The heat, on top of half a bottle of raw spirit, had been too much for him. The victim of their attentions was Ortiz, the Spaniard, whom the man with a rifle had stumbled on under some raspberry canes.

Georges watched this scene without moving. But Madame Duvernois who had also been watching, walked down to the burning house directly the German soldiers had turned away. First of all she bent over and looked in, then she went down on her knees and said a long prayer.

The German boy who had been sick, and was feeling better for it, saw the woman kneeling there and was puzzled. They had done what the older man had thought was a good idea. Something had to be done with the fellow. But as he watched the kneeling woman he felt doubts. He wanted to cry and to get away from the other men.

'You are looking a bit blue, chum,' said one of them and held out a bottle.

'No thanks,' said the boy and soon afterwards, saying something about wanting to eat, he wandered away. He began to feel sure that they had done wrong. 'Forget about it,' he said aloud. But he was never able entirely to forget.

The story of what had been done was whispered among the German troops. It was received by some with shrugs and by others with incredulity. When it reached the Feldwebel he sought out Private Braun, the man who had found Ortiz under the bushes, had beaten him ineffectually and then originated the plan of throwing the wounded man into the fire. Braun listened to his non-commissioned officer with surprise and shifted uneasily on his feet.

'No. I know nothing about it. I had nothing to do with it,' he said. And in fact though he knitted his forehead with the effort, he could not remember.

The Feldwebel was turning away when Private Braun called him back: he had remembered.

'There was a corpse lying in the street. Someone said we oughtn't to leave him there and I remember I did lend a hand to throw him in.'

'Irregular behaviour. And you see they make an atrocity story out of it. You stick to the rules, Braun, or you'll get yourself in trouble.'

And for the rest of his life Private Braun was convinced that he had been reprimanded for getting rid of a corpse in the most sanitary way.

Old Rouault had not gone to the *lavoir*. He found a spade and went back to the cemetery. There he dug a grave and buried Zafferelli's body. Later on he would put up a wooden cross with the corporal's identity disc nailed to it.

The first business at the *lavoir* was to get a meal for the children. Several buckets of potatoes were dug in the fields, washed and peeled, a fire was made and they were put on to boil.

During the afternoon German soldiers had rounded up the animals grazing in the fields, and driven them off for butchering by the army cooks. But a young bull had broken away and had been shot and left lying in a field. Now Lucien,

26

the butcher, skinned the carcase and carried it to the *lavoir*, making several journeys.

'Mustn't blame me if it's tough. Not slaughtered and bled the proper way . . .' he excused himself as he distributed joints to the women. They crowded round the fire, holding their bits of meat and beginning to squabble. But they were brought to reason by Madame Thomassin who appeared suddenly carrying a galvanised iron cauldron.

'You can't all be cooks. Give the meat here and I shall make a communal stew for everyone. Some of you go off and scrounge some carrots and onions. And someone find some salt.'

It grew dark and the slope to the west of the *lavoir* was dotted with glowing spots. From one or another, flames would still suddenly shoot up and grow into a blaze where sparks had reached and set fire to an outhouse or fallen on a faggot stack.

When Madame Thomassin was satisfied with her stew, women crowded round her cauldron and she ladled out pieces of meat and carrots and potatoes into the wooden-handled washbowls that the women kept in the *lavoir* and which now were all they had to eat from.

The bowl of stew was passed from one scared child to another and sent back to be refilled.

Fear is exhausting and as soon as they had some warm nourishment in their bellies, the younger children fell asleep. Their parents stayed awake watching the glowing piles of embers that marked their homes. Georges Roux sat apart watching and brooding.

About midnight two German soldiers wandered down towards the groups of women and old men. One of them held his companion round the neck to keep his balance. The other called out that they wanted some French women. Pierre Lanfrey stood up, but La Fouine, who had wandered down from the church in search of food, forestalled him. She was very drunk: not unusual with her at that hour. Always a reddish brown, sinuous and shiny, both her colour and the agility of her movements seen in the firelight reminded Georges of a red centipede. She started towards the soldiers and called out: 'I'm a French woman if you want one. And I've got the pox too and I'll give it you for nothing.'

The German soldier who had called out, seeing her raddled face confronting him, recoiled and tried to turn away, but his companion, hiccoughing, was anxious to remain.

'Don't be shy,' called La Fouine and went after them as the more sober soldier dragged his friend away. Catching up with them, she put her arm round the drunk soldier's neck, and then grabbed his free arm. The three staggered back towards the village swaying to right and left as the more sober German first pulled one way and then La Fouine pulled the drunk man the other.

Suddenly the roof of Lorcey's barn fell in, great flames shot up illuminating the German soldiers in their greenish uniforms with trousers tucked into high boots and La Fouine clinging to one of the drunk man's arms, while his fellow tried to wrestle him away from her.

'Someone stop the wretched woman,' cried Marcelle Duvernois, but no one moved or seemed to hear her words. Georges Roux was the first to laugh. A moment later the watching crowd yelled and La Fouine and the pair of soldiers disappeared round a bend in the path pursued by catcalls. Darkness suddenly fell and the laughter and hooting stopped abruptly as though cut off. The younger women who had laughed loudest began to whisper their disapproval and the older men who could remember La Fouine when she had been a pretty girl, spat in disgust.

Few of the grown-up people got any sleep that night. They sat in pairs, or groups, making plans. Most of them decided to go and stay with relatives in another village and the arguments were usually about which brother or sister, uncle or aunt, or rich cousin they could rely on for, if not a welcome, at all events temporary shelter and food. Some of them firmly decided to stay on at Dorlotte. Chief among these were old Conduchet, whose farmhouse had not been burned down as it was full of German wounded at the time when the incendiary squad came round, and Pierre Lanfrey who thought that he could rig up some kind of tent. Actually he was staying because he felt that he might be useful to the village. He was the only man who, because of knowing a few words of German, could hope to restrain the invaders.

In his early life Pierre Lanfrey had been a sailor. Then, after losing his right hand, he had qualified as a pilot and because of having to pilot many German ships into the African ports, had made friends with German ship's officers and picked up a smattering of their language.

Next morning they discovered that their plans for leaving the village could not be carried out. Those parties that set off confidently down the road were stopped by German military police and were told that they could not leave the village without permits. It turned out however that there was no one in the village with power to issue a permit. All the officers had gone down the road to Blaye and were quartered there. Most of the German troops had also left the village.

Just a few villagers were able to get past the military police and make their way to the forest and through there to Belmont. But it was the same thing there, and they could get no further. There was however shelter in Belmont and bread to be had so long as the supply of flour held out.

CHAPTER TWO

When Georges Roux went to the church next morning he found La Fouine there as usual. She was praying; her hut had been burned and she had had no breakfast. Georges had brought with him a saucepan full of boiled cabbage and two pig's trotters that he had chopped off one of the Adjoint's pigs which had been shot by the Germans the previous morning on their arrival.

Georges offered La Fouine a trotter and cabbage. Then, while she ate, he said:

'You cry over the Boches when they come in to pray, but you don't care for the chap in the crypt.' There were tears running down La Fouine's scarred cheeks while she gnawed at the boiled trotter.

'They will all burn in fire everlasting,' she said.

'Maybe they will. Maybe they won't,' said Georges. If he could persuade La Fouine to look after de L'Espinasse, he was certain she would not betray him. But he knew that she did not like him coming to the church.

'Knock on the door of the crypt and say: 'The virgin is here to help', and give him the other trotter and the cabbage,' said Georges.

'He'll be damned on the day, just like the others,' said La Fouine with her mouth full of cabbage.

'Maybe so. But he's a Frenchman and one of ours,' said Georges. 'I've got to go now.'

'What about tomorrow?' the woman asked.

'I'll bring food so long as I can scrounge any,' said Georges. That settled the question.

There had been a sharp fall of rain before dawn. Those women for whom there was no room in the *lavoir* moved about wretchedly trying to shelter wet and wailing babies with sacks. Later that morning many of the houses had stopped smouldering because of the rain and were cold enough for their owners to stir the ashes and find what could be found: melted spoons, twisted forks. In most cases the cellar of the houses and sometimes their contents had escaped unharmed.

Once the fallen tiles, chimney pots and plaster had been shovelled aside and the entrance uncovered, a cellar offered shelter from rain and often such riches as pots of jam, a jar of potted goose, bottles of treasured wine sometimes cracked by the heat, a sack of scorched haricots or lentils.

The village stank like a burning rubbish dump in which the smell of burnt woollen clothing and the ammoniacal odour of burned leather predominated. Even the calcined stones at the corners of the ruins stank of the piss which had soaked into the limestone for ten generations. A few days later a smell of rotten meat came from the burned fowl houses and rabbit hutches when their inmates had not been completely incinerated. But the stench of their former possessions did not deter the owners, who poked and prodded, exclaiming with joy or sorrow when they dis-interred an unbroken cup, metal buttons that could be used again, or an incomplete set of brass weights which had not melted though the shallow pans of the scales were distorted almost out of recognition. Soon beside the houses little rows of such treasures were laid out.

The rain made Marcelle Duvernois remember her vegetable garden, which was not attached to her house, but across the road from the *mairie*, close to the church. A week earlier – in a different world – she had planned to plant out the winter salads: *scarole, endive frisée de Meaux* and *laitue brune d'hiver*. It was high time they were out of the seed bed and where they would remain.

When she had gone into the garden by the side gate, something attracted her attention to the rows of bush fruit. She walked over quickly to investigate and Corporal Simon looked up at her. He was barely conscious, but at what seemed like long intervals to him, he realised that a woman was looking at him.

'Water,' he murmured.

Marcelle put down her trowel and went down to the fountain and came back with a wine bottle washed out and full of cold water. She looked carefully to see that there were no Germans in sight, then she went down on her knees, held up Simon's head and put the bottle to his lips.

'Keep quiet. I'll get you out of here. I'll manage it somehow.'

The injunction to keep quiet was unnecessary. Corporal Simon had sunk back unconscious.

Marcelle went back to the seed-bed of salads and began planting out, but looked up sharply whenever a party of soldiers or an army vehicle came along the road.

After two hours she saw what she was waiting for: a German ambulance. It slowed down as it turned the corner coming towards her, because the road between the ruins was littered with tiles and a stone wall had collapsed outwards. Marcelle sprang out into the road, stood in the middle of it and raised her hand. The ambulance driver reined up his horses and a spectacled interne, sitting beside the driver, asked her in French what she wanted.

'There's a wounded soldier hiding in the bushes there,' she said, pointing.

'A stretcher case?' asked the interne.

'Yes.'

'Come on, Karl,' the interne said to the driver. Marcelle showed them where Simon was lying. They lifted him carefully on to the stretcher, carried it to the back of the ambulance and slid it in. 'Thank you, Frenchwoman. You did

32

the right thing,' said the interne. Marcelle flushed and went back to planting out her *scaroles*. She had nearly finished when Georges Roux came down the road with a bucket and a shovel.

'That boy is always up to something. I wonder what it is now?' she asked herself. He went to the house where the wounded man had been thrown into the flames and began raking about.

Georges found two hands with the fingers charred and gone, and one foot. He shovelled them into the bucket and then skimmed off the top layer of ashes with charred bones among them. He spent some time sorting out fragments that he thought were human and kept a look-out for the metal identity disc which at last he found and put in his pocket. While he was at work an army lorry drove up and the driver sounded the horn. Five German soldiers who had been waiting round the corner drinking in the Bistro belonging to the widow Zins – one of the four buildings not destroyed – came running up. Four of the men climbed up over the side of the lorry, but the fifth man noticed Georges and called out:

'Hi! What's this boy up to?'

'I'm not waiting,' called the driver and revved up his motor. The soldier reluctantly ran to the lorry and climbed in after his companions.

'Look at that boy,' he said.

Georges had not turned his head or looked up. After the lorry had driven off Marcelle came down and joined him. Together they walked up the street to the cemetery, picking their way among the heaps of tiles that had cascaded off roofs. They stopped while Georges fetched a spade he had hidden among the artichokes.

He dug a hole beside the grave in which Rouault had buried Zafferelli. Into this he poured the contents of his bucket and then covered the ashes with earth. Marcelle said a prayer, and Georges said that he would come back next day and put up a wooden cross and nail the identity disc to it.

'You are a fine fellow, and I thank you. You did the right thing,' said Marcelle echoing the German interne's words to her.

Before they parted, she held out her hand and they shook hands in silence. Georges would have preferred to have done the disagreeable but necessary job alone.

There had not been a priest living in Dorlotte for five years – not since the scandal of 1909 when Father Gérome had married his young housekeeper after getting her with child. No one had hired the presbytery garden; it had run wild, so it was a good place to hide in and when three days later a new company of German infantry marched into the village and stacked arms up by the cemetery, the children and many of the women hid. Sylvie Turpin chose the Presbytery garden. She was a brunette of fourteen with dark hair and dark languishing eyes and a complexion like a ripe nectarine. Until a week before, she had been a lively and adorable little monkey, but in the last few days of terror and suffering, she had developed the sweet sympathies of a woman. She came to the Presbytery garden because she wanted to be alone. But someone was there before her: Georges Roux was sitting on some stones which had once been a wall of the priest's house.

Sylvie was astonished to see that he was, or had been, crying. He was a tough boy a year older than herself. Instead of running away and telling her girl friends about Georges's tears as she would have done only a few days previously, Sylvie went up and stood in front of him and asked:

'What is the matter?'

Georges looked up at her and said at once:

'It's my tom cat, Hercule. I can't find him anywhere.'

Sylvie said nothing.

'He may have been killed by the Boches, or may have run off because of all the strange people and the noise. I shall go to the forest to call him. But of course he may have gone in any direction. You know him well, Sylvie. What do you think he would be most likely to do?' Georges looked up as he said this and saw an odd expression on her face.

'You know something, Sylvie. What is it?'

'No, I don't. But please don't go looking for him, Georges. I can't bear to think of you wandering in the forest, calling your cat. It's dangerous with the Boches everywhere. And it's a waste of time.'

'You do know something.'

'No, I don't, Georges. How could I?'

'Swear on the name of Jeanne d'Arc that you know nothing.'

If Georges had named any of the saints, or even the Virgin, Sylvie might have lied to him. But she had a cult for Jeanne d'Arc and since the German invasion had been hoping to have visions herself and become the heroine who would save France, side by side with Papa Joffre. Sylvie would not swear and she hesitated for a little while.

'Promise you won't revenge yourself if I tell you.'

'Tell me.'

'No, Georges. Not unless you promise to do nothing.'

Sylvie squatted down in front of him and took both his hands in hers.

'All right.'

'Hercule is dead.'

'Who killed him?'

'Joseph.' Georges tried to spring to his feet but Sylvie held him tight.

'Tell me everything.'

'You know how hungry everyone is?'

'You mean Hercule has been eaten?'

Sylvie nodded.

'How do you know?' asked Georges.

'Mathilde boasted to me yesterday: she said, "Do you know, Sylvie, we had jugged hare today." Of course I told her that I didn't believe her. Nobody has a gun – and Joseph isn't much of a hunter. Then it came out. He had killed

Hercule and they had jugged him like a hare.'

Georges sat silent, his face dark with anger. At last Sylvie said: 'It's not like ordinary times. When a man's children have nothing to eat . . .'

'Yes. I understand.'

Sylvie put her arms round his shoulders and kissed him. 'Don't be too unhappy. I love you.' Then she let go of him and ran out of the wild garden. Georges did not move but sat thinking. If he minded so much losing only a cat, how much pain there must now be in the world.

It was an anonymous act. Nobody ever knew who did it or why. Madame Blanchard went to ask Julie Cange to return the Canterbury hoe that she had borrowed. Like other people who had nowhere to go, Julie had gone back to live in the cellar of her cottage. She had been using the hoe to clear away rubble near the entrance.

Julie did not seem to be there and did not answer when Madame Blanchard called out to her. Then she noticed a queer smell. She looked into the cellar and saw a bloody footprint on the second step. She walked back then to her own cellar and fetched matches and a candle and went back to see for herself. Blood was everywhere. Julie and her three children had been stabbed. The baby's head was cut off. Julie herself was fully dressed. She had been stabbed several times.

Madame Blanchard went at once and told Pierre Lanfrey. He fetched old Lorcey and Michel Fournier the roadman, and the three men fetched the bodies up. Pierre went over to Marcelle Duvernois's garden and discussed it with her and she agreed to go into Blaye and tell the German general. She knew where he had billeted himself. The sergeant of military police stopped her at the bottom of the hill, but she browbeat him into letting her go past. She was able to see the general at once – the woman of the house, a friend of hers, went in and told the general that there was a woman who must see him and then showed her in. The general was a tall, tired, elderly man with a pale face, sitting at a desk. He pushed down his spectacles and looked at Marcelle from over them.

'Sit down and tell me what I can do for you,' he said. She explained that a woman and her three children including a baby in arms had been massacred in a cellar. As their houses had been burned, many people had been living in their cellars.

'I don't believe it,' said the general. 'A propaganda story.'

'Come and see for yourself. They have just brought the bodies up out of the cellar.'

The general stood up, took his cap, and went out to where his car and the driver were waiting. He opened the door, got in, and told Marcelle to get in after him, and they were driven to Dorlotte. During the drive neither of them spoke.

The bodies had been laid out on two sheets of galvanised iron and covered with a tarpaulin belonging to the road man. The general walked up over the rubble and Pierre removed the tarpaulin. The general examined Julie's body, asking old Lorcey to turn her over on her face and then back again. After that he examined the bodies of the children and went and looked into the cellar.

'It has been done with a bayonet, used as a sword,' he said to Pierre. 'It looks like the work of a homicidal maniac. In time of war it is so difficult to be sure. Who was the woman? What was her reputation in the village? Did she consort with German soldiers?' Pierre Lanfrey replied – the general's French was better than his German, and the general took notes. Then he spoke to the military police and gave some orders.

'If the murderer can be found, he will of course be put on trial. Of course he may be French. One cannot make charges of atrocities without complete evidence.' The general turned to Marcelle Duvernois. 'Thank you, madame, for reporting these murders. You did the right thing. I will see that you are given what protection I can. Don't be anxious. German soldiers are not monsters. A very puzzling incident.'

The general got into his car. Marcelle and Pierre stood

watching him drive away.

'I seem to have wasted my time. The murderer may be French – one of the many homicidal lunatics who live in this village,' said Marcelle.

'Nonsense. You did very well to have rubbed his nose in that filth. It is the only way to get them house-trained. He knows it was done by one of his men and that he is responsible for their behaviour.'

'We had better have the funerals this afternoon because of the rats,' said Lorcey.

But Madame Zins at the Bistro said that the bodies could be locked up in her still room until a coffin had been made. She gave the wood for the coffin too.

During the remainder of the occupation the military police sergeant made a habit of stopping at Pierre Lanfrey's cellar every morning and asking if he had any trouble to report.

Georges had lost count of the days of the week and he was surprised when he went to the church to hear the sound of a congregation inside. It was Sunday. But the villagers would not have gone to a service as there was no priest. He slipped in and saw that it was packed with German soldiers. A German army chaplain was conducting a service for the soldiers of Christ.

The funeral of Julie Cange and her children would take place that afternoon and it occurred to Georges that their murderer, who had stabbed her several times with his bayonet and had beheaded her baby, might be among the crowd in front of him. To Georges's surprise the soldiers were singing hymns. He had never heard hymns being sung in church before. And after that the chaplain was celebrating the mass. And then the soldiers sang again. Georges had to wait until they had trooped out and he could find La Fouine and hand her the basket he had brought, with a pot of haricots boiled with leeks and garlic, and a bag full of greengages. He stood at the back while he waited, thinking that he wanted nothing to do with the God they were praying to, whichever side He

38

favoured. When he had found La Fouine he went out. If he could have locked the church door and thrown in a kilo of those incendiary tablets, it would have turned the tables!

Pierre Lanfrey saw Georges coming out of the church and intercepted him.

'Are you a believer, my lad?'

'No.'

'But you go to the church every day.'

Georges pouted and shrugged his shoulders. 'I take La Fouine a bite of food sometimes. She lives in the church.'

'Do you know what the German general said when he saw that baby with its head cut off, and the two other children and Julie stabbed three times with a bayonet?'

Georges looked sourly at Pierre, waiting.

'He said that they might have been murdered by a Frenchman – a homicidal lunatic.'

Georges laughed. It was a curious, unexpected laugh, more like a frog croaking than a boy laughing. Then he said:

'There will be plenty of homicidal lunatics around soon.'

Pierre said no more and Georges went off up the road.

'That boy Georges Roux may turn out a fine man. Who would have thought a boy of fifteen would take on the job of keeping a semi-imbecile, syphilitic woman of fifty alive?' Pierre reflected. He was puzzled.

In the middle of the night the inhabitants of Dorlotte, crouching in cellars, or sleeping in out of the way corners under trees, were woken by the clatter of horses' hoofs, the cracks of whips and shouting of drivers, by the grinding noises of heavy motors, by bugle blasts and by the rumour of many men.

At each corner in the village a military policeman, heavily cloaked and waving a lantern, stood by to direct traffic.

Georges, who seldom went near his home, was sleeping in the Presbytery garden. He woke to hear the beating of hoofs, the rattle of motor lorries, grinding gears. There were guns, heavy artillery – and it was going north. Georges got up and made his way stealthily to the corner by the *mairie* and the church where two cloaked military policemen were walking up and down waiting for the next artillery train. Near him was a tall figure watching: Pierre Lanfrey.

Georges bent down and moving only when the police were not looking in his direction, reached where Pierre was standing.

'They are going north. Do you think they are pulling out?' he whispered. The older man nodded and put a finger on his lips.

The noise of straining horses and the cracks of whips came up the hill. They stood silently watching for an hour or two. It was a big movement. It could only be a retreat.

Suddenly a horseman galloped up, pulled round by the church, dismounted, cast his eyes round and seeing Georges outlined against the night sky shouted: 'Hi, you there! Hold my horse.'

Georges ran down and took the bridle. The German officer, with a large haversack on his back, ran into the church. One of the military police had followed and took the bridle.

'What are you doing here, my lad?'

'Look there,' he said, and as the German looked he slipped away round the corner of the church porch.. Suddenly everything was brilliantly illuminated in a blazing light from the belfry. Georges could keep in shadow close to the church wall but Pierre and two groups of people watching were revealed.

The officer who had run in came out and he and the military policeman stood gazing upwards. Soon it was obvious that the wooden structure of the ancient spire had caught fire. Later it would collapse into the transepts. Very soon La Fouine and a young man in a black soutane came out. The Germans busy watching their handiwork did not notice him as he turned a corner into the shadow. Georges joined him.

'He set the belfry alight as some kind of signal; they are pulling out.'

De L'Espinasse wanted to complain: Georges had shut him up in the dark, had handed him over to a crazy religious maniac, had fed him on a starvation diet of boiled vegetables. He had been deprived of wine, spirits and tobacco – but at the moment there was not an opportunity to say all this. For he was within fifteen metres of a German officer and German military policeman. He had trusted to this wretched small boy and now that it seemed the enemy were retreating, he was in desperate danger of being arrested and carried off as a prisoner to Germany. He glared indignantly at Georges but it is impossible to glare effectively while hiding in a dark corner. And he was frightened by seeing Germans so close. The moon rose and Georges made de L'Espinasse walk round to the other side of the church. He became aware of the older man's fear and tried to reassure him.

'There's nothing to worry about. The Boches are all on the road. All the fields down here are empty. Go and wait in one of them until their retreat is over.'

'How do you know it is a retreat? They may be pulling back here to reinforce their line somewhere else.'

'I think they are pulling back everywhere,' said Georges.

'You don't know. You can't possibly tell," said de L'Espinasse peevishly.

'Our *poilus* will be here soon after dawn,' said Georges with absolute confidence.

'The Boches may be drawing them into a trap as they did in Alsace,' said de L'Espinasse. He was annoyed with himself for entering into an argument with a mere child.

'Anyway, you will be perfectly safe if you stay here in the fields outside the village. I've got to get back now.' And before the lieutenant could expostulate, Georges had nodded and was running back to the village.

'Damn the boy. He doesn't seem to think that I may be hungry. What wouldn't I give for some hot coffee and a fine

41

cognac,' he said to himself bitterly. After all he was an officer in the Air Service. It was the boy's *duty* to prevent his being taken prisoner and he ought to devote more attention to looking after him.

The tramp of the enemy infantry sounded horribly close. Georges joined the group of old men, women and children who had gathered round Pierre Lanfrey. The moon had risen and in its light he could see many villagers standing on heaps of rubble that had been their comfortable houses before the Germans had come. There they stood: a few old men, old women, a few younger ones and some inquisitive children watching those who had ruined them depart. They did not speak but stood watching silently. And the German columns went in silence except for the heavy tramp of their boots.

Georges was right. By dawn all the German troops had disappeared along the road through the forest. As the sun rose four or five 75 shells were thrown into the village by the French artillery. Two of them hit the church and made holes in the roof. The spire had already collapsed and La Fouine had found other accommodation. Two shells fell in the Presbytery garden but did no damage. After the first explosions most of the villagers dived into their cellars. Pierre Lanfrey and Georges, who had stayed out waiting for the first sign of the reappearance of the French army, did not bother. Then, as no more shells burst, curiosity brought up most of those who had taken refuge. They were in time to see a company of French cyclist scouts pass through the village. Soon afterwards came companies of infantry, many of whom called out and waved to the villagers. Some of the younger women waved in return but most stood dumbly watching.

Old Lorcey had fought in the war of 1870 in the Dragoons and had been wounded in the foot. Now he stood at attention with his hand at the salute as though he were a general inspecting troops.

About the middle of the afternoon a field kitchen drove

up, turned off the main road and pulled up by the fountain.

A bell was rung and the army cook shouted: 'Soup and sausages for everybody,' as the astonished villagers approached. It was true and a crowd gathered quickly. Another vehicle drew up behind the first one. From it army loaves were distributed. The first comers stood round drinking bowls of hot soup. Behind them others waited for the bowls to be emptied so they could have their turn.

'You never made anything as good as this, Mother Zins,' called old Conduchet who certainly had not gone short during the occupation since the Germans had not burned his farm or killed his rabbits.

However he drank up the soup quickly and handed back his bowl to be filled for someone else. After the soup they were each given a sausage and a slice of bread. And to finish up, half a glass of red wine.

The men sipped it slowly, scarcely believing in it. The women dipped crusts in it and gave them to the children.

'It seems we haven't been entirely forgotten,' said Pierre Lanfrey.

'No indeed,' said Madame Blanchard angrily. 'And I for one am grateful.'

Old Madame Eglantine Constant, Veuve Turpin Lanfrey – Pierre's first cousin twice removed, and Sylvie's great-grandmother, hobbled up, rested her hand on the kitchen counter and said to the cook:

'I am the oldest inhabitant of Dorlotte. I was a young woman in 1870, and remember when the Germans came then. And I wish to give thanks for our deliverance. It is a day of rejoicing.'

The cook was overcome with emotion. He took hold of the old gnarled fingers and kissed them.

'I embrace you in the name of the army,' he said solemnly.

'Are you coming back again, or is this all we can expect?' asked Marcelle Duvernois, breaking in on the historic scene.

43

'I shall be back tomorrow and here every day at eleven o'clock until the emergency is over. Now a distribution of dried milk for the babies.'

The cook was as good as his word. Every morning the villagers trooped down to the fountain and bread and stew were handed out, though the numbers waiting for it decreased rapidly as many of the people left the village. For several days there was tremendous confusion. Nobody who could stay with relatives, or who could afford to hire a room in Blaye, or Revigny, or even so far as Bar, wished to stay another night in a cellar.

Georges's mother had pneumonia and Pierre Lanfrey succeeded in getting her taken to hospital three days after the liberation. Georges stayed in the village and heard of her death a week later without undue emotion.

Every few days parties of women and children left the village when they had been able to find shelter elsewhere. About thirty remained. Pierre Lanfrey and his family, old Lorcey, Michel Fournier, old Rouault, Eglantine Constant Veuve Turpin Lanfrey, Madame Blanchard, Madame Turpin and Sylvie, Georges Roux, La Fouine, the innkeepers Madame Zins and Georges Muller and his wife, old Conduchet and his large family of married daughters (their husbands were in the army), his youngest daughter Germaine and his grandchildren.

Lieutenant de L'Espinasse had vanished without saying goodbye, either to Georges Roux, or to La Fouine.

The kitchen stopped coming but the army continued to supply the village once a week with bread in the form of huge round loaves which later were concocted of a wartime mixture of wheat, rye and tapioca flour. The colour of the bread was grey, but it tasted good and had the advantage of not going stale though sometimes it went mouldy.

In all that belt of France between the Marne and the Aisne and from Vitry and Sermaize to the middle of the Argonne – in fact from the line of the Germans' furthest advance to that where they dug themselves in and were to remain until near the end of the war, there was an absence of livestock. The demand for horses, cattle, sheep, goats, rabbits and poultry was far beyond what could immediately be supplied.

Marie Durand and her old alcoholic, semi-imbecile father lived outside the village, to the north. This had not prevented their little farmstead from being burned down, but Jeanne had saved the life of their draught ox which happened to be lying in a willow spinney near the stream during the German invasion. Marie kept him there tethered, during the occupation, taking him bundles of green meat and sugar beet pulled up from one of old Conduchet's fields.

Having the ox enabled Marie to set herself up as the village carrier. Twice a week she drove him at a fast walking pace into Blaye, executing commissions and taking out and bringing back parcels in the narrow tumbril which he drew.

CHAPTER THREE

During the German occupation of Dorlotte, lasting only ten days, the inhabitants had lived as though in a dream. They had scuttled for shelter, scraped for food, helped each other, been mean but more often generous, but all the time they had been paralysed, watching events that were beyond their comprehension and powers of response. A large number were suffering from shock.

With the departure of the enemy, they awoke from a nightmare to find themselves surrounded by proofs that the nightmare had indeed been real. The village in which many of the women and all the children had spent their entire lives, had been transformed into a collection of scattered calcined stones and heaps of rubble. But because the nightmare had been real they looked at each other with a new knowledge when they awoke. They had been welded together, had become precious to each other because with the destruction of all their material possessions, with equality of ruin, all that was left to them was each other and themselves. Their neighbours were all that remained to them of their previous lives. They did not formulate this, but all of them were aware of it and for the future it governed their behaviour. Jeanne, Pierre Lanfrey's wife, was one of the first to become her ordinary self after the Germans left. Three days after the liberation she insisted on going into Bar-le-Duc, though for much of the way she had to go along the edges of fields and by paths through the woods, as the road was jammed with army vehicles and the military police turned back civilians.

'You'll have to look after the children, Pierre. Expect me

when you see me. If I can't get Brigitte settled in a good place I may stay a day or two. And I want all the money you've got.'

Pierre gave her six hundred francs in notes from the money belt that he wore next to his skin.

'Mind you I shall spend every centime and buy all that I can get on credit too. There is bound to be a most awful shortage for months to come.'

Pierre nodded and set to work shovelling rubble into a basket which was the only receptacle he had. By the middle of the afternoon he was breaking off work to watch the road from Bar. He stood on the high ground among the ruins of his house and looked down the dusty winding road that led to Bar. A company of soldiers came in sight marching two abreast to allow for the passage of army trucks. A battery of seventy-five millimetre guns came next, then a dispatch rider on a motorcycle, but no sign of Jeanne. The church stood high above the road and opposite the two couchant stone lions that flanked the steps leading to where the *mairie* had been. Then Pierre turned his eyes northwards to where the rumble of guns marked the front, now stabilised in the forests beyond Ste Menehould. The only buildings left to interrupt his view were old Conduchet's farmhouse and his barns. Here and there was a wall standing as high as the first floor. But these would have to be pulled down. Already Pierre was finding it difficult to remember exactly what this collection of ruins amid their smiling gardens had looked like before they had been burned down. He looked back down the road to Bar and then he decided that Jeanne would not be coming that night and made ready an evening meal of soup with haricots, tomatoes, leeks, courgettes and peppers. No meat in it, alas. Then he went back to watch the road. Just before sunset he chanced to look down the road to Blaye and there was a woman pushing a wheelbarrow up the hill. It was Jeanne. He ran to meet her. She dropped the handles of the wheelbarrow and stood waiting for him, red-cheeked,

47

perspiring and out of breath.

'What are you doing on this road? And with a wheel-barrow!' he exclaimed.

'An army driver gave me a lift as far as Revigny. I've pushed this damned barrow ten kilometres. My God, I'm tired.'

Pierre took a loop of cord out of his left-hand pocket, slipped it over the right-hand handle of the wheelbarrow, put the hook through it, and pushed the loaded barrow up the hill. Jeanne, who didn't seem so tired after all, was bursting with excitement.

'I'm longing to show you what I've got: a mattress, six blankets, a quilt . . .'

'What about Brigitte?'

'That's turned out all right. She's a clever girl and has won the hearts of all. Your sister has found her a job as a nurse-maid and Madame Salmon wants her to stay on to look after the children for another fortnight until we've got things straight.'

'Well that's a relief for the moment.'

'Then I've got saucepans, a coffee pot, chicory, spoons and forks, some cups and mugs . . . I can't remember everything. Oh I've got soap! Just think. Soap; and soda . . . Darling, isn't it exciting? It's like setting up house all over again!'

Pierre began laughing. After a time he said:

'So you are glad we are ruined, darling?'

'Well we may as well make the best of it. I shan't make the mistakes I made last time.'

Marcelle Duvernois, on her way back to Blaye after a day's work in her garden, saw the new wheelbarrow and came over to speak to Pierre and Jeanne as they were unloading it. The two old men, Lorcey and Rouault, stopped in the street to watch. They were on their way back to their cellars after a day's work in the fields lifting potatoes with forks. There were no horses to pull the potato-lifter. It was already nearly twilight.

Jeanne saw them standing there and called to them: 'I've bought a new coffee pot. Come and help christen it!'

They hesitated, drew near, wiped their earthstained hands on the seats of their trousers before shaking hands, and even then Rouault decided that his hand was too dirt-stained and at the last minute held out his wrist to Marcelle Duvernois. She laughed at him and then imitated his action, holding out her wrist and rubbing it against his.

'How can we greet each other like that, old friend? It's like savages rubbing noses.' Jeanne went into a peal of laughter and Rouault, looking at Marcelle with a twinkle, opened his gnarled fist and grasped her hand.

'Not but I wouldn't like to rub noses and anything else with thee,' he said. 'If thou hadst a mind to it.'

'Mine is always cleaner than anyone else's but cold for shaking,' said Pierre, exhibiting his steel hook.

They laughed. Laughter was something they had almost forgotten and not yet got used to.

'It looks as though you meant to stay with us,' said old Lorcey to Jeanne, pointing to her new acquisitions.

'Yes, our cellar is fine. And Pierre plans to put in a skylight so that we shall not live by candlelight – and a trapdoor to keep out snow in winter.'

'Your Pierre is a brave bunny who likes a warm burrow,' said old Rouault, winking at Lorcey, who responded with a scowl. He did not think that even so mildly improper a remark should have been made in front of Madame Duvernois. He had been embarrassed too by Rouault's remarks about rubbing noses. So now he sipped the coffee and said:

'Coffee's good. Your health, Madame Lanfrey.'

'Delicious. Well now I must get back to Blaye before it's pitch dark,' said Marcelle.

'Here comes another battalion,' said old Lorcey, whose hearing was remarkable in an old man. It was true. They could hear the sound of three hundred men marching out of step growing louder.

49

Then, possibly because they saw the lights at the top of the hill, the regimental band broke into the tune of *Sambre et Meuse*.

Lorcey and Rouault picked up their forks and went off before the soldiers should make crossing the road impossible. Marcelle waited until the battalion had passed through the village. The band stopped playing before they had reached the crossroads. The moment of gaiety was over.

'There has been a lot of fighting in the Grurie Wood,' said Marcelle.

'Yes, it goes on,' said Pierre.

'There were any number of trains of wounded, waiting end to end on the line above Revigny,' said Jeanne.

Marcelle shook hands with Pierre and on an impulse kissed Jeanne, and then went down the hill. Jeanne and Pierre spread the new mattress on the cellar floor by the light of a lantern and then stowed away her purchases wherever they would be safe from damage.

'Come along, you brave bunny,' said Jeanne.

Georges Roux dug up his father's old gun, apparently none the worse for burial. But shortly afterwards he buried it again as the postman, who had reappeared, told him there was a decree that all firearms in the zone of the armies had to be registered with the military authorities. Postman was concerned because his gun had been taken away and broken up by the Germans. He was one of the keenest sportsmen in the district; he was worried because he didn't know where he could pick up a gun that suited him and get it registered in time for the shooting season that was going to start. So he asked Georges about his father's gun, but Georges, who didn't want to part with it, told the postman that it had 'disappeared'.

There had been no cellar in the Rouxs' old cottage, and Georges decided to build himself a hut in the garden. Since there was a shortage of timber of all kinds, he planned to build it of stone. Pierre Lanfrey lent him the wheelbarrow when he wasn't using it, and Georges carted big squared stones from nearby ruins whose owners had gone away. In theory the hut was to be built from the stones of the Rouxs' burnt cottage, but Georges thought it a good plan to use other material while it was available. He might want to rebuild the house later on, so he kept his own property in reserve.

Marie Durand brought out a sack of quicklime from the builder's in Blaye, and there was sand for free in the pit down the lane. So Georges mixed a primitive mortar which would at all events stop the wind from whistling through the joints of his masonry.

One morning a battery of 75s came up the hill and halted on the corner. It was midday and the midday meal was due. Soon the men were crowding round the kitchen, carrying their bowls and mugs. They were served with haricot soup, bread and a quarter of *pinot*. After they had eaten their ration they were given half an hour's rest. Some lay down on the ground, one or two went into the church, others wandered round the village.

Georges was at work. He had not stopped for lunch and was busy fitting stones of the same thickness into his wall when he heard a sound behind him. An artilleryman was watching him. He was tall, thin and handsome with a long brown face, a slightly hooked nose and dark eyes. Georges nodded to him and went on working.

'What are you building?' asked the soldier.

'A wall.'

'So I see. But what is it for?'

'I need some place to sleep in, at night.'

'Why are you making it of stone?'

'The Boches couldn't destroy the stones. There are plenty of them. And not much else.'

'Was that your old home?' asked the soldier, looking at the mass of rubble under the trees.

'Yes.'

'Where's your father?'

'He's in the army.'

'And your mother?'

'Dead. She died in hospital.'

'How old are you?'

'Fifteen.'

'Do you ever read books?'

'No.'

'You ought to.'

'But there aren't any. They were in the houses and all got burned.'

'Stupid of me not to think of that. May I give you this one?'

'What is it?'

'Poems.'

'Are they religious?'

'Not very.'

'All right then.'

The artilleryman held out his hand and Georges took a tattered little book from him. A bugle sounded. The soldier said: 'I feel happier since I have met you.' Then he saluted and turned to run back to the crossroads. Georges put the book down on his folded jacket and went on working.

He was at work on the job when Sylvie came into the garden and went up to him. It was a hot day and Georges had taken off his shirt and was wearing a pair of cotton trousers. Sylvie said:

'But you are building a house!'

'There wasn't a cellar and I want somewhere to sleep when the weather turns cold.'

'How big is it going to be?'

'Just a tiny cabin. Two metres by one-fifty. But I may add another room in front, later on.'

'But it's wonderful, Georges. Nobody else in Dorlotte has thought of building yet.'

52

'Well, most people have cellars that they can sleep in. We hadn't.'

Georges noticed that for some reason Sylvie looked troubled. So he put down the little hod he had made for holding mortar and turned to her.

'What is the matter, Sylvie?'

'I don't know if I've done right, Georges. It may make you angry. But I wanted to please you.'

'Well, what have you done?'

'I found Hercule's skin in Joseph's shed. So I took it. It is so beautiful. And I've tanned it with wood-ashes and brought it for you. I hope you will like to have it and it won't give you pain.'

'Let me see.'

Sylvie unrolled the blue apron in which the cat's skin was wrapped and spread it out on the grass. Georges sat down beside it and began stroking the fur. Then he picked up the skin and buried his face in it.

He looked up at Sylvie but could not speak, so he nodded his head again and again.

'So I did right, Georges?'

He nodded again and put the skin down and began stroking it and looking at it, and Sylvie sat beside him and stroked it too.

'You have made me very happy,' he said.

'I must go now.' Sylvie got up and Georges jumped to his feet and put his arms round her. Her skin, her hair, her scent all inspired him with a sudden physical longing and he pressed her body close to his and held her tight. Then, because his desire had come on him unexpectedly and unplanned, he let her go and drew a deep breath. Sylvie had run back a few steps. 'I love you, Georges. You have made me very happy too. I must go now. Grandmother expects me.'

'Come again soon,' said Georges. He spent a long time stroking the skin and rubbing his face in it, before he went back to laying the stones on his wall.

Joseph was the ne'er-do-well of Dorlotte. As he had only one small field of his own left, he went to work for Monsieur Conduchet, but he was a poor labourer and often got into trouble with his master.

Seed corn would soon be wanted. The Germans had burned down all the corn stacks; who could tell when the markets would reopen, or when supplies could be got from further south? But old Conduchet's corn stacks, in his farmyard fortunately, had been spared, just as his farm had been because the house was full of German wounded, waiting for the ambulances, and to have burned them down would have been unsafe. If he could get them threshed he could sow his own fields and sell the rest at high prices to neighbouring farmers. But as it might be weeks before the threshing machine came to Dorlotte, he went back to the days of his father, brought out an old flail and had two new ones put together. He had luckily a fairly modern winnowing machine for cleaning seed corn and he told Joseph to get it ready. Joseph had to take it to pieces. Then when he was putting it together, one of the bits would not slide in. He took a hammer to it. It broke, for he was forcing it in upside down.

Conduchet's rage was such that he hit the younger man in the face and ordered him never to set foot on his land again. As Joseph was in his employer's debt for a whole month's wages and for flour and faggots, he could expect nothing. He did not dare return home to face his wife.

'Fair fucked out,' he repeated over and over again. And there wasn't a place in Dorlotte where he could get a drink. He owed money to Mother Zins and to that bastard Muller. Well he could go to Blaye – and maybe he'd never come back to Dorlotte again. Such were Joseph's unhappy thoughts. He was seen leaving the village in the middle of the morning by the roadman, Michel Fournier, who was filling up potholes in the surface of the road up the hill with spadefuls of earth and turf. It was a quite useless proceeding, but it showed that he was on the job. Michel knew that Joseph should have been at the farm where the need for seed corn was urgent.

'Hullo, I says to myself, what's up with Joseph? Being sent with a message somewhere, or got himself into trouble? He didn't stop to pass the time of day, so I rumbled that it was not an urgent message.' So Michel reported himself as thinking to Pierre Lanfrey when he went up the hill to fetch the cigarettes he had left in his coat pocket.

Joseph did not reappear, but the next day the policeman from Blaye, whose job had almost stopped with the arrival of the military police, came out to Dorlotte on his bicycle. He was fifty and not accustomed to much exercise, so he got off the machine at the bottom of the hill and pushed it up, stopping twice for a rest on the way. At the top he saw Pierre Lanfrey.

'Can you tell me where I can find that fellow Joseph d'Oex?'

'Why, is he in trouble?'

'I want to have a talk with him, that's all.'

'Well, he was away yesterday. I don't know if he has come back. He works for Conduchet. I'm told they had a bit of a row.'

'Well, Monsieur Lanfrey, I don't mind telling you, because I know you won't let it go any further, but Joseph has let himself in good and proper.' Pierre waited and the Sergent-de-Ville said, lowering his voice: 'Joseph was seen to go into Mère Richard's little bistro – and then to pop out again quick. Mère Richard was in the yard hanging out washing. She never saw Joseph. But when she came back, the drawer in which she keeps her money was empty. Over a hundred francs, she says.'

'Circumstantial evidence isn't all that good. What about the exact time?' asked Pierre.

'Don't be silly. It stands out a mile. Of course the people who saw Joseph hadn't got stopwatches. Not but that I would narrow it down in cross-examination. But when I've had five minutes with Master Joseph, he'll spill the beans. I shall have a full signed confession. I've been run about by the military police so I'm glad this came along, I can tell you. Well, I'll see what Monsieur Conduchet has to say. He looks like my best bet.'

Directly the policeman was out of sight, Pierre went to find Marcelle Duvernois and told her the story.

'That awful man Joseph. What an imbecile!' she exclaimed.

'We can't let him go to prison. There's that wife of his and they haven't a bean – and three children,' said Pierre.

'Yes, I see something will have to be done. What do you suggest?' said Marcelle, putting down her trowel.

'Well, there are two things. First we must find Joseph and keep him hidden so that he doesn't "spill the beans". Then we must get Mère Richard to withdraw the charge.'

'She won't do that unless she gets her money back. And perhaps not even then. She's a mean old stick. A thoroughly bad woman like a lot of them in Blaye.'

'Well, if Joseph hasn't spent it all, we'll make him give back what's left – and we'll have to have a whip round in the village.'

'Can't you get Georges Roux on to the job of finding and hiding Joseph? That boy's a splendid fellow. You know about the fellow in the crypt? Well you get hold of Georges and find Joseph and keep him out of the reach of the law and I'll tackle Madame Richard. What a bore the whole thing is!'

Before the invasion such a conversation would have been inconceivable. But suffering produces a new morality – and with it a sense of personal responsibility. Both Pierre and Marcelle had taken for granted that it was their duty to defeat the ends of justice. Not for the sake of Joseph – who deserved all he got – but for the community of Dorlotte. If Joseph went to prison his miserable wife would have to go out looking for soldiers in order to feed her children. Altogether it would be a bad business.

Madame Duvernois walked into Blaye that afternoon, taking a large sum of money knotted up in a silk stocking which she had not had an opportunity to wear for five years. She had time to take all her money with her to the cemetery so it was not lost when her house was set on fire.

'Well, Madame Richard. I've come to have a word with you in private.' La Mère Richard was surprised and led her into the parlour.

'You'll have a glass of my mirabelle?' Marcelle accepted the drink. The more she could get Mère Richard to lay out, the more reluctant she would be to let her depart without having made a bargain.

'Absolutely delicious. Just what I needed after my walk. May I take another glass? You must give me the recipe.'

La Mère Richard poured out another glass rather reluctantly. She wondered what was coming.

'I've heard about your loss and I've come to make restitution. How much was it exactly?'

'I told the sergent it was over a hundred. But I've reckoned up since and it was exactly ninety-seven francs and twenty-seven centimes.' La Mère Richard was scrupulously honest, to the exact centime.

Marcelle pursed her lips and said: 'I have the money here and I am empowered to make restitution – but on one condition: that you withdraw your charges against Joseph.'

'Oh, but I can't do that. I have gone to the police . . . I have sworn . . Besides he is a thief. He ought to be punished.'

'Let me say one thing. We in Dorlotte have suffered . . . weaker heads than Joseph have gone crazy. He has a wife and three children. They had nothing to eat for several days . . . only boiled potatoes. The children crying from hunger. Then do you know what he did? He caught a cat and they ate it jugged, like a hare . . .'

Mère Richard smiled. 'They do that in the cheap restaurants in Paris. I'm told a cat isn't half bad.'

'You realise that if you drop the charge against Joseph you get your money back now? If you persist you will have to go to court, pay Maître Surlot, and Joseph will have spent all the money. You'll be a lot out of pocket.'

'He ought to be punished.'

'He will be. We in Dorlotte will take care of that.'

'But what shall I say to the sergent?'

'Tell him that you found it afterwards in another drawer. You had forgotten that you had locked it up.'

Mère Richard smiled again. 'He'll be awfully angry, and he may not believe me.'

'Give him a bottle of anis. That will put things right. He can't force you to bring a charge.'

'Well, it's wrong. But I will do it purely for your sake, Madame Duvernois. I do it to help you. I can guess how you feel. I am a woman too.'

'Ninety-seven francs and twenty-seven centimes, Madame Richard?'

'And I'll charge you for the bottle of anis. That's fair, isn't it?'

'We won't quarrel about that. And I am very, very grateful,' said Marcelle and counted out the money.

Mère Richard watched through the window as she walked away. 'Who would have thought that Madame Duvernois had that oaf Joseph for her lover! Even I, at my age, could find someone better than that!' she said to herself. She realised that until the case was withdrawn and could not be reopened, that she would have to keep her mouth shut. But after that! What a fine bit of dirt about those people up at Dorlotte! Her friends would love it.

Georges looked up from his building at Pierre and asked: 'Have you come for your barrow, M. Lanfrey?'

'No. Something else. Joseph is in trouble.'

'I'm glad to hear it. But it's not news. He's always in trouble.'

'I mean real trouble. With the police. The damned fool stole money out of Mère Richard's till.'

'He stole my cat too and killed him and ate him. I hope he gets sent to prison.'

'He will be if the sergent finds him.'

'I can guess where he ought to look.'

'That's why I came. I want you to find him and make him keep in hiding. The sergent would arrest him if he found him today. By tomorrow the danger may be over.'

'I don't want to help Joseph. I would rather show the policeman where to look.'

'Remember, Georges, Joseph has a wife and children. If he goes to prison they won't have a penny to live on. The only way she could live would be to go with soldiers.'

'Funny taste they would have. But why should I mind? I tell you that bunch of devils ate my cat. I would like to see all of them in jail. Straight, I would.'

'Have you ever heard, Georges, that you should return good for evil?'

'Do you mean so as to get on the right side of God?'

There was a silence. Then Georges went on : 'I listened to the Boches singing hymns and praying in the church. And Julie Cange and her babies were lying outside, not yet buried. And I thought that if they could please God by singing hymns after doing that, then I didn't want anything to do with Him . . . but you don't believe in all that rot, do you, M. Lanfrey?'

'Well, I don't actually believe in God . . .' Pierre hesitated and seemed embarrassed. He went on : 'But I do believe that one should return good for evil.'

'Nobody else does. There wouldn't be a war. We should just give the whole of France to the Germans if we all believed that. Anyway, what does Joseph matter to you? He hasn't done you any harm. He hasn't eaten your cat.'

'Well, Georges, you may be right about good and evil. I don't really know. I certainly wouldn't give France to the Boches and I would be fighting now if it weren't for this.' Pierre held up the steel hook and the empty sleeve fell back exposing the steel shaft. He saw that he must try another tack – perhaps a more truthful one, or at any rate less idealistic.

'I feel that since the invasion we in Dorlotte are all one family. We must stick together. I don't care about Joseph, the man, but he belongs here.'

'Dorlotte would be better off without him,' said Georges.

'Probably it would. But we have got him and we have to stand by him. Marcelle – Madame Duvernois – feels just as I do. So while I came to try and get you to give Joseph a warning, she has walked into Blaye and is paying Mère Richard back the money if she agrees to drop the charge against Joseph.'

'Good Lord! How did she get the money out of Joseph? Hadn't he spent it? He won't be where I think he is, unless he has bought himself a bottle or two. Absinthe what's more.'

'No. We haven't either of us seen Joseph. Marcelle is paying the money out of her own pocket. I shall squeeze what I can out of Joseph and we'll have a whip-round to make it up. If everyone gave a franc or two, it would probably cover it.'

Georges sat on his stone wall thinking and said nothing and Pierre Lanfrey stood silently watching him. At last Georges asked: 'Would you be doing the same for me, if it were I who had stolen the money?'

'Yes, Georges.'

'But I haven't a wife and children. And don't you think that if I stole, I ought to be punished? That I ought to suffer for it?'

'I think that all of us in Dorlotte have suffered enough. And our sufferings aren't over by any means what with the winter coming.' Georges sat for some time longer in thought. Then he looked up and said:

'All right, M. Lanfrey. I'll find Joseph if I can and keep him out of harm's way until tomorrow. I think that you and Madame Duvernois understand things better than other people. I don't know whether I agree about Joseph. But I'm on your side and will be ruled by you.' He stood up and they shook hands.

Georges wheeled Pierre Lanfrey's barrow to the sandpit

that afternoon, loaded it with sand and only then went to look behind the bushes that grew at the back, where there had been an older working. As he expected Joseph was there, lying on his back, his fly buttons undone, snoring. There was an almost empty bottle of absinthe beside him. Georges went up and inspected him critically. He lifted one of Joseph's arms and let it drop. The unconscious man did not stir and the noise and tempo of his stertorous breathing did not alter. Georges left him and wheeled the barrow load of sand back to his cabin. He had long known that when Joseph went on a drinking bout, which was about every six weeks, he went alone to the sandpit and stayed there until it was over. He always went out of doors, except in very cold weather, because if he were at home his wife would snatch the bottle and as likely as not drink half of it and start knocking him and the children about.

Later that evening, as dusk was falling, Georges walked over to Pierre Lanfrey's. The policeman was standing, holding his bicycle, sometimes putting a foot on the pedal and then thinking of some last thing he wanted to say and taking it off again. Pierre stood smiling inscrutably and listening. This had been going on for half an hour. Georges did not hesitate but walked up to the two men. 'Can I have the wheelbarrow first thing tomorrow morning? I'll bring it back by ten o'clock,' he said.

Pierre nodded.

'Hullo, young feller-me-lad. I wonder if you can help me? You know Joseph d'Oex, don't you?' said the sergeant.

'Yes, sergeant. And I have a complaint to make against him.'

'That's interesting.' The sergeant reached for the notebook in his breast pocket. 'Well, what is it?'

'He stole my tom cat and killed him and they ate him as jugged hare.' The policeman burst out laughing.

'There were exceptional circumstances,' said Pierre Lanfrey. 'It was during the German occupation.'

61

'Exceptional circumstances! I want to see him punished for it,' said Georges.

'You'll see him punished all right. But I shan't add cat-eating to the charge against him. If anything makes the judge laugh it always makes him more lenient when he passes sentence. I've noticed it scores of times.'

'There will have to be an indemnity for such incidents during the German occupation,' said Pierre Lanfrey. Both he and the policeman were near laughter.

'Well, I bet you Joseph gets off. That bastard always does. Anyway, I shall never speak to him again,' said Georges.

'When did you see him last?' asked the sergent.

'I haven't spoken to him since I found out about my tom cat. Oh, the time I last saw him? I'm not quite sure of the time. But he was dead drunk. Georges held out his hand and the sergent shook it, and Georges walked off, his face dark with anger.

'Fine young feller. Wanted to bring a charge about a tom cat! Damned funny. But I've heard he stood out well, when the Boches were here. . . . Well, it's getting dark. I'll be back on the job tomorrow.' The sergent held out his hand to Pierre who shook it. Then he mounted his bicycle and freewheeled down the hill.

Except for the whip-round to which old Conduchet contributed three times as much as anyone else, the incident of Joseph's larceny was closed.

After the fortnight that Madame Salmon had promised to keep her, Brigitte was fetched home by her father. She was a tall, very beautiful girl with a rosy complexion, fair hair and blue eyes, who at sixteen was almost physically mature. As she had a strong character and did not hesitate to say what she thought, she seemed almost like a grown-up woman. She loved her father and when he appeared unexpectedly, she flung her arms round his neck. Pierre worshipped her, which was perhaps the reason why she was the only person who caused him real unhappiness.

62

Pierre had walked out most of the way to Bar-le-Duc. Now he and Brigitte were being driven back with a cartload of young pigs being delivered to old Conduchet. Conversation was hardly possible. Before they started home she had asked her father about the details of the German occupation and had flushed with anger. On arrival she followed her mother down into the cellar, lit by two candles, where Pierre proposed that his entire family should spend the winter. Brigitte scrambled out scarlet with rage and turned on her father fiercely.

'Papa, I think that you are insane. How do you expect anyone to live in that hole? And why should you? The whole of France is wide open to us. We can go to Marseilles, to Lyons, to Bordeaux. You can get a job anywhere now all the men have been called up for the army. Why wait for the Boches to come back here, which is quite possible? I at all events shall go back to Bar. Madame Salmon will be pleased to have me until I can get a job.'

Pierre turned away to hide his feelings and Brigitte went on: 'Explain, please, why you want to stay in this hole in the ground with my mother and sister. It's damp. You'll die of cold. What possesses you?'

Pierre found that he could not say that he was staying partly because the poor and the old and the mothers with children who had nowhere to go, would need someone like him who could speak for them to the authorities. He said quietly:

'I know it seems awful. It is awful. But the place belongs to me and I've got to tidy it up.' Brigitte almost spat at him and he went on: 'Of course you are free to go back to Madame Salmon, if you prefer. But promise to keep in touch You must write to us every week.'

'Tidy up a rubbish heap! I am sure, Papa, that you could earn good money anywhere. I expect they would be glad to have you as a pilot in Algiers again – or in any French port. We could live in Africa until the war is over.'

Pierre felt that he could not argue with this vehement creature. He smiled awkwardly, waved his steel hook and went off to look for some boards to knock up a rabbit hutch. Madame Blanchard was being given a doe rabbit by her cousin in Blaye and had nowhere to put her where the rats would not get at her.

Jeanne, who had been listening to her daughter's outburst, turned on her directly Pierre was out of earshot.

'What a way to talk to your father, you wretched girl! You ought to be ashamed. Don't you understand that he feels it is his duty to stay? A duty to help rebuild what has been destroyed and to stay and help the people who have lost everything.'

'If you talk about duty – I should say that a wonderful man like my father would do a lot more for France by taking a job as a harbour pilot, or come to that as a schoolteacher, than by shovelling up a lot of rubbish. Anyway I had to tell him what I think.'

Jeanne secretly wondered if Brigitte were not right and this made her angry as she knew the thought was disloyal.

'You conceited girl! Nobody expects you to do anything. You weren't here when the Germans came, so you can't understand what your father feels and what I feel too. You are selfish and disloyal.'

'So I am a disloyal daughter because I want my father and mother and my little sister to live through the winter without catching pneumonia. I won't say any more.'

Ten days later when they had heard that Madame Salmon would be pleased to have her, Brigitte got a lift back to Bar. Pierre stopped Doctor Bergeroux at the crossroads as he was driving to a confinement in Givry and the doctor called in on the way back to pick up Brigitte.

CHAPTER FOUR

Until the invasion, Eglantine Constant, Veuve Turpin Lanfrey had been a quiet, dignified and almost immobile figure, living in her two-roomed cabin. In one room she cooked, ate, spent all her time and slept. In the other room she stored the few possessions she had acquired in a long life. She was dressed and had breakfasted and had sat down to go on with the piece of lace she was making, when a German soldier flung open the door and shouted: 'Heraus!' at her.

Eglantine took off her spectacles, put them in their case, put the case in her bag, rolled up the lace and put that in her bag, stood up and 'made an arm', lifting her elbow. The German who had been watching her pointed to the door. Eglantine pointed to her arm and the German came in, took it and helped her outside. She stood outside while they set fire to her cabin and watched it burn. The sight took fifteen years off her life – an effect which she demonstrated immediately. A young German lieutenant saw her and came up and apologised to her in French. He was very sorry indeed, but orders were orders and there was no help for it. Eglantine turned on him and said: 'I remember 1870. I was still a handsome woman then though I was over forty. A German soldier who was billeted in our farm asked me to give him a kiss. Do you know what my reply was? I'll whisper it.'

The German, amused and condescending, bent down to the old woman and Eglantine smacked him on the face as hard as she could.

'Yes, that was my reply to you barbarians!'

She spent the first night of the occupation in the communal

wash-house, the next four days in Pierre Lanfrey's cellar, after which she walked alone to Conduchet's farm leaning on two sticks and timing it so as to arrive as old Conduchet was sitting down to the midday meal with his two married daughters, his unmarried daughter Germaine, his daughter-in-law Bette, his four grandchildren and two of his farm labourers who always ate at their master's table in the middle of the day. Old Conduchet stood up and embraced her. 'Lay a place for my aunt,' he said.

'I am glad you remember that I am one of your family. No, I shall not sit down unless you agree to turn your rabbits out of the stone house they occupy and let me live in it until I get a house of my own again. I would not ask you for it except that I am too old to live underground. I shall have to put up with it for eternity very soon.'

'But my dear aunt – where shall I put my rabbits?'

'Put them in a cellar. Rabbits are used to burrows.'

'I would do anything to oblige you but . . .'

'So that's settled. Your mother was my favourite niece, so I have a right to your rabbit hutch!' Whereupon old Eglantine sat down at the table, burst out laughing, and took a spoonful of soup.

She stayed on and supervised while the rabbits were put into new quarters and the building in which they had been living was scrubbed out and the earth floor swept clean. Monsieur Conduchet found a portable stove which had been lying unused since he had given up keeping sheep ten years before : it was for the shepherd's hut in the lambing season – and he and Achille Durand installed it. His daughters brought a bed out of the attic and an old armchair. Eglantine gave her new abode time to dry after the scrubbing, and moved in next morning. All she had in the world were the clothes she was wearing, and the bag containing her spectacles, the piece of lace she was making and the bobbins for making it – and her purse containing three francs and sixty-two centimes in copper.

Once installed where she could live, if not in comfort, at all events without fear of illness from living in a cellar or death from exposure, Eglantine began to take a part in village life far greater than before the invasion. Her first act was to offer a good home to Sylvie Turpin, her great-grand-daughter. Sylvie was only too glad to get out of the over-crowded cellar in which she and her mother and sister were jammed. A pallet made of an old door raised on stones and covered with a palliasse of straw was installed for her in the rabbit mansion. She found her great-grandmother very good company and in a short time picked up more about the love affairs of the preceding seventy years in the village than she could quite keep track of.

'How is young Emile making out?' the old woman asked her great-granddaughter one day. Sylvie could not think of any young Emile; then she remembered: 'Oh, that little boy. His mother took him with the rest of them to lodgings in Bar.'

'I mean Emile Carré, you goose.'

Emile Carré was sixty, a hopeless alcoholic, but to Eglantine he was a young man. Sylvie stared and laughed.

'His house is burned down like everyone else's. But you know the privy there is at the bottom of the garden? It's next to Celestin Roux's garden. Of course his house was burned also.'

'Of course I do. One of the wonders of the village. The Carrés had a large family and Jules Carré, the father, made a privy with six holes of different sizes, so all the children could do their business at the same time before they were sent off to school. Why, I can't have been in it for fifty years and more.'

'Well, it's still there and the Germans didn't burn it. So old Emile has laid planks along the bench over the holes and straw on top of that and he lies there all day I believe.'

'Somebody ought to look after him. He has never done any real work after he came back from shepherding in the Vosges. His girl married another fellow and he went off as a shepherd and stayed away twenty-five years. That's when he got the wolfskin he's so proud of. I always liked the boy. But ever since he came back he's never done a stroke of work. Always reading books. He had a big box of them. I suppose they have been burned. He's probably lying in that privy without a bite to eat. You go and see how he is, dearie. Take Brigitte Lanfrey or one of the other girls with you.'

Sylvie always thought of Emile Carré as a hedgehog. He had a hedgehog's sharp little eyes buried in his face, a long snout with a tip to it that moved a little and a furtive way of looking this way and that. And then there was his dirt: ingrained dirt. Impossible to get rid of it. Hedgehogs are extremely dirty animals: it's all black in between the quills. Because of course they can't lick themselves clean like cats on account of the sharp prickles. And just as a hedgehog rolls himself up and is completely uncommunicative, so it was with Emile when he had passed out with the drink.

Sylvie went to the Lanfreys and found Brigitte reading a book. But when she told her that Eglantine had said they must look after Emile, Brigitte refused point blank. 'I've got more important things to do than look after a disgusting old drunkard. It's not anybody's responsibility but his own. And anyway I'm not staying in this hole: I'm leaving for Bar as soon as I hear from Madame Salmon.' Sylvie had to go elsewhere. Finally she, Suzanne Leblond and Julie Fournier took on the task of looking after old Emile – cleaning up his converted privy once a week and taking him a basket of food, and if they could get hold of one of his shirts, they washed it.

The old man tried to be sober on Thursday, the day when the girls came. He would totter out into the open air and Sylvie would pull the straw off the bench with the six holes in it, carry it into the garden and set it alight while Suzanne and Julie came with bundles of clean straw brought from Conduchet's stack yard, taken when the farmer wasn't looking.

One day the old fellow misbehaved. Sylvie was in front, the other two girls a long way behind. Of course Sylvie had seen them as long as she could remember. Her father's, her uncle's, men doing pipi, not always against a wall. Those of the boys her own age and sweet little boy babies. Then horses and donkeys that let them hang down ever so far, like black rubber hose pipes for filling a cistern. And then when Georges had kissed her after she took him the cat's skin, she had felt it round and hard, pressed against her, in spite of his cotton trousers and her frock. That was something altogether different, and though she had run away, she thought about it with excitement.

And then this! Why is what is beautiful in one man, hideous in another?

'Eh! What's going on here? None of that, Emile. You mind your ps and qs when we girls are here. See!'

Suzanne might have been talking with equal confidence to a vicious horse in its stable, or to a boar pig in its sty.

And old Emile, blinking his eyes rapidly, murmured:

'I know, I know. Didn't mean any harm.'

'They send men to prison for that, you horrid old beast. And before Sylvie! She's too good to live on the same earth as you bit of old filth.'

'Shut up, Suzanne,' said Sylvie for Emile seemed suddenly terrified. And Sylvie went on: 'It's all right, Emile. We are good friends, only do be nice, won't you?'

Suzanne wasn't appeased. 'All right, if Sylvie says so, you are forgiven this once. But if there's any more of that I'll tell my Grandpa and he'll come and give you a hiding.'

Old Emile was still trembling, so Sylvie said: 'Tell us how you killed the wolf while we are changing the straw.'

Georges had finished his little cabin. He had roofed it with a thick thatch of rye straw. There was no window and the hurdle he employed as a door when he was out was seldom used at other times There was no fireplace, but acting on a tip from Michel Fournier, the roadman, he had provided himself with a large bucket pierced all round with holes, in which he burned charcoal and bits of old charred beams and rafters taken from the ruins. On this he could cook his supper and roast chestnuts. In the evenings Sylvie often visited him, bringing as an excuse a couple of eggs she had stolen, some home-dried prunes, a bag of haricots and a couple of slices of pork belly she had been given, or allowed to take from the huge kitchen in Conduchet's farm.

'Before the Boches came, I killed two pigs at Michaelmas and they lasted till Christmas. Now I kill a pig once a fort-night and we are always short of bacon!' the old farmer complained. But his gruff manner was belied by a twinkle in his eye. He took pride both in his stinginess – he had a reputation for driving the hardest bargains in the district and for counting every centime – and in his generosity as the sole survivor and representative of the open-handed days of yore. And he seemed never able to make up his mind for which quality he wished to be renowned.

After bringing Georges her little basket of loot, Sylvie often lingered in the cabin. There were no chairs, but Georges had made himself a couch of pine branches laid on a frame of rafters. On this he had spread a thick layer of straw and then sacking. Sylvie and Georges would sit side by side on this in the dark, lit only by the glow of the brazier until Georges put his arms round her and somehow they lost their balance and found it more comfortable lying in each other's arms. They kissed, long and passionately. But that was as far as their lovemaking went. For Georges was aware that he was older – already a man – and that Sylvie was a mere child and in need of his protection. Sometimes her emotion overcame her and she clung to him desperately, her young body crying out to his for the act of love. But though Georges was himself fainting with desire, he always managed to control himself, and when Sylvie had somewhat recovered he would pull her on to her feet and accompany her back to the rabbit mansion.

Winter came. Every day when the ground was not frozen hard, and there was no snow, Pierre Lanfrey was at work with his wheelbarrow, shifting rubble. The roof and upper floors of his house with the division walls had fallen inwards so that there was a great mound of tiles and plaster and stone walls, burned rafters, ends of joists, together with broken bedsteads and the relics of household goods and furniture. All this had to be moved away before he could get to where he hoped to put a skylight in the floor over the cellar. It was slow work for a man with only one hand. Pierre worked slowly and methodically, sorting out such squared stones as could be used again when it came to rebuilding his house.

He often paused to pick up some familiar object, melted and distorted by the heat. Some things had survived and might come in useful. So he would pick out two metal and stone-ware casters, all that was left of a favourite armchair, or some long nails that could be hammered out straight and used again. When his barrow was full, either of squared stones or of rubbish, he would slip the hook that was his right hand through the loop on the barrow handle, then lift and, staggering a little, wheel it to where in the garden stones were arranged, or rubbish dumped.

Pierre had become the representative of the village. There were constant complaints, usually of unequal treatment by the authorities, and all such were brought first of all to him. He would listen quietly, sometimes ask a question, and the trouble often ended and went no further after he had said: 'It would be better for you to think it over before taking any action.' He would add: 'I will think about it also.'

Occasionally he was determined, vigorous, even fierce. He heard, before anyone else, that the authorities were planning to order the evacuation of the whole village – to save money spent on services – and he at once drafted a letter which, signed by almost everyone left in the village, he sent to the Préfet and to the Deputy for the department and to three Paris newspapers. In it he pointed out that Conduchet, Zins and Muller had perfectly good houses. The evacuation could therefore be only partial and the services now given to the village would still be required for those households. He also asked if there was any law enabling the civil authorities to evict French citizens from their own property. The inhabitants of Dorlotte would fight the case in the courts. The military authorities did not object to them and had been helpful.

When winter came many hectares of sugar beet had to be left to rot in the fields, as there was not enough labour to lift them. Even if the village had not been burned it is doubtful if the whole crop could have been harvested as all the men of military age had been mobilised, most of them not until just after the wheat had been got in. And after the destruction of the village, many of the older men and the women who might have lent a hand had moved away. Those that remained found the task of coping with a troglodyte existence left them with little energy or time for field work.

Old Conduchet went out and worked all the daylight hours. Georges, who had sworn never to work again with Joseph, and Conduchet who had sworn never to employ the wretched fellow again, worked side by side with him until the first hard frost came and caught the roots, making them worthless. While it lasted Georges earned good money, as old Conduchet paid him a man's wages.

'You work faster than Joseph and cut the tops as accurately as I do. I would be ashamed to pay you less.'

The sentiment was gratifying and Georges was pleased – but he knew that Conduchet did actually pay him less. Joseph was entitled to a litre of free milk and to potatoes and swedes and faggots of kindling wood, privileges that Georges did not get. But a hard frost came early and the owners of the fields of sugar beet saw one of their main sources of income ruined : the frost-bitten blackened roots stood in dark rows in the fields until they could be ploughed in, the following spring.

What was a ruinous loss for many men was plenty and paradise for the wild swine. They came out – sounders of half grown *marcassins* led by the old sows, and solitary fierce old boars – in droves from the forest and rioted in the fields. There were few men with guns and fewer with permits to use them.

By January enough permits and guns had been obtained and old Conduchet organised a wild boar shoot. It was held on a Sunday as is usual and also because the older boys would be available as beaters.

While working beside his employer, lifting sugar beet, Georges had told him about the existence of his father's gun and Conduchet had managed to get a permit for it. Thus he was able to go among the guns and not with the beaters. The day broke fine and cold: at ten o'clock the two parties had assembled in Conduchet's farmyard. The guns were: Conduchet, Lorcey, Michel Fournier, Dufour the postman, Achille Durand (one of Conduchet's labourers), Rouault, Muller and Georges. Conduchet and Muller each had two dogs, Fournier and Dufour one. There were twelve beaters: ten boys, captained by Rousillon who had a gun but no permit, and Joseph who had neither. Pierre Lanfrey had been invited but did not come. In any case he had no gun and with his one arm could not fire one. Everyone was impatient. 'We are all here. What are we waiting for?' was repeated by different people several times.

Georges stood with the guns. He felt shy but it was a great moment in his life. And then suddenly, as old Conduchet gave the signal to move off and Muller's dogs, which were not on the leash, bounded forward with ecstatic cries, everything became terrible. For he suddenly realised that the cartridges he had brought with him were not loaded with buckshot. His number six would scarcely pierce the skin of a wild boar. The situation was appalling and in desperation he said to Achille Durand, the man who was nearest to him: 'My cartridges aren't loaded with buckshot.' Achille was not a bad fellow, but he was not noted for tact.

'Our Georges here is setting out to shoot wild boars with birdshot.'

Georges's plight and his childish ignorance and incompetence were exposed to all the sportsmen of Dorlotte.

'Well, it's no good your coming with the guns. You go with the beaters, my lad,' said Muller.

'What's your trouble? No buckshot cartridges, Georges? I've not got many myself but I'll lend you a couple,' said old Rouault.

'You keep those if you've not got many. I'll take care of Georges,' said Michel Fournier, taking a box of twelve out of his bag. 'If you get a wild boar with every one of those I'll not ask you to pay me back.'

Laughing and joking they went along the road to the forest. When they got near it, old Conduchet called a halt, and ordered Muller to put his dogs on the leash.

'They stay at heel without. I've trained them myself,' said Muller.

'If you don't do as I say, you'll have to go with the beaters,' said Conduchet.

'That's a fine way to talk. Thinks he's the Emperor William, does he?' grumbled Muller, but he took a piece of cord out of his pocket and slipped it through the dogs' collars, and they went on.

Michel Fournier was chuckling in high glee and whispered to Rouault: 'Conduchet overheard what Muller said to the boy about going with the beaters and he has ticked him off properly.'

Georges went into the forest feeling as though he were treading on air.

The beaters were lined up along the road running through the forest, spaced twenty-five metres apart and waiting to move until the guns had got into position. Led by Conduchet and keeping well away from the forest, they walked down the side of a field of what had been sugar beets but which

74

were now rows of blackened stumps. In two places there were wide saucer-shaped depressions where the wild swine had wallowed in communal mud-baths. Conduchet stopped. He had arranged that the men with dogs should alternate with those without. One by one they stole silently across the field to enter a ride cut through the thick undergrowth of the forest, parallel to the road. Each dropped out at an interval of about sixty metres from the man behind. Georges had been put at the far end of the line, furthest into the forest. Next to him was Michel Fournier, then Rouault, then Conduchet. He had hardly taken up his position, standing a little way back from the ride, when a whistle sounded. It was the signal for the beaters to start. An immensely long wait followed. Georges could hear the beaters thwacking their sticks against the bushes and trunks of trees and giving shouts and catcalls designed to frighten any creatures that there might be. A hare appeared on the edge of the wood, saw Georges and ran back. Suddenly at the other end of the line there was a shot, followed quickly by three more. Georges stepped forward to look, but Michel Fournier put a finger to his lips and made a gesture for him to stand back. There were suddenly four shots, coming almost simultaneously from Rouault and Conduchet and Fournier's dog gave a trembling whine, which was followed by the yelps and bayings of Conduchet's dogs which he had released. Fournier released his dog and turned and ran into the forest and Georges at once followed his example. The dogs were baying and howling and from their cries he could tell that the boar was moving diagonally across the line. Georges struggled desperately to burst through the undergrowth to head him off. But he could see nothing. Suddenly the character of the forest changed and Georges almost fell out of the undergrowth into a clear space in which large oaks and chestnuts were growing. In front of him was a large dark animal with the three dogs surrounding it. One of them – Fournier's bitch – flew forward and caught hold of the boar by the ear. It was impossible to shoot because of the dogs.

75

Suddenly the boar stopped and jerked backwards throwing Fournier's bitch over his shoulder onto the ground in front of him.

There was a howl of pain as the boar ripped the dog with his tusks, and next moment the animal had disappeared behind an oak followed by the other two hounds. They dared not tackle it. Before Georges reached the bitch, Fournier was on his knees beside her. 'Pierrette,' he said and touched her. Georges could see that her back was broken as she tried to drag herself towards her master. Old Fournier felt her body gently. Then he stood up, picked up his gun and shot her. The charge of buckshot broke the skull and death was instantaneous. The old man slung his gun over his shoulders and regardless of the blood soaking her fur and the brains falling out of her head, picked up the dead dog and walked slowly back towards the village. He clasped her awkwardly in both arms in front of him as a man carries a baby. Occasionally he shifted his burden to his left arm so as to be able to wipe away his tears with his right sleeve.

Georges waited. He felt that the day's sport was over and had no wish to continue. Yet he thought that perhaps he should try and overtake the other two dogs and the wild boar. But as he stood uncertain, one of Conduchet's hounds came limping out of the forest, followed soon after by the other. Georges went back to the end of the ride where the guns and beaters had gathered. Muller had shot a sow and Achille Durand a fine *marcassin*, or half-grown boar. The legs of the dead swine were tied together. Two poles were cut from the undergrowth and hanging from them the game was carried back to the village.

The problem for people living in cellars through the winter in Northern France is to keep warm. When it was not raining they lived above ground during the daytime, each group having its hearth with a log fire burning where the women cooked and round which the children huddled. Even in a hard frost they could keep warm outside unless there was a fierce wind. But when there was driving rain or snow, it was impossible. They put up little shanties of sacking or sheets of corrugated iron in the back of which the children squatted and in the mouth of which there burned a brazier made out of a big pail with holes knocked in the sides. On this the women cooked.

But a brazier cannot be taken down into a cellar because of the poisonous charcoal fumes. At nightfall the women filled a number of litre wine bottles with hot water – one for each member of the group, and these had to last till morning when the embers of the log fire could be blown up, or in bad weather the brazier lighted.

In the first months they found enough fuel in the ruins of their homes: charred beams and rafters, bits of outhouses. Then fuel began to run short and they turned their eyes to the forest.

Georges was working at carting sand one beautiful morning at the beginning of winter when the postman stopped to ask where he could find Madame Pierron.

'Madeleine? She's down in the forest with all the other younger women,' answered Georges.

The postman had a paper which she had to sign: some relative had sent her some money. He would have to take it back. Georges, however, persuaded him to come to the forest. He would show him where they were working and it would save Madelaine Pierron from having to walk six kilometres to the post office and back. There was no proper office at Blaye. So the postman bicycled down the hill to the forest with Georges standing on the step and holding on to his shoulders. When they reached the forest, Georges jumped off and the postman dismounted and they walked down the path to the clearing.

There had been a frost that night, but the sun was shining and in the brilliant light the fallen oak leaves sparkled and the big trunks of the larger trees threw long white shadows of hoar frost. In the distance they saw old Rouault with a gang of women clustered round a felled oak tree. They were hard at work. Two with a crosscut saw were cutting off the top of the tree, others with hand saws were cutting the bigger branches into logs and two with billhooks were lopping off the smaller branches for faggots. None of them looked up or noticed the postman and Georges until they were quite close.

'Madame Pierron, Madeleine,' shouted the postman. A young woman of about twenty-five looked up, and laying aside the heavy axe with which she had been splitting the larger branches already sawn into logs, walked up to them. Her face was flushed, her arms bare. She had tied a kerchief over her head, from underneath which fair reddish ringlets had escaped down the back of her neck. She was wearing a pair of men's boots too big for her and her skirts were belted up to the knee showing a pair of sturdy bare calves. Her forehead and face were wet with perspiration and grains of sawdust had stuck to it here and there. Madeleine's eyes flashed and she showed white, even teeth as she smiled and asked:

'What is it, Monsieur Dufour?'

'Someone's sent you some money. Sign here.'

'That will be my old granny in Troyes. It's too bad of her. She goes short herself to help me when I don't need it.'

Old Rouault hobbled up to them.

'See my team of woodmen? These girls work like men,' he boasted.

'And what are you doing, old friend?' asked the postman.

'I'm making the withies for faggots,' and Rouault pointed to where a few dozen wands of hazel were laying.

'Where did you get the saws and axes?' asked the postman.

'Michel Fournier went into Belmont and they lent us the crosscut and what we needed. There are decent people living there who are always ready to help.' This was a reflection on the inhabitants of Blaye, who though living nearer than Belmont were not.

'The women are a lot of evil-minded bitches and the men are tom cats,' was what the people of Dorlotte said of them. Then as M. Dufour, the postman, lived in Blaye, Rouault said to be friendly:

'Your daughter's over there, haven't you noticed?'

A young woman was sitting on a stump a little way apart giving the breast to her baby.

The postman's face lit up with pleasure and he hurried over to greet her. Near her an older woman had lit a fire and was warming up soup for their midday meal.

Georges saw all these things going on with his eyes. He stood watching, but the scene made no impression on him at the time. It must however have sunk in, for a year later it all came back to him in every detail and he reflected that he had seldom seen women so happy, or a young woman more beautiful than Madeleine Pierron with her sparkling eyes, brushing the grains of sawdust out of her eyebrows and off her red cheeks and laughing before she took the postman's pencil and painstakingly signed her name. What went almost unnoticed at the time and seemed perfectly natural had become idyllic when remembered on the battlefield.

It was getting dark when the party of women came back, some dragging branches and others carrying faggots on their shoulders. Their voices went ringing through the frosty air as they chattered and then called out good night as they separated.

For the rest of the month Marie Durand was fully employed carting logs to every cellar where they would be needed. Before the snow came everyone had a woodpile which was carefully covered over with bits of tin or sacks weighted down with tiles to keep it dry.

It was a wet day with driving rain but a warm westerly wind. Georges had been digging sand for Pierre Lanfrey who had wheeled several barrowloads up the hill. They had

79

expected the rain to stop, but after two hours they were so wet that they decided to knock off work, and went out onto the road to walk up the hill to Dorlotte. Georges was wheeling the last load of sand.

Suddenly the shrill sound of trumpets rang out; then with the clatter of hooves, General Humbert's mounted bodyguard came riding towards them, on the way from advanced head-quarters to the rear. Lean brown horses, streaked with almost black patches where they were wettest; riders in long blue cloaks with phrygian helmets covered in blue cloth; young men with hawklike features down whose backs hung dripping tresses of horsehair and by whose sides hung long straight cavalry swords. The horsehair tresses hanging from their helmets gave the clean-shaven youths among them the aspect of Amazons. Here and there one of the horsetails was dyed red. They rode with a careless clatter down the road and Georges pushed the wheelbarrow on to the verge and he and Pierre Lanfrey waited until the squadron had passed by. Georges was suddenly inflamed with a military ardour he had never felt before, and gazed at every detail of their equipment as they walked their horses down the steep hill. When they reached the bottom the trumpet blew again and turning the corner of the road to Blaye, the squadron broke into a trot.

'That's beautiful. I would like to be one of those,' said Georges.

'You would be damned lucky if you were – advertising the war and dodging it – without being looked on as a shirker, which is what they really are,' said Pierre.

'Why do you insult them? They are splendid,' said Georges.

'For every one of those beautiful creatures there are a thousand wounded men hanging from the barbed wire, who die in torture and cannot be rescued. Those playboys know even less about real war than their general,' said Pierre savagely.

Georges digested these words as he walked beside Pierre

who was now pushing the wheelbarrow. Of course what he had said was true, and yet the boy could not forget those superbly romantic figures clattering down the hill and feeling his blood stirred by them – and a wave of pride because he was a Frenchman and soon he would join the army and be fighting to free the soil of France.

The winter was mercifully mild, yet the misery of women, young and old, crowded with babies and old men into cellars difficult to warm and even more difficult to ventilate, was very great. It was almost impossible to dry clothes once they got wet. But when there was a clear day with a wind, the whole area of the village of tumbled heaps of stone and rubbish, fluttered with garments of every sort, hung out on washing lines strung from one improvised post to another. And then when a storm or a shower came along, the women rushed out and snatched them down before they could get wetter than they were.

There was a shortage of everything – and then after years of grasping meanness, of exacting every centime that it was possible to squeeze out of his neighbours, old Conduchet suddenly became the most open-handed and generous man in the village. Everyone who came was entitled to a bale of straw once a week. Everyone who had not his own store of potatoes could come and fill a basket when the long pile, protected with straw under the earth against frost, was opened one day in the week. Everyone could have as many swedes as they wanted. And to some Conduchet personally gave a few eggs, and on special occasions a fowl, or a rabbit. And in spite of the fact that he had been a byword for close-fistedness nobody was surprised at his generosity and nobody was profuse in thanks. It was taken for granted, and that is how the old farmer liked it. He would have been embarrassed by thanks and have thought something had gone wrong.

So somehow, in spite of the misery, they managed, by helping each other. When Madame Thierry had a high fever,

Jeanne Lanfrey took the baby, Elise Turpin took Suzette aged three and Marcel aged four, and Marcelle Duvernois brought out medicine from Blaye and went in every morning and gave the sick woman some hot soup and tidied the cellar and emptied the slops. And then after Marcelle Duvernois had gone back to Blaye, Suzanne Leblond, or Julie Fournier, would look in last thing and see the invalid was comfortable for the night. There was, however, astonishingly little illness. Being out in all weathers during the daylight hours and working themselves to the bone seemed to keep them as healthy as gipsies.

CHAPTER FIVE

Spring came and with it many of those villagers who had lodged with relatives, or had taken rooms in the neighbourhood, came trudging out along all the roads that led to their former homes and gardens. By ten in the morning the village was alive with people digging and hoeing, or shovelling the debris of their homes into heaps that could one day be used for rebuilding or carted away. Soon smooth and neatly raked garden beds with little pegs, marking where parsnips and onions and leeks had already been sown, formed a curious contrast to the piles of rubbish and the heaps of stone – the homes to which these gardens belonged. With the advent of the gardeners, Dorlotte took on a positively gay and joyful look – particularly at midday when neighbours joined in groups and picnicked together.

One day when Georges was working with Pierre Lanfrey, there was the loud hammering splutter of an aeroplane engine and a little Morane monoplane fighter shot past very low down. The pilot waved and the plane disappeared into the sky over the forest near Belmont. In two minutes it was back, very high up so it seemed to them and then, as they watched, it dived towards them, pulled up, executed a perfect loop and then, without pausing, another half loop, rolling right side up when at the top of it. By then the little plane was again over the Belmont forest, but they could see it turn towards them and then come buzzing back. A power dive followed and the plane flattened out not twenty metres over their heads and disappeared in the direction from which it had come. It did not reappear.

'Your airman, I suppose,' said Pierre.

'He's very different when he's in the air,' said Georges.

There was a silence while Pierre turned back to levering up a block of stone that was too heavy for them to lift, and Georges pushed and guided it where it was to go. Then he said:

'So it was worth saving his life after all.'

Pierre was shocked at the implications of this remark.

'You don't mean that Georges. You would save anybody's life. You would have done the same if he had been a German.'

Georges looked at him and thought. After a time he said:

'I might have done then. But not now.'

'I think that you would, whatever you say,' said Pierre.

'No, I would let him burn. And that goes for a lot of Frenchmen too.'

'Who?'

'The fellow who murdered Jaurès for one. The men who made the war. And a lot of our generals.'

'If the circumstances arose . . .' began Pierre.

'They won't arise, worse luck. Those fellows keep themselves out of harm's way,' said Georges.

'Yet the other day you would have liked to have been in the bodyguard of one of them.'

'I think General Humbert is all right. He's holding the Boches.' But in his heart Georges knew there was a contradiction as there always must be in a war. His patriotism was intense and his feelings had been stirred by the general's bodyguard riding their horses down to Blaye. He would give anything to be one of them. At the same time he felt a vitriolic hatred for the war and for those who directed it. A hatred which did not prevent his longing for victory, for revenge and a desire to fight himself.

In the early summer the Germans launched an offensive in the Argonne and the sound of the guns became almost continuous. Every day either the French or the Germans made an attack during which fifty metres were captured, only to be

84

recaptured a few days later. The numbers of killed and wounded on the Argonne front ran into thousands. The road to the north echoed to the shuffle of exhausted troops being hurried along like flocks of sheep to the abattoir. Once again the sidings of the junction at Revigny were filled with hospital trains, end to end, packed with wounded men whose need to reach a hospital had to be delayed until there was a lull in the fighting, since shells for the artillery and cartridges and hand grenades for the infantry were the first priority.

Whatever they pretended, whatever courage inspired them, the people of Dorlotte were frightened. At any moment the French army might again be routed and the Germans come swarming back upon their heels. What was the point of growing rows of vegetables in their gardens if the new peas and the salads were to be eaten by invaders? But though all were afraid, none of them would admit their fears to each other, or let them interfere with their plans for reconstituting their gardens and one day rebuilding their homes. Some of them had already knocked together rabbit-hutches and wired in chicken runs, even though rabbits and chickens were almost unprocurable.

And those who got a breeding doe rabbit recognised that it would be a crime to kill and eat her progeny until their neighbours had one to breed from also.

One balmy day in early summer Captain Maurice Bloch marched at the head of his company of the Chasseurs Alpins in their full knickerbockers, but with steel helmets on their heads, instead of their big bérets, up the hill into Dorlotte.

He halted his men by the crossroads, ordered them to stack rifles and then led them round the village, or a part of it. He then stood on the steps of the ruined *mairie* and addressed them as follows. Georges Roux and Pierre Lanfrey had stopped work in order to listen.

'I have halted you here, my boys, not to give you a rest, but so that you would look about you and that these ruins should teach their lesson. Hatred. You will harden your hearts and go into the battle determined to kill and revenge the innocent, and the devastated homes of France, on the barbarians. Each of you has a bayonet. Before many days it must run with blood. Give no mercy. Remember the sufferings of our people living among these heaps of stone. The enemy awaits us and La Patrie relies on you to drive these monsters from her soil and to liberate Alsace and Lorraine. Blood is a good manure. Let German blood fertilise the fields of France. I have said enough. To arms. March.'

The soldiers who had been resting, squatting on the ground, or leaning against the bank enclosing the church, and hoping that their captain would go on gassing for an hour, rose to their feet, picked up their rifles, formed ranks and marched out of the village.

'Wow! That was something like!' said Georges, who had been impressed by the earnest savagery in Captain Bloch's little speech.

'Would you feel happier if you knew that a village in the Rhineland was going to be laid waste like Dorlotte?' asked Pierre.

'It would be only justice,' said Georges.

'Nonsense. It would only be more cruelty and more injustice, added to what has already been committed,' said Pierre.

'But surely you would be glad to know that our men were in the Rhineland?' asked Georges.

Pierre laughed. 'My God, that will be a happy day for us all!'

In the early summer a notice from the prefecture announced to the people of Dorlotte that huts would be erected in the village for all those who agreed to have the cost of the materials deducted from the sum eventually due to them as compensation for war damage. The buildings would be erected by an English benevolent society free of charge. This led to a good deal of discussion. It was, old Lorcey said,

86

'buying a pig in a poke'. The price of the materials was cheap. But what would the huts be like? And who could tell whether the English workmanship would enable them to keep out the weather? On the other hand old Rouault, who was a realist, pointed out that compensation for war damage was problematic. If the Germans won the war they would never see a centime of it. But if they accepted the huts, they would be getting some of it now. The Germans might come and burn them down later. But at least they would be getting what they most needed until then. Nobody would guard against defeat.

In the end practically all the villagers living either in Dorlotte, or in the neighbourhood, applied for the wooden huts to be supplied under these terms.

The huts themselves looked all right on paper. They were designed as one, two, three, or four-roomed buildings, and were adapted to the needs and numbers of a family. One old woman living alone could not put in for a four-roomed hut.

Bitter discussion broke out as to the priority in which they should be allotted. Marcelle Duvernois had put her name down first and was at the head of the queue, but it was felt that it would be an abominable injustice if she, who had a perfectly good lodging in Blaye, should get a hut before Madame Turpin with her children squashed into a small cellar, or Joseph d'Oex. Pierre Lanfrey was consulted and, after argument, his advice prevailed, although he pointed out that it would result in his being third on the list. Pierre said that those families who were actually living in Dorlotte should have priority over those living outside, and that, among them, priority should go by the number in the family needing to be housed. He admitted that this was hard upon old people living by themselves, but he thought the needs of children should come first. There was some growling, but his opinion was accepted.

When all this had been thrashed out there was a delay, and in ten days the whole proposal was forgotten. Then one morning, when everyone was helping in the hayfields, a lorry drove up and the first anyone was aware of were heaps of pine joists and the prefabricated sides of frame houses, dumped near the sites of the first huts due to be erected.

Next morning a lorry with eight young foreigners arrived and, with incredible speed, started putting up one of the huts. They were dressed in grey uniforms and looked curiously agile – like so many monkeys. Next day they engaged Georges Roux and old Rouault to help and a few days later they were joined by two elderly French Territorials in uniform – skilled carpenters in civil life, whose job it would be to put in the windows and hang the doors. The two territorials spoke with a Breton accent, were stand-offish, and took a room for themselves in Madame Zins's bistro. Everyone in the village rubbed their eyes and came to have a look.

'Why aren't they in the army?' was the obvious question which everyone asked about the young Englishmen.

Pierre Lanfrey had already asked the question of the representative of the prefecture and had the answer.

'The English have not got compulsory military service, and these boys belong to a pacifist religious sect.'

This was not good enough for Eglantine who had a strong prejudice against the English – the hereditary enemies. 'They have got us into a war with Germany, by pretending to be allies, and it is just another example of their perfidy for them not to have compulsory military service. Then their royal family is German. Their Queen is the aunt of the Emperor William.'

'I believe that Queen Victoria died some time ago and that the King of England is her grandson,' said Marcelle Duvernois in ironical tones.

'It is the same vicious breed. I know her son Edward sucked up to us, but it was only because he found that French girls were better in bed – more shame to them,' said Eglantine.

'It is no good fighting the Hundred Years War over again. And even that was before your time, Madame,' said the postman. This was thought to show a lack of politeness.

'I think they are shirkers and ought to be sent to Coventry,' said Muller. But Madame Turpin took him up short.

'Both you and Eglantine have roofs over your heads and can afford to talk like that. But the rest of us are thankful that they are building us huts out of good quality wood. I for one shall be glad not to spend another winter in my cellar.'

At first the English were quartered in Blaye and were brought out in a motor lorry. But then they built themselves one of the three-roomed huts in the Presbytery garden and lived entirely in the village. After that everyone got to know them and made friends. Madame Blanchard was glad to get a job to go in and cook their midday meal. There were eight of them, but only two could speak French. They were tidy, fresh-faced boys.

The one who spoke good French was unlike the others: a small unkempt figure, in spectacles, a clumsy and hopeless carpenter who hit his fingers with the hammer when he drove in a nail and could not saw down a pencilled line. The secret nailing of tongued and grooved matchboarding remained, for him, forever secret. But when any villager came to ask a question, or to make a complaint, this incompetent, called Bruce, was always summoned and as there were continual requests about the details and the progress of the building, he soon became the unofficial liaison officer of the *équipe*. Bruce could speak French well and, what was more unusual, could understand what the villagers said in the local accent.

An angry old woman would appear and begin to jabber at one of the young Englishmen: her rage would mount as he failed to reply. Then there would be a shout for Bruce and he would arrive with his dark brown wavy hair full of sawdust and a bloodstained rag wrapped round his left thumb, his gold spectacles awry, and in less than two minutes he and the old woman would be laughing and when he took off his spectacles, she would insist on taking them out of his hands in order to wipe and polish them carefully for him on the cleanest corner of her apron and then go off chuckling with a story to tell. 'That boy Brus! He's a rascal! One can't lose one's temper with him!'

'He gets away with it! I can never keep my face straight,' her crony would reply.

Within a fortnight of their going to live in Dorlotte, the village had taken the English boys to its heart: that is to say the older women who formed public opinion and were the censors of morals had done so. Their approbation took a practical form they supplied the *équipe anglaise* with vegetables and fruit.

Madame Blanchard, who cooked the midday meal let it be known what would be wanted and arrived with her basket loaded with produce culled from the village gardens. Madame Thomassin would supply broad beans and new potatoes and Madame Turpin lettuces and red currants one day, Madame Leblanc carrots and a cucumber the next and so on, turn and turn about throughout the week. They were never allowed to run short. Thus the people of Dorlotte provided more than half the food for eight hungry young men – free of charge. For when Madame Blanchard was asked about payment, she scouted the suggestion.

'Everyone is only too happy to help.'

The English boys were never told whose courgettes or haricots they were eating; none of the donors claimed recognition for her generosity. The gifts were anonymous: a self-imposed tax upon the village.

Eggs were a different matter and so was the fowl provided on one occasion for a distinguished visitor. They had their market value and were paid for.

As soon as Pierre Lanfrey's hut was finished, Brigitte arrived home and said that she was going to stay. She did not volunteer much information, but did say that it was no fun being a girl on one's own with all the soldiers about. She had decided to pass an examination to enable her to be trained as a school teacher and brought back a lot of books with her and worked steadily.

Her arrival made Pierre very happy, but the other girls and women in the village said she was stand-offish. Only once did she have a quarrel with her father, which was on the subject of Georges Roux.

'Why is that hideous boy always hanging about? And why do you encourage the horrible creature?' she asked her father one day after Georges had borrowed the wheelbarrow.

Pierre turned on his daughter angrily. 'Don't speak like that about one of my friends. Georges is the bravest man or boy in the village. I admire his character.'

'Do you mean because he pulled that airman out of his plane with a pitchfork?'

'That is only one occasion on which he showed courage.'

'Well, Papa, you must admit he's hideous to look at and he's so dirty that he smells unpleasant.'

'Brigitte, I'm ashamed of you. What can he do in these conditions?' Brigitte pretended to go back to her book. But she was in tears.

On one occasion when Pierre was hammering brads into the sole of an old boot with his left hand while he held it down on a stone with his hook, Georges was standing beside him watching. Every little while he would wipe his nose on his sleeve and spit. Suddenly Brigitte said to him :

'Don't do that. Use a handkerchief.'

'I haven't got a handkerchief,' replied Georges.

'Well, don't wipe your nose on your sleeve. It's a disgusting dirty habit. And don't spit either.'

Georges looked at her in wonder. Pierre, secretly amused, pretended not to have heard this exchange. That evening Georges cut the tail off his shirt and used that as a handkerchief until he could get hold of something better. He deeply resented Brigitte's criticism of his habits. At the same time he was impressed by the way in which, almost alone among the village girls, she kept herself spotlessly clean. Soon afterwards

Georges began to imitate the English boys who used to wash themselves behind a bush in the Presbytery garden in a bucket of water taken from the fountain.

Brigitte liked her father's other favourite: the young Englishman Bruce, even though his personal habits were not quite up to her bourgeois standards. But although he would scratch himself in public, his manners to other people were always perfect. Georges on the other hand would laugh rudely, without any consideration, if someone made a silly mistake. One day she turned on him after he had guffawed because old Rouault thought that India was part of America.

'If Pierre and I laughed every time you said something idiotic we should never have time to do anything else.'

Georges put his tongue out at her. This made Brigitte laugh. 'What a polite little boy you are! And what do you think you will be like when you grow up? You'll be able to spit and swear and hit girls and women as much as you like. Won't you be pleased with yourself?'

Georges hated her.

Bruce was forced to take up a sideline because it was needed in the village. Madame Blanchard arrived one morning hobbling and complained: 'I shan't be able to come tomorrow because of my legs.'

'You had better show them to me,' said Bruce. Madame Blanchard gave him a look, but she saw that he was serious and said that she had sore places as big as five centime copper coins and that they were spreading. Then she pulled up her skirt and rolled down her thick cotton stockings and unwound a dirty bandage.

Soon Bruce was dabbing the sores with cotton wool dipped in boiled water out of the kettle and then smearing the sores that covered her fat legs with a grey ointment. Next morning she came to work. The treatment was repeated and in four days she was cured. Bruce's reputation as a doctor was immediately established and every few days he was called upon to treat septic sores, paint tonsils, bandage cuts, and adjudicate on sprains and possible broken bones and any disease which involved sending the patient to the hospital. However, when Aline Muller, one of the prettiest girls in the village, consulted him because her monthly was ten days late, he sent her off with a flea in her ear.

'I know nothing of women's diseases – but is there perhaps a simple explanation of your trouble?'

It was the men and the older women who became fondest of Bruce. The pretty girls pouted a little, while they admitted that he was an honest fellow. He had never made a pass at any of them.

Brigitte liked him and Sylvie became devoted to him. She had been bitten by one of the postman's ferrets when they were ratting in the stackyard. The wound was slight but the whole arm swelled up and when she went to Bruce she was feverish and it was a mass of throbbing pain. Bruce examined her arm, washed the wound, sent her to bed and gave her some tablets of a pain killer and some sleeping pills. His first visit to his patient lying on her pallet in the rabbit mansion brought him into contact with Eglantine Veuve Turpin Lanfrey. Sylvie was lying with her hair tangled, her face flushed, her young bosom exposed. She was in a high fever. Her great-grandmother had hobbled out to hang some clothes on the line. When she came back she saw the young Englishman leaning over Sylvie, taking her pulse with his left hand while a large gold watch lay open in his right.

The old woman watched him like a hawk, knowing that she was unobserved. Then Bruce stood up, put the watch in his pocket, pulled out a bottle of pills and looking about for a glass of water, saw her.

'Perhaps, if you gave them, Madame, Sylvie would swallow these more readily,' said Bruce.

Eglantine's prejudice against the English was wiped out by the first sight of him. It is hardly an exaggeration to say that she fell in love.

'He has a heart. He really cares about the little one and he loves France. Not stupid either,' she said, talking to Conduchet and his daughters that evening.

Bruce had observed the cobwebbed rafters, the earth floor, and one or two holes in the roof of the rabbit mansion and that evening he went round to see Pierre Lanfrey and said that Madame Eglantine ought to be put on the list for a hut – if she would agree, as it was unfit for a woman of her age and for a delicate girl who was lying in a high fever with a touch of septicaemia. Next day Marcelle Duvernois persuaded Eglantine to put in for a one-roomed hut. Bruce talked solemnly to the head of the relief mission about the brave old woman of eighty-eight and almost by the time that Sylvie was out of bed, her great-grandmother's hut had been built and would be ready for her to move into, when the windows had been put in and the door hung.

Eglantine announced that she was going to give a house-warming party and invited twenty of her closest friends. The hut was four metres square but there would only be Eglantine's armchair, a folding bed, the stove and two kitchen chairs to take up floor space. She herself sat in the armchair, next to the stove which had been brought from the rabbit mansion. The company consisted of ten old or elderly women, six girls and younger women. Brigitte Lanfrey had refused to come. Her father was annoyed with her and said: 'Well, I shall have to go myself.' Besides Pierre there were old Lorcey and Michel Fournier, Georges and Bruce. All of them were uneasy and on their best behaviour; none knew what to expect. Old Lorcey did not take off his béret, but Michel Fournier took off his képi and held it out as though begging for alms. Sylvie offered them sweet biscuits out of a tin and glasses of sweet white wine. Pierre Lanfrey asked Madame Blanchard what furniture she was choosing from Le Bon Gîte and a discussion started in subdued voices. After half an hour Michel Fournier and old Lorcey left and soon only ten people remained and the room seemed relatively empty. Shortly

94

afterwards Bruce suggested that Germaine Conduchet should sing them a song. She blushed, laughed, said it was absolutely impossible. Bruce appealed to Eglantine who smiled and said: 'I can't make her sing if she doesn't want to.' Then she muttered to herself: 'And I can't give the child a voice if she hasn't got one.' However, just as Bruce was giving up, Germaine pulled her dress down, stood upright and sang – not very well. However, she was applauded but refused to sing again. She only knew one song. Then Eglantine said: 'I used to sing. You should have heard me when I had my teeth.'

'Well, we'll hear you now without them. You don't need teeth in order to sing. You need a good ear and you never lose that.'

Eglantine laughed – not coquettishly, but genuinely amused that she should be asked to sing. Then she began.

> Fishing for mussels
> I don't want to go, Mummy.
> Fishing for mussels
> I don't want to go.
>
> The boys from Marennes
> Take hold of my basket, Mummy,
> The boys from Marennes
> Take hold of my basket.
>
> When it's me that they hold
> Are they being good boys, Mummy?
> When it's me that they hold
> Are they being good boys?
>
> They stroke me and poke me
> And say pretty things, Mummy,
> They stroke me and poke me
> And say pretty things.

So fishing for mussels
I don't want to go, Mummy,
Fishing for mussels
I won't go no more.

Eglantine had a pure and sweet voice. At eighty-eight it was not strong and she did not over-exert herself, but kept within her power. Soon everyone in the room was laughing, or smiling with a touch of wistful regret that the world it called up before them had vanished. Bruce felt this perhaps more than anyone in the room, but he could see that Sylvie and Georges were under the same spell as he was himself.

'Another song, please,' he pleaded.

'In a little while. I must rest my voice. It is a long time since I sang.'

'Well, while you rest your voice, I suggest that we others play a game of blind man's buff – "colin maillard".'

The company was astounded. None of the older ones had played a game of any kind since they were children. They gaped, but with secret delight, and Bruce was at once told that he must be Colin and was blindfolded. He noted carefully where Eglantine was sitting because he did not want to blunder into her. But his difficulty was, in such a small room, and with so many people, not to catch someone whenever he stretched out his arms. However, by exaggerating his clumsiness, Bruce succeeded in not catching anyone for a full minute. Then Madame Blanchard was pushed into his arms from behind by Georges. Bruce investigated her anatomy very thoroughly and finally announced: 'Sylvie Turpin'. This brought shrieks of delighted laughter. He released Madame Blanchard and the game went on.

Next time he caught Pierre Lanfrey. He felt him carefully, found the steel hook and said: 'Either I'm in a butcher's shop or it's Pierre Lanfrey.'

But Pierre refused to be Colin. His hook might hurt someone if he started swinging it around. And if he didn't he would never catch anyone with only one arm. So Georges deputised for him. Confusion and screams of consternation followed his vigorous attacks. When he caught Germaine Conduchet, he reversed Bruce's joke and pretended to think she was Madame Eglantine.

When they paused out of breath, Sylvie was told to give them all a little glass of plum brandy and as they sipped it, Eglantine said that she was ready to sing again.

This time it was a little song of separation which brought the women thoughts of their men fighting.

> Nightingale you sing
> Among the leaves so late.
> You never have to part
> From your most happy mate.
> But I, in my distress
> Quite broken is my heart.
> My mistress I must leave
> And in despair we part.

Soon afterwards the party broke up. Bruce heard Sylvie whisper to Georges: 'No, impossible. Not tonight,' and saw Georges nod sullenly and walk off. Bruce thanked his hostess and kissed her hand and she caught hold of his hair and drew his head to her and kissed him on each cheek. As he was walking back to the mission hut he heard Georges in front of him singing a verse of an army song: a folk song that had come into existence during the last month or two, and they were still fighting and dying in the Grurie wood.

> In the woods of the Grurie
> Today is too much glory.
> The Lady's Well, The Wishing Well
> Tears flow as I those names do tell.

He hung back so as not to overtake the boy and as he waited

before reaching the mission hut, he heard the guns throbbing and then the earth shook with the explosion of a distant mine.

One morning Georges arrived with the news that Madame Blanchard's husband had been awarded the croix de guerre for extreme bravery in action. When Bruce went back to the hut a little early for the midday lunch he found Madame Blanchard in the kitchen mashing potatoes. He congratulated her on her husband's honour. The pale faded woman looked at him queerly: the look that an animal gives the drover when it finally rebels: the desperate but somehow blank look of an overdriven cow.

'First they give you a war cross, then they give you a wooden cross and two metres of ground to go with it,' she said and bent over, hiding her face in the saucepan and began mashing the potatoes furiously. Bruce said nothing and went away.

In the autumn the Crown Prince of Prussia, commander of the army in the Argonne sector of the front, started another intensive attack. Once again the road running north through Dorlotte was jammed with munition waggons to serve the guns and with troops marching to replace those killed and those being brought down wounded by rail. Many regiments of Algerians and Moroccans were sent up and the olive-skinned men with oval faces cast curious glances at the ruined village with its sprinkling of brand new huts roofed with interlocking tiles. They must have felt that they were getting near to their destination. For a third of their number it was indeed final.

One evening a battalion of Frenchmen who were almost dead beat came along the road. It was led by the commanding officer and his lieutenant, walking and leading their horses on which were perched two crumpled but somehow perky figures – soldiers who would otherwise have dropped out.

After them marched, limped or shuffled an exhausted

throng of soldiers, their horizon blue uniforms turned white with dust. Near to the side of the road stood Clementine Rouillac, Sylvie and Madame Duvernois, waiting to cross the road when there was a break in the ranks of the soldiers.

Suddenly in the middle of one of the fours of marching soldiers there appeared a figure capering, a figure wearing a top hat instead of a steel helmet, a crazy incredible figure of pantomime.

Seeing the three women standing beside the road, he took off his top hat, gestured with it and shouted: 'Think of me when you get your next fuck.'

Clementine started forward and began a furious harangue. 'Do you think that you are men? I've seen better sheep going to the slaughter house. You are fools and cowards. That's all you are. Murder, murder, murder that's all men are good for. Don't dare talk to me about fucking. Not till you have the guts to stop the war.'

The clown with the top hat was already out of earshot, gambolling and capering along, drunk, or drugged and waving his top hat while he addressed his speeches to the empty air. But some of the younger soldiers, hearing Clementine's curses, turned their faces white with dust towards her.

Sylvie and Marcelle Duvernois took Clementine by the arms and dragged her back, away from the road. By then she was weeping and saying through her sobs: 'Those fools going to be slaughtered like sheep.'

Marcelle held the crazy woman in her arms but Sylvie looked at them stonily.

'I would not show what I felt. Those women have no pride.' But in spite of her condemnation, the scene was one which she remembered all her life.

M. Dufour, the postman, stopped by the ruins of the Roux house and hesitated. Then he went up to the stone hut that Georges had built. He was sorry to find Georges there: he had

99

hoped he would be at work with the English. But Georges was expecting Sylvie.

'Good morning, Georges. Here's a letter addressed to your mother. I had better give it to you.' He handed Georges the letter and went off quickly. He knew what it contained.

> . . . . your husband, ROUX, Celestin
> on the FIELD OF HONOUR
> died in defence of our COUNTRY
> in the sector of ST. MIHIEL
> 15 OCTOBER 1915.

When Sylvie arrived five minutes later she found Georges lying on the ground with his face buried in the grass. She called to him, knelt down beside him, questioned him. Georges only said:

'Papa is dead.' And when she tried to console him he said:

'Go away. Leave me alone.'

Sylvie left him, wondering if she should fetch Pierre Lanfrey, but in the road she almost bumped into Bruce, who saw that the girl was crying.

'What's wrong, Sylvie? Can I help?'

'Georges's father has been killed. He's very unhappy and won't speak to me.'

Bruce pushed through the bushes to the stone hut. Georges was sitting on the couch staring in front of him.

'You know that my father has been killed?'

'Sylvie told me.'

'I shall volunteer at once. I shall make them pay a hundred lives for his. Kill, kill, kill!' Georges started up. 'Yes I shall volunteer at once,' he repeated. Bruce put his arm round Georges's shoulders.

'Come with me. We'll hear what Pierre has to say.' They set off with Sylvie following unnoticed behind.

'What did you come for?' asked Georges.

'There is a lorry to be unloaded. But it can wait.'

When they reached Pierre's hut near the crossroads, they saw that he and his wife Jeanne were talking to Marcelle Duvernois who kept clasping and unclasping her hands, which was noticeable because she was a woman of very few gestures. Seeing Bruce and Georges coming, Jeanne came towards them, almost as though she wanted to warn them away. 'Louis has been killed. Marcelle's husband,' she explained to Bruce.

'And Georges's father . . .'

'They were in the same company of reservists with other men from Dorlotte.'

Georges went up to Madame Duvernois and said: 'My father also. Perhaps in the same attack . . . St Mihiel.'

'Yes,' she replied. She embraced Georges, kissing him first on one cheek and then on the other. And then she suddenly burst into loud sobs, clutching Georges tightly. Tears began streaming down her face and her whole body was shaken. Between her sobs she exclaimed: 'Both. Both together. The two of them.'

Bruce turned away from the scene. It seemed to him unbearable. But Pierre, Jeanne and Sylvie watched it without expression. After what seemed to Bruce a very long time, Georges released himself from Marcelle's embrace and said:

'I must go now and help Bruce. There is a lorry waiting to be unloaded.'

When they were alone together Jeanne said to her husband: 'I have never seen Marcelle in tears before.'

'It was for Georges that she was weeping. Not for her own loss. For that she had fortitude,' replied Pierre.

Next day the news came that four more men from Dorlotte had been killed in the same attack. Each of the families of these men had moved outside the village and having found good lodging and work had not elected to come back. It was for this reason that the news of their deaths had been delayed. In a single attack in the St Mihiel sector, six of the older men of the village had been killed – six out of a total of nineteen reservists from Dorlotte in that company. All six were married men, aged between thirty and forty-five.

Their wives and children were not there to weep over their loss, but all four had some relatives in the village: one was old Rouault's only son, another had a married sister, one an older brother, all of them cousins and aunts. Everyone in the village had known them, had worked with them or drunk a glass with them when the day's work was done. The village became silent. After the first discussions of the news, its inhabitants avoided each other. For some months they had been able to ignore, even if they could not forget, the war. And then, in the best days of the year, when the fruit was ripe, came this sharp reminder of how vulnerable the village was.

'There will be no men left if this goes on much longer,' the women muttered to themselves.

'And not only in Dorlotte, but in the whole of France.'

And a few of the more independent-minded said fiercely to themselves, 'Somehow it must be stopped. At all costs it must be ended.'

A fortnight after the news of her husband's death, Marcelle came to Pierre Lanfrey and asked:

'Will you buy the vegetables growing in my garden?'

Pierre looked at her enquiringly and asked: 'Are you leaving us?'

'Yes. I was only keeping things going here until Louis came back. There is no point in it now.'

'What are you going to do?'

'I have taken a position as a matron in an orphanage. That is if they take me. There has to be an interview.'

After half an hour's talk about her plans, Pierre asked: 'What are you doing with the hut the English have built for you?'

'I shall sell that. And the land too.'

'I don't want the land. But would you sell me the hut?'

'Yes, most willingly. For whatever they knock off our war damage compensation.'

'No, Marcelle. That's not business. I'll pay you that and twenty per cent more, with a down payment of a thousand francs.'

Marcelle laughed for the first time for some days.

'You'll never make a businessman, Pierre. Surely when he has a widow anxious to sell – and there are no buyers, a businessman ought to make the most of the opportunity. Think again.'

Pierre put out his left hand and tapped her on the shoulder. 'Better accept, while you can.'

'All right. I accept. But what do you want to do with my hut?'

'I am going to set up a general stores. I shall take your hut down and put it up again, here by the crossroads.'

'Well, the village needs a shop like that more than anything. I would have given you the hut, if I had known what you wanted it for.'

'Unfortunately for me, you didn't know and it's too late now. The bargain is struck.'

Marcelle turned away laughing, but Pierre called her back. 'What do you want for the vegetables growing in the garden? Of course they are to be left until they are ready.'

'I'll throw them in, Pierre.'

'You may regret it. But I'll accept them.'

Next morning she waited for the car in which the English were giving her a lift all the way to Vitry-le-François. Pierre and Jeanne came out, talked and shook hands. Marcelle wrote at intervals asking news of the village.

A week later Bruce was astonished to hear Madame Blanchard say to him: 'That Madame Duvernois has behaved disgracefully. It doesn't surprise me. I always knew she was an interfering woman, thinking herself much better than the rest of us. She was always talking about the village, but she didn't care about it at all. I think that it ought to be stopped.'

'Whatever are you talking about?' asked Bruce.

'That Madame Duvernois. She has sold the hut you built for her at a profit. You didn't put it up for nothing in order to line her pockets. It ought to have been taken away and allotted to someone else. And now she has left the village for good and all.'

'You ought to feel sympathy for her. Her husband was killed and I suppose nothing seemed worth while any longer,' said Bruce severely:

'She's not the only war widow in France,' retorted Madame Blanchard.

While she was there everyone in Dorlotte had respected Marcelle, had gone to her when they were in trouble and had taken her advice. Now because she had left Dorlotte they were criticising her on all sides.

Even Eglantine said: 'Well, I think that she ought to have stayed in the village. She was always talking about it and hinting that people's duty was to the village. And now she has walked out and left.'

'I am sure she didn't do it for money,' said Sylvie who was listening.

'No, darling. I don't think so either. I don't know the details. But there could be nothing underhand if Pierre is involved.'

'Or Marcelle either,' said Sylvie.

'No. I don't suppose so. There would not have been any talk if she had stayed here.'

'No, they would not have dared,' said Sylvie.

After hearing the talk about Marcelle, Bruce wondered what the villagers would be saying about him and the other English boys in another few weeks when the work was finished and they had left. 'Every cracked tile or warped board will be an instance of English perfidy, incompetence or fraud,' he reflected. Bruce was however wrong. Although they had been called shirkers, dodging military service, no hostility to Bruce and his companions developed after their departure, but rather the reverse. They became, or at any rate Bruce became, a legend. The reason why Marcelle Duvernois was condemned and the English boys remembered with affection was because public opinion in Dorlotte was formed by women – the great majority of its inhabitants. Women enjoy criticising another woman unfairly and tearing her character to shreds but are notoriously lenient to young men. There was also a class animus against Marcelle. She was better educated and she and her husband had more distinguished manners than those who now attacked her. It was noticeable that those who spoke of her most virulently were those who had gone most frequently to her for help. Her detractors learned however not to say anything against her in the presence of Georges Roux who would spit on the ground and say :

'You make me vomit, you dirty cows.'

'What was Georges's father like?' Bruce asked Pierre Lanfrey one evening when they were looking at the sunset before saying good night.

'Well, you know George's mother was an alcoholic, a coarse woman too, a whore, but not one in great request. This was a bad background for the boy who worshipped his father – and his feeling was returned. Celestin was a small, ugly little man. Georges is certainly his son. He was very quiet and gentle – and intelligent. But his intelligence had never got him anywhere. He was one of the poorest men in Dorlotte. Dressed in rags, a hired labourer all his life. But he had at some time in his life – when he was in the army probably – read books. He surprised me once by quoting Molière. But he was remarkable. Any intelligent labourer can be an anarchist or an extremist of some sort in politics. It seems almost inevitable. But Celestin would only discuss the possible. If a communist revolution had been possible he probably would have been in favour : as it wasn't, why waste time pretending that it was? And you know that shows a high critical intelligence in a man who has suffered from exploitation and grinding poverty. . . . On the Dreyfus case, he always believed that truth would out and justice be done. He never doubted or forgot.'

'What about you?' asked Bruce.

'I am ashamed to say that I thought it didn't matter. I was sick of the Affaire. I think that being a sailor makes all these political affairs matter less. What one realises are the eternal forces that man has to contend with. And the need for every man is to do his duty, as your Nelson said. So that the Dreyfus Affaire seemed to me to be just a landsman's squabble. Celestin made me see that I was wrong. He believed that it was a moral turning point for France. I don't know what he would have said about things today.'

A fortnight later news came that Jacques Turpin, Sylvie's father, had died in a prison camp in Germany. His death left her bewildered by what she did not feel, rather than heart-broken by what she did. While she had been living with Eglantine she had almost forgotten him. And what she remem-bered of the thin, narrow-chested, impatient man were his sarcastic remarks and sudden angry orders. Telling her to sit up straight, to stop licking her spoon, biting her nails and scratching her head. And to sit frozen with shame and rage when he said: 'What have I done to be afflicted with these damned little savages?'

Sylvie knew that her father belonged to a class above that of the Dorlotte labourers – that he was an educated man. She herself wanted to live up to his standards. But she could not understand why, with his insistence on good manners, on politesse, on civilised behaviour, there had always been angry voices in her home – while with her great-grandmother there was always exquisite restraint and the smoothest understand-ing and sympathy.

Eglantine had never spoken a word to her about Georges, but she knew that the old woman liked him. Her father would have forbidden her friendship, for Georges's family belonged to the lowest of the low. Her father would have been wrong.

The war levelled everyone, and Pierre, whom her father respected, would have told him that Georges was the finest young man in the village.

Anyhow her father was dead: the argument she had been imagining would never arise. Yet the knowledge that it would have done, made her feel that her grief was hypocritical.

The last but one of the huts had been built and the English would be leaving when they had completed that and had done one or two little odd jobs: tiling one or two huts that had been roofed with inferior felt when the supply of tiles had run out.

Bruce and Georges Roux were carrying a load of matchboarding from where it had been dumped in the road to the site where it would be used. Another load of thicker floorboards was on its way from the railway siding, but they finished carrying the light boards before the expected load arrived and sat down on a heap of stones to wait.

'What are you going to do when we leave, Georges? Work for old Conduchet?' asked Bruce.

'No, it's the wrong time of year. He won't need any extra labour until the summer.'

'Well, what will you do?'

'I shall volunteer for the army. I'm nearly seventeen.'

'Do you want to kill Germans or be killed by them, or lose an arm or a leg?'

'One has to take one's chance. I shall have to be a soldier anyhow.'

Bruce was silent. Suddenly Georges asked: 'What about you? I heard that the English now have compulsory military service, so you will have to go into the army when they catch up with you.'

'I shall refuse. You see, Georges, I think that war is wrong. It only leads to this.' And Bruce pointed to the heaps of rubble all round them.

'What's the good of talking? You can't do anything about

it. Everyone says it's wrong. But we go on fighting because we can't do anything else.'

'I can refuse to fight. I can go to prison rather than put on uniform if necessary. I think it is wrong to kill other men.'

Georges looked at him. First he grinned, then his expression changed and he looked stern. After a pause he said: 'If our men up there,' and he jerked his head towards the north, 'felt like you there would be nothing to stop the Germans coming and burning our villages and doing whatever they pleased.'

'There may be men who feel as I do in Germany,' said Bruce.

'Bah! They wouldn't stop the others. You haven't seen Germans. I have. These huts are only being built because the French Army protects you. If they weren't there holding the Germans, we could not build these huts. So fighting the Germans and building the huts is all part of one job. You are able to pick the one you prefer. But someone has to do the butcher's work. The soldier up there is saving our skins and you show your gratitude and understanding by telling him that he is doing something wrong. I shall volunteer.'

Bruce said no more.

The lorry loaded with floorboards drove up. Bruce and Georges helped the driver and his mate to unload it, and after they had driven off, they carried the floorboards on to the site and stacked them neatly next to the matchboarding.

For a few weeks after the departure of the English the question of Georges's volunteering was shelved. For Pierre Lanfrey had asked him to help him take Marcelle Duvernois's hut down and make the necessary alterations to enable a shop window to be put in one side, and then to re-erect it and to equip it with a counter and shelves. Most of this was work that Pierre could not do with his one hand. It involved, after demolition, taking the frame of one side to pieces and redesigning it so as to give a clear space for the window and yet make it strong enough so that the purline, taking the rafters and the weight of the tiles, should not collapse.

Pierre thought that this could best be done by making the whole length between the top of the window and the eaves into a big box girder. However, he kept the central upright.

When the shop was finished it had to be stocked. There would be bars of soap, brushes, brooms, household flannels, reels of cotton, pins and needles, nibs, pencils, pens, notebooks, blotting paper, spices, oil, vinegar, flour, lentils, haricots, sardines and tinned fish, corned beef, sugar, jam, treacle, condensed milk, bottles of sweet wine, port, vin ordinaire, rum, grenadine, boxes of cigarettes and tobacco and postage stamps. All of which was a lot to be crowded into a hut four metres square. Most of the stock would have to be stored in the cellar which had sheltered Pierre's family the first winter of the war.

Paying for the stock was a problem. Most of the goods had to be obtained on credit – but that involved either charging high prices or making less profit.

The sun shone, but shower after shower swept the ridge of Dorlotte and during the afternoon every shower brought its rainbow – sometimes of brief duration, sometimes lasting after the rain had stopped falling. The sky perhaps was still full of suspended drops of spray.

A busload of civilians drove up and stopped at the crossroads during one of the showers, but no one got out. Apparently they were waiting for the rain to stop. Pierre Lanfrey, who was preparing the foundations for his shop, was braving the weather with a sack thrown over his shoulders. He looked up. Someone was tapping the window of the bus and waving at him from inside. Owing to the rain and the light, he could not see who it was, or what might be wanted. Reluctantly he straightened his back, propped his pickaxe against the wheelbarrow and strolled over towards the bus. As he did so the last vicious spray of icy driving sleet passed and next moment everything was sparkling with diamonds and steaming. The sun was hot.

The door of the bus opened and an elderly man got out,

followed by a second and a third and then more. Pierre recognised them and rushed forward. 'Leblond! Fournier! Camus! Dujardin!' They were the hostages that the Germans had taken for the good behaviour of Dorlotte while they were burning it. Other villagers had seen the group and came running up.

Leblond began explaining. 'One fine day the Boches discovered that we were hostages for a village which they had not got possession of. An economy drive perhaps! So they arranged to send us back through Switzerland with the help of the Red Cross.'

'I wanted to stay in Switzerland, but the damned Swiss would not let me,' said Hugonin crossly. 'They have more food there than they know what to do with,' put in Camus.

'Are you all back?' asked Pierre. Some faces seemed missing.

'No, alas! Jacques Turpin . . . he died of consumption. And Constant is in hospital with arthritis.'

Soon they had all eagerly dispersed, going to look for their wives and families in the new huts perched about among the ruins.

The return of the hostages was a nine days wonder in Dorlotte. Wherever they went groups of women and gaping children formed about them and they were asked the same questions by everyone in the village until they got tired of repeating :

'Not all of them are that bad. The German guards were sensible family men. It wasn't their fault. But there was never enough food. We were starving. Leblond used to catch rats and make them into pâté. . . . Look out he doesn't keep it up now he's back on his job as charcutier! And then we nearly froze to death with cold : hardly any heating – one coke stove in a huge room. That's why poor Jacques Turpin got tuberculosis and Constant was crippled with arthritis so he could hardly walk. Jacques was spitting blood. They were taken to hospital. And then the week before we were sent back through Switzerland, we were told he had died. We others are lucky to be survivors.'

A theme on which all the returned hostages were ready to talk was the wealth of Switzerland.

'The cream! They don't know what to do with it! Chocolates everywhere! Charcuterie and then soup and fish and steaks and fresh salads and every kind of cheese and fruits and coffee! If one lived for a week in Switzerland one would burst with overeating! Hugonin asked to be allowed to stay but they would not let him. He said he had enough savings to bring his wife over. But they would not let him.'

The return of the hostages added to the manpower of the village and they were soon at work on their old jobs. Fournier, the cobbler, soon had a thriving business. Leblond's wife had been urged by everyone to start a tiny charcuterie. But she found it could not pay unless she killed a pig every week. And she could not slaughter and handle a whole pig by herself. Now there was her husband to undertake buying and slaughtering the pig, scalding and singeing its carcase and cutting it up. And she could make the sausages, pâtés, rillettes and boudins : delicacies that up till that time could only be procured by a visit to Blaye and bought at a shop which did not inspire confidence in its products. And then there were joints of salt pork and fresh pork and lard. Leblond's return and his charcuterie gave Dorlotte renewed self-confidence.

When the war was over they would stop eating ammunition bread and have a baker of their own.

Georges had enjoyed working with Pierre at transforming Marcelle's hut into a village shop. He had been invaluable : Pierre with only one hand and a hook could not have done the work alone. He wanted to pay him what he had been earning with the English. But Georges, who knew that Pierre would need all his capital to buy his stock, refused to take money.

'Credit me with the amount and I'll take it out in groceries after you've started business,' he suggested.

'All right. But I shall charge you wholesale prices.'

This was excellent in theory but in practice it meant that when Georges wanted to buy a kilo of sugar or a box of matches he usually had to buy them from Brigitte, who served in the shop and did the book-keeping. Brigitte disliked Georges whom she still thought of as a parasitic hanger-on who exploited her father's good nature, and she regarded Georges's right to buy at wholesale prices as an act of un-businesslike charity on the part of her father and not as the payment of wages due. She disliked it all the more because it involved her in looking up the price paid for a batch of articles and doing a long division sum to arrive at the wholesale price of, let us say, a packet of pins, which Georges happened to want to buy.

Soon suspicions had arisen on both sides : Brigitte believed that Georges was selling his purchases at cut prices, a centime or two lower than they were marked in the shop, Georges believed that Brigitte had done her sums wrong and that she was overcharging him. Neither of them dared call in Pierre to adjudicate between them as they knew how such bickering would distress him.

CHAPTER SIX

A little two-seater Hispano-Suiza, painted light blue, raced up
the hill into Dorlotte, braked hard and swung round by the
church and was pulled up sharply. Two officers in the uniform of the Air Service, got out. They were both tall men
and it had been a tight fit.

'This is the place, Bertrand : my torture chamber. I was
shut up in the crypt of that church for ten days. I was in
frightful pain, with a dislocated ankle and a cracked collar-
bone, lying there in the dark, nowhere to wash, nowhere to
shit, fed once a day on boiled cabbage or potatoes, cooked
without butter, usually without salt. The damned church was
full of Germans praying and singing hymns. It would have
been as much as my life was worth to sneeze. I can tell you
I was terrified out of my life.'

'Where did you actually crash?'

'In a field just down the lane. We'll have a look presently
and see if anything is left of the plane. The engine wasn't
worth salvaging, I was told. The Germans had buried poor
old Denis, but we dug him up again.'

'What made you take shelter in the church?'

'It was that idiot boy. He ran up to the plane with a
pitchfork and prodded at me. I thought he wanted to murder
me and he did tear the lobe of my ear owing to his clumsiness. But it turned out he was trying to rescue me. There was
a battle going on. Bullets whizzing everywhere. The Germans
were coming into the village. I told him that I must hide
somewhere. You see with my ankle I couldn't run away into
the woods.'

'So he hid you in the church?'

'First he shoved me into a bullock wagon and covered me with grass, then took me into the church and locked me in the crypt in total darkness, and that was almost the last I saw of him. He left me to the mercies of a crazy old woman: a religious maniac with V.D.'

'How do you know?' asked Lieutenant Bertrand.

'Well to crown it all, she gave me a dose.'

Lieutenant Bertrand L'Ormesson burst into laughter.

'You are a card. Maurice. You say she was a crazy old woman, how old was she really?'

'Old enough to be my mother. And ghastly to look at, what's more,' added de L'Espinasse in a complaining tone.

'What on earth possessed you?'

'I got so bored. And in the dark all cats are grey. So one day when she brought me my disgusting mess of turnips, I grabbed her and pulled her into the crypt. She squealed like a young girl; luckily the church was empty. Afterwards I was afraid that she would turn me in to the Germans, so I repented and we went down on our knees together and said prayers. . . . God it was a farce.'

'Really Maurice, you go too far. It's not decent. And in a church.'

'That was the whole point really. You know that I am an ardent Catholic. I got a kick out of it because it was in a church. But my God I was in a pickle when I got out.'

'They sent you straight off to hospital, didn't they?'

'I had an ankle that had to be broken to be reset – I can still feel it when I do a left hand Immelmann – a cracked collar bone: that still hurts when I laugh, and V.D. on top of it all. And was I peppered and was I poxed! My God I was in a condition! Grounded and seven weeks under treatment. Colonel Barès tore me off a strip . . . I thought he wouldn't let me fly the Nieuport when we got it.'

Maurice de L'Espinasse stopped and whistled, and nudged his friend. 'There's a pretty bit of skirt . . .'

Sylvie had just passed them carrying a bucket from the fountain.

'Come along and show me where you were shot down,' said Bertrand as his friend seemed inclined to turn back and follow Sylvie.

'All right. I don't really know whether I can find it. Talk of the devil – I think that is the boy with the pitchfork there, stopping to talk to that bit of skirt. Come along, Bertrand, I'll get him to introduce us. We may have some fun.'

If Sylvie had seen the officers approaching, she would have hurried away as she was shy and like the good village girls avoided being spoken to by strangers in uniform. But she had her back to them and Georges was looking down and drawing something on the ground.

'Forgive me breaking in – but I think that you are my friend with the pitchfork. I was hoping to see you,' said Maurice. Then as Georges stared and recognition came and Sylvie looked up in alarm:

'Introduce me please to the charming young lady.'

'This is Lieutenant de L'Espinasse, who was hidden in the crypt of the church. This is Mademoiselle Sylvie Turpin.'

'And may I introduce the distinguished pilot, Lieutenant Bertrand de L'Ormesson?'

Sylvie smiled and held out her hand. De L'Ormesson, a tall young man with almost colourless eyes like glass marbles, and with yellow hair, bent over it and kissed it.

'I see that you have won the croix de guerre since I last saw you,' said Georges. His eyes had been fixed upon the red and green ribbon since de L'Espinasse introduced himself and his friend.

'It was awarded Maurice after his fourth confirmed aerial victory,' said de L'Ormesson.

'I was lucky because my victories were confirmed. Other men who have done better get no credit because their victories, which are often over Germany, haven't been witnessed,' said Maurice. He was speaking so generously because of the presence of de L'Ormesson who had claimed five German air-craft shot down, but had only been credited with two.

'I wanted to see the place where Maurice was shot down two years ago and where you, I believe, rescued him from his blazing plane,' said de L'Ormesson.

'You stuck me with your damned pitchfork and pulled me out like a piece of toast that has fallen into the fire,' said Maurice.

'It was lucky he had a pitchfork with him or he couldn't have reached you,' said Sylvie.

Maurice turned to her with a flashing smile. In it she read sympathy, delicacy and understanding. She looked back at him for a moment. He was a head taller than Georges, a thin and extraordinarily handsome man, with an oval face, curly dark hair and green-gold eyes like a cat's, or as Sylvie said to herself, a tiger's. She had never seen a tiger. And she was looking into the eyes of one of the heroes of the war – a man who had shot down four of the German fliers.

'Well, it's down the lane. I believe that some bits and pieces are still there, rusting in the ditch,' said Georges.

'I must be going, good bye,' said Sylvie, waved her hand and ran off. Later she reproached herself for impoliteness.

The three men walked down the lane and Georges held up a wire stretched across the gateway so that the officers could duck under it. 'I seem to recognise that bit of wire. Tension-ing, interplane, wire, piano, steel,' de L'Ormesson said with a laugh. In the ditch on the far side of the little meadow was a lump of rusty metal half-concealed by comfrey and water forget-me-not. Pushed into a gap in the hedge was a tangle of wires.

'I could never understand it. They hit us first shot,' said Maurice. The two officers discussed it professionally and Georges did not understand until de L'Ormesson said:

'I'm sure it wasn't a shell. You were carrying a grenade, weren't you?'

'Yes.'

'Those grenades were pretty primitive. The pin shook out and it blew the plane to bits.'

'The curious thing is that I have never thought of that. I took it for granted, that when we sighted them, they sighted us and shot us down.'

'It was you who flew over Dorlotte and then looped the loop, wasn't it?' asked Georges.

'Oh yes, I thought it might be the boy with a pitchfork standing beside a man with a wheelbarrow. Quite a nice little kite for its period. I'm flying something much better than that now. The latest Nieuport. Beats the daylights out of their latest Fokker.'

'The English are getting something pretty hot: the Sopwith,' said de L'Ormesson. They had got back to the little car.

'By the way, what's happened to that old woman that was in the church – La Fouine I think you called her and with good reason?' asked Maurice.

'She was taken to hospital and hasn't come back,' said Georges. He was embarrassed.

'Best place for her,' said Maurice. The two officers fitted themselves into the car.

'Well, I'll be back soon and we'll have a long talk,' said Maurice, suddenly genial. Georges swung the starting handle. The engine fired and Maurice drove off with a roar. He winked at Bertrand. Georges had not seen the wink, but he stared after the car until it disappeared. He was puzzled, but could not put his finger on what it was that was wrong.

Maurice was as good as his word. This time he came alone and brought a present with him: something that few people in Dorlotte had ever handled, and nobody since the war: a large box of expensive chocolates made in Switzerland. He stopped to ask Michel Fournier where he could find Georges and was directed to where he was marking out foundations for the new room he planned to build in front of his stone hut which would become the toolshed of the new house. Georges looked up surprised and greeted Maurice politely, while the latter pressed the box of chocolates into his hands with the words: 'Thought you might like to share them with that pretty sweetheart of yours.'

Georges said to himself: 'So that's why you have come back.' But to Maurice he said only: 'This is unexpected generosity.' Maurice asked Georges what he was doing.

'Well I've been working with the English building the huts. But their *équipe* has packed up. I thought of volunteering, but Pierre Lanfrey says that with my experience in building I ought to apprentice myself to a carpenter, or to a mason, until my class is due to be called up.'

'You ought to volunteer at once,' said Maurice.

'Well, Pierre thinks that if I survive, it would be good to have a trade to come back to.'

'If you volunteer, you get immediate advantages. Besides I might be able to get you into the Air Service. In that case you would get training either as a woodworker or as a mechanic, engaged in maintenance. Far better for you to volunteer immediately.'

Sylvie suddenly came round the corner and was on them before she was aware.

'Oh, excuse me. I've brought the milk. I'll come back later.'

But Maurice had risen. 'I am enchanted to see you again, Mademoiselle. Please take one of these chocolates. I brought them for you.'

Sylvie took one and stayed.

'I have been telling Georges that if he volunteers for the army now, I may be able to get him into the Air Service. Wouldn't it be an ironical twist if he were to become my mechanic?'

Sylvie clapped her hands, and bounced up and down with excitement like a small child – not at all a young lady trying to preserve her dignity.

'If he looks after your aeroplane he will be at Vassincourt and you can both come over very often.'

Maurice smiled at her enthusiasm.

'I will get my great-grandmother to invite you to one of her parties,' said Sylvie.

'Your great-grandmother?' asked Maurice. He wondered for a moment if the girl were making a fool of him.

'I live in the same hut with her. She is wonderful. At eighty-eight she sings better than any girl in the village and we play games on the floor taught us by that Englishman, Brus. Hunt the Slipper. It's such fun.'

'I know it's something to do with the motor, but what exactly does a mechanic do?' asked Georges.

' A fighter aeroplane such as the Nieuport which I fly, needs six men. The pilot who flies it, the riggers who look after everything except the engine and the gun, and the mechanics who look after the engine and all mechanical parts and the armourer who looks after the gun. Between them they keep the aeroplane in perfect condition.' As he talked Maurice kept helping himself to the chocolates.

'I expect it would require a long training before I was good enough for that,' said Georges. He did not like to say that the war might be over and de L'Espinasse killed long before then.

Maurice wondered why he should be talking to these two little peasants. The girl was so sweet and soft as butter – and if he could get the boy out of the way, it would be easy for him to have her, and an amusing change from the whores at Chalons. He was not the only one to ask that question. Old Emile saw the three talking as he passed by, going as he did every week to buy himself three litre bottles of *marc* at Muller's drink shop.

'Sniffing round our little Sylvie already. An officer too, in uniform. Damn the fellow,' he muttered to himself.

Most of the chocolates had disappeared when Maurice looked at his gold wrist watch. 'You volunteer straight away and I'll do what I can to get you into the Air Service. I've got to be back on duty at the airfield in half an hour. Au revoir, Mademoiselle, and good luck to you my boy.' The two children stood up and shook hands. Maurice lifted Sylvie's hand to his lips and touched her fingers with his tongue.

When he had roared off in his little racing car, Sylvie turned to Georges and said 'It's too wonderful. I can hardly believe it. You would be working at Vassincourt and not going into the trenches. And he is so tremendously smart.'

'I don't believe it. I shall talk to Pierre about it,' said Georges.

'It's only natural that he should do everything he can for you, because you saved his life,' said Sylvie. Georges shrugged his shoulders.

'I don't understand it,' he said.

'His moustache tickles,' said Sylvie. But she said nothing about his touching her fingers with his tongue.

That evening Georges went and talked to Pierre Lanfrey in his new hut. In the porch there were strings of onions and garlic, dried haricots, several rabbit skins and garden tools. Then, in the living room, glowing with warmth from the kitchen stove, were Jeanne and the two children. Georges was given a chair and Pierre took off his reading spectacles.

'I am going to volunteer. Lieutenant de L'Espinasse came out today. He says that if I volunteer he will get me into the Air Service. He talked about my becoming his mechanic and looking after his aeroplane.'

Pierre who had first seemed resigned to a futile conversation became suddenly interested.

'I can't think that he was serious. It would take you a year working in the shops to qualify – if you ever did. The lieutenant may be killed any day. Or the war may even be over before you get a job as a mechanic.

'But if I work hard, and if he wants me?' said Georges.

'Why should he want you?' asked Pierre.

'I don't know. He's so friendly and different all of a sudden.'

'Mysterious,' said Pierre.

'Sylvie thinks it is gratitude because I saved his life.'

'It has taken him some time to show his gratitude.'

'Well, I think I had better volunteer and ask to be put in the Air Service,' said Georges.

'Everyone wants to get into it to avoid going into the trenches,' said Pierre.

'I know. But Lieutenant de L'Espinasse said he would get me into it.'

'I think it is most unlikely that he could exert any influence. If he were a cabinet minister, or a minister's mistress, or someone high up in the production of munitions, it might be credible. But that a mere lieutenant in the Air Service, a man who is actually risking his life, should have influence in France seems to me incredible,' said Pierre. There was a silence while Georges thought about this. Then Pierre continued: 'Of course if it were possible, nothing could be better. But I don't believe in it. I think you had much better apprentice yourself to the mason in Blaye, and learn the trade until you are called up. Then, if you survive the war, you can go back knowing there will be no lack of work for the next dozen years – every village in France will want its war memorial. And the gravestones for those who can afford them.'

'The idea of becoming an aircraft mechanic appeals to me more,' said Georges.

'One is certain. The other in my opinion is highly unlikely.'

'Sylvie is thrilled at my becoming a mechanic. She imagines me already installed at Vassincourt, looking after the lieutenant's machine.'

'So Sylvie plays a part in this childishness, does she?' asked Pierre.

Georges did not answer and Jeanne called them to the table on which she had put a saucepan of steaming soup.

Next morning Georges walked into Blaye, got a lift from a wholesale grocery van which took him all the way to Chalons. There he volunteered.

CHAPTER SEVEN

With the departure of Georges Roux, the village of Dorlotte began to see a great deal of Lieutenant Maurice de L'Espinasse. On his first visit Sylvie greeted him warmly as an old friend and took him at once to see Eglantine. The old woman was fascinated by his good looks, his height, his distinguished family name, his polished boots and polished manners. She did not realise that he had been mentioned in newspapers not only throughout France but all over the world, as a fighter pilot of the Air Service who had shot down four German aircraft – that is confirmed victories. Her unawareness of this, and Sylvie's only partial awareness of his fame endeared them, quite genuinely, to Maurice.

He had said to himself only a week before that Sylvie was as sweet and soft as butter, that with the boy out of the way it would be easy for him to have her, and an amusing change from the girls in the Chalons whorehouse. But now that Georges had gone he made no effort to seduce her. A kiss, a brotherly squeeze, a flirtatious tickle – that was all. For Maurice had begun to fall in love – not with Sylvie – but with innocence, with purity, with the village of Dorlotte and above all with Eglantine herself. Besides which there was another reason – a medical one. Back at the airfield Maurice sought out the priest and made a longer and more genuine confession than was usual with him.

Confessions were part of the routine of the fighter pilots' lives. It was their habit to confess and receive absolution at frequent intervals.

At this date – late in 1916 – the tactics of airfighting with the machines then available were only beginning to be worked out. It was not until Boelcke and then Richthofen appeared with the 'circuses' that the principles of mutual defence and of co-operation came to be accepted. Maurice belonged to an earlier period and he owed his victories and his survival not only to his brilliance in aerobatics, but to his individualism. He was not a good comrade. If he saw one of his squadron caught in a dogfight with three or four of the Luftwaffe, he did not sail in and take a hand. He liked being alone and watching high up for the enemy below. It was when he saw a German plane alone that he pounced. After an enemy formation had been split up, either by a squadron of French fighters or by accurate anti-aircraft fire, he would watch for an enemy who had been shot up or badly shaken and was leaving the fight. and then dive onto his tail and hunt him down. At first Maurice received reprimands for his lone wolf methods – but as his score of confirmed victories mounted and his reputation grew, he was allowed to fight in his own way. Although eventually promoted to the rank of captain, he never would become a commandant or squadron leader.

Whenever possible he avoided flying over the German lines. As far as was possible he fought over and behind the French lines. He was afraid of German flak, although extremely confident when engaged with enemy aircraft. This was more logical than the general attitude of despising flak and treating enemy aircraft with respect. Maurice hated to expose himself to the dangers of chance. He trusted in his own skill. No doubt the early experience of being shot down in the Maurice Farman was partly responsible for this fear of flak – only perhaps the Farman had been blown up by the grenade it carried.

For a number of reasons Maurice de L'Espinasse was not very popular among his fellow-pilots, partly his jealousy of better men like Navarre . . . . partly his reluctance to go headlong to help a comrade.

He was, even his admirers admitted, and they had the best

reason to know, mean about money. He left the bar before it was his turn to stand a round of drinks. He was often without small change, and what was worse, for those admirers who were of an analytic turn, was that this meanness was obviously due to indifference or contempt. Maurice de L'Espinasse thought the other pilots of no account. One exception had been de L'Ormesson to whom he had appeared genuinely attached, but de L'Ormesson had not returned after a dogfight over the German lines and none of the younger pilots drafted into the squadron had replaced him. Maurice lived in an ivory tower and incurred the dislike which is usually extended to such fortunate individuals.

Exceptions to this dislike were Stanislas Lebreil and Raoul Meissonier – the rigger and the mechanic who looked after his aeroplane. With them Maurice was on much closer relations than usual between officer and ranker. He talked to them as though they were his brothers. The friendship was strictly professional, limited by a common preoccupation with compression, piston rings and magnetos. He treated Meissonier with a genuine respect which he did not feel for any of the officers: the respect a boy shows to his elder brother.

'Have you any news of Georges yet?' Sylvie asked Maurice the next time he went to Dorlotte. For a moment he did not know what she meant and his blank expression led her to add: 'Has he been drafted into the Air Service?'

'I have heard nothing so far. These things take time,' replied Maurice.

'Why should they? Have they replied to your application?'

'No, it always takes a long time before they reply.'

'Wouldn't it be best if you went to see someone in the Ministry of War and got him to give an order for Georges to be transferred to your unit at Vassincourt? After all you are someone of importance and have the entrée everywhere.'

Sylvie's persistence was tiresome. Maurice could only promise to write again and to ask the advice of the officer in charge of personnel.

When he had told Georges that he ought to volunteer he was being quite sincere; it was what he would have done himself. And when he had said that Georges ought to get into the Air Service he was being equally sincere. It was the finest, the youngest, the most adventurous and exciting branch of the service. It had the greatest future. It was good advice, but when he went on to suggest that he might be able to arrange that Georges should be drafted into that service he was indulging in a fantasy which was delightful and flattering to himself. It was pretending not only to Georges and to Sylvie, but to himself that he had powers and an influence which he had not got and that it was impossible that he ever should have.

And then the idea that Georges might one day become the mechanic servicing his aeroplane – that was surely a harmless and amusing dream. It was not his fault if those little peasants took it seriously. The whole conversation with them both had been delightful – an almost idyllic interlude.

But when he had left the village it did not for a moment occur to him that he was bound by a promise to do something in order to try to make Sylvie's childish dream come true. And now that he was being questioned and worried he felt aggrieved with her for taking that amusing fantasy seriously.

She seemed to think that the object of his existence was to keep Georges out of the trenches!

On the third occasion that Sylvie began talking about getting Georges transferred, he began to wonder whether he could get somebody to write him out a refusal on a paper with an official heading so that he could show it to her and put a stop to the absurd business. But before he had decided anything, he was stopped in the road by Pierre Lanfrey, just as he was getting out of his car.

'Excuse me, but I believe that you are trying to get Georges Roux into the Air Service', said Pierre.

'What do you want to know?' replied Maurice impatiently.

'Have you had any reply to your application?'

'Nothing definite.'

'To whom did you address your application?'

Maurice was astonished by this question and felt himself getting angry. But he hesitated. He knew that if he told Pierre to mind his own business and not ask impertinent questions, it would make things more difficult for him in the village. So he controlled himself.

'The officer in charge of personnel, headquarters of the Air Service, Paris. Such an application has to go through the usual channels. It will be dealt with by an officer on his staff.'

'Thank you, lieutenant. I will write to the officer in charge of personnel myself. A letter signed by some of those who have known Georges all his life may possibly help to achieve our ends.'

'It might be disastrous,' said Maurice.

'I don't see how it could hurt Georges.' said Pierre. He lifted his steel hook in a salute and walked away. For some reason the sight of the hook frightened Maurice. It was an evil omen.

Sylvie greeted him with: 'Pierre has had such a good idea. He is going to write a letter signed by several of the men here backing up your application. That will show that it is not that Georges wants to escape going to the trenches.'

Maurice did not repeat that such a letter would be disastrous or try to get her to persuade the man with the hook to abandon his plan. He realised that he had now got to make an application, or his failure to do so might come out. He would make it as colourless as possible. It would be ghastly if the story got round! Everyone would laugh at him and Colonel Barès might be furious. His reputation was bad enough as it was without his giving himself the airs of God Almighty! Pierre Lanfrey knew perfectly well that a letter such as he had suggested writing would be pigeonholed and would lead to nothing. He had made the suggestion in order to see what effect it had on Lieutenant de L'Espinasse and to judge whether the lieutenant had in fact made any attempt to get Georges diverted into the Air Service. He concluded that he had not and that he had encouraged Georges to volunteer simply in order to get him out of the way.

Emile Carré avoided meeting most of the grown-up people in the village. If he did meet someone face to face he passed by silently and grunted unintelligibly in reply to greetings. With the children it was different. He would wave a bottle, sometimes laugh and nod his head. But he took special care to avoid meeting Pierre Lanfrey, always taking a roundabout route so as to avoid the crossroads when he went to Muller's to buy drink The reason for this was that Pierre was, in Emile's opinion, the most intelligent man in the village and he was an intelligent man himself. Pierre had read books too and in the past years had sometimes borrowed one from him. Emile did not mind what Joseph, or Muller, or Achille Durand thought about him. They were like beasts in the field. But when he met Pierre he felt ashamed of being an alcoholic who had done nothing during the last fifteen years and he was seized with bitter despair and hatred of life.

Pierre guessed that something of the sort was the reason that Emile avoided him and he was a good deal astonished when looking up from his carpentering – he was making wooden brackets for a shelf in the shop – he saw Emile Carré leaning on his stick, watching him.

'Good day, Monsieur Carré.'

'Good day, Monsieur Lanfrey. I would like to have a bit of a talk. Can you come along to my place where we shan't be interrupted?'

'Whenever you like, Monsieur Carré.'

'In half an hour's time?'

'All right.'

Emile had fixed half an hour so that he should not have to endure the strain of remaining sober longer than absolutely necessary.

Emile sat on the couch inside his home, Pierre sat on the stump of a tree that served as accommodation for visitors.

'Haven't seen you to speak to for a long time. Don't know how it is: as one gets older one goes out less and less,' said Emile who was embarrassed and could not get to his subject.

'You wanted to talk to me. About yourself or about someone else?' asked Pierre.

'Oh, not myself . . . . some of our little birds. . .'

'Was it about Georges Roux by any chance?'

'Yes, about Georges and about our little Sylvie . . . his little Sylvie, I should say.' Then as Pierre said nothing Emile went on: 'That officer fellow. He persuaded Georges to volunteer. Now he's coming here a bit too often.'

'I agree. But he seems to be behaving quite correctly.'

Emile spat through the opening of his shed, but well to one side of Pierre.

'Sometimes I ask myself why he is so correct,' said Emile. 'There was a hillside in the Vosges with rocks and heather full of vipers. I used to watch them to find out about them. I once saw a viper eat a fieldmouse. First he paralysed it, but without killing. Then he bubbled saliva all over it before swallowing it, still alive. That's what our officer is doing with little Sylvie.'

De L'Espinasse's behaviour, which Emile Carré described as the salivation of his victim, Sylvie herself regarded as neglect. For the lieutenant seemed to prefer the company of Eglantine to that of her great-granddaughter. He would drive straight to her hut and often alight carrying a cardboard box tied with a pink or a blue ribbon which contained sweetmeats of a kind unprocurable in wartime except by the very rich or the greatly privileged. Eglantine would bring out a bottle of *prune* or *framboise* and the smart young officer and the old peasant woman would sit eating cakes and sipping liqueurs while she told stories about the games the girls used to play seventy-five or eighty years before, or how the country weddings used to last four days and all the young men and

128

girls would seize the opportunity to indulge in wild flirtations and petting.

One of the reasons for de L'Espinasse's neglect of Sylvie was that the doctor at the base had managed to scare him. He had only agreed to allowing him to leave hospital by putting all towns and villages where there were brothels out of bounds and telling him that any sexual intercourse would result in such severe illness that he would be either grounded for months or invalided out of the Air Service. For some weeks after this de L'Espinasse kept to a strict regime and avoided Sylvie.

However, on one of his visits Eglantine was absent, having gone over in person to complain to her nephew that his young heifers had got loose and after straying into her garden had eaten half a dozen of her cabbages – a misdeed for which she demanded reparation. Maurice de L'Espinasse tapped lightly and then, as usual, pushed open the door to save Eglantine from getting out of her armchair and coming to open it. Sylvie was alone in the room and had been brushing her hair. She was wearing only a petticoat and camisole.

The young officer in his spotless uniform walked up to the embarrassed girl who was saying:

'My great-grandmother will be back in a minute. She is at the farm.' Maurice stroked her hair and asked unexpectedly:

'Will you come for a few days with me to Paris?' Sylvie blushed. She was tongue-tied. She expected the officer to kiss her and, at that moment, she would have found the strength to repulse him. But instead of embracing her he stepped back and said:

'You haven't ever been to Paris, have you? We could have a gay time together. I'll go up to the farm now and greet your great-grandmother. I've got to get back to the airfield. Think it over and meet me in Georges's little cabin tomorrow. I'll be there at three o'clock and you can tell me what you have decided. I'll be seeing you, my beauty.'

De L'Espinasse had of course no serious intention of taking Sylvie to Paris. But it was delightful to make her eyes go round with surprise and to pretend that he was seriously inviting her. It was a game, a delightful innocent game which filled her with excitement and anticipation. And the idea gave him a kind of nostalgic yearning for the golden age of fairy tales when such things were possible.

In sober fact he knew that he would look damned silly with a young peasant girl of her age tagging along with him in the music halls, restaurants and nightclubs. Even if he bought her some expensive clothes which he could not afford, she would not know how to behave. And how those stuck-up pilots in the Cigogne Squadron would stare if he ran into any of them on leave! He would be the laughing stock of the airfield. Besides, when he did manage to wangle a pass for Paris, which would not be yet awhile with the colonel in his present mood, he would have the pick of all the prettiest women in the capital.

No, Sylvie was strictly spare time: a rustic idyll. And to tell the truth he was a bit ashamed of having embarked on such a crude affair as the seduction of an unsophisticated village girl who had never had a manicure, or been to a fashionable hairdresser in her life.

Part of the charm of seduction is difficulty and though Maurice had not read *Les Liaisons Dangereuses* he knew as well as Laclos that the most innocent girls are the most difficult to seduce.

For that reason he had pointedly ignored Sylvie on his visits to her great-grandmother so as to induce a feeling of pique in her. And while he surmised that his uniform and reputation and a box of chocolates might be an insufficient bribe, the promise of a trip to Paris in his company would be irresistible. So it proved. As he had not made any physical approaches, or laid hands on her except for a careless stroking of her hair since the day on which he had kissed her hand, Sylvie was able to tell herself that her relationship with the famous airman was one of the most innocent friendship.

The choice of meeting place – Georges's stone cabin – was also a clever move. For Sylvie it was associated not simply with Georges but still more as the place for making love.

Sylvie was waiting and had fallen into a daydream when she heard the popping of the little Hispano-Suiza as it pulled up and then was driven off the road behind the shelter of the plum-trees in the Rouxs' garden, where it would be hidden from the eyes of passers-by. A minute later Lieutenant de L'Espinasse had entered the cabin and as she had risen to her feet, he caught her to him and gave her a kiss. Then letting her go, threw himself down on the couch and drew Sylvie down beside him.

'You'll come of course. . . . But we can make plans so much better lying in each other's arms.'

When Emile was sober not only his hands but his whole body shook and trembled, and it needed a full glass of spirits before he was physically capable of the actions on which he had decided in the rare moments of sober reflection. And so, when he pushed himself off his plank bed and sat up, his first action was to pour a large tot of marc into a mug, then, before tasting it, hastily push the bottle out of sight and out of reach under the mattress on his bed, before swallowing the spirit that would restore him. He shook himself and waited until the shaking had stopped and then set out for Eglantine's hut, taking a circuitous route to avoid being seen by anyone in Conduchet's farmyard and hesitating before crossing the road so as to be sure that there was no one belonging to the village on it. When he came in sight of Eglantine's doorway, he sat down under a blackcurrant bush and waited for nearly twenty minutes. Then the door opened and the old woman came out and went round behind it, for her bladder was weak and she had to empty it at frequent intervals. Directly she was out of sight, Emile stole forward and entered the hut and a moment later came out carrying Georges Roux's old shotgun, which he had left with Sylvie to look after when he volunteered. It was a quarter to one and everyone in the village was eating the midday meal, so Emile got back without being noticed by anyone except Clementine Rouillac with whom he came face to face as he stepped out onto the road.

'You did give me a fright! Going shooting, Emile?' she asked.

'Rats. They run over me at night and gnaw holes in my sheepskins. I've tried traps, but they are getting too cunning.'

'Are they real rats, or the ones you see after drinking two bottles of marc?' asked Clementine in the most innocent tone.

'I don't see rats when I have the horrors. I see half-witted old women. That's the worst of all. They are horrible,' said Emile and walked on.

'What a beast the man is. I've never done him any harm,' Clementine exclaimed and soon afterwards her old face puckered up and tears of self-pity rolled down her cheeks.

'I've no one. Nobody in the world to defend me. Anyone can insult me and maltreat me as much as he likes,' she said loudly, regretting that there was no one to overhear her words or see her tears. They were wasted without an audience.

Emile went back to his habitation, hid the gun under the mattress and retrieved the bottle of marc. He was drunk that night.

Emile heard the car stop, then the sound as it turned off the road and bumped over the grass in lowest gear and stopped behind the shelter of the plum-trees. He pulled Georges Roux's gun out from under the bench and tottered with quick little steps round to Georges's stone cabin. He had scarcely seated himself on the couch when Maurice de L'Espinasse appeared. He stopped short and stared at the hunched figure in front of him. Two men could not have presented a greater contrast.

Maurice in his clean, pale blue long-skirted tunic, breeches cut tight round the knee, polished gaiters and boots, and his képi, stood for a moment dumbfounded in the bright sunlight looking at the crumpled old man in his incredibly soiled and ragged clothes, with his grimy face, dark with dirt that was relieved only by his unshaven white bristles, sitting where he had expected to see the fresh and exquisite figure of Sylvie.

'What are you doing? You have no business here," said Maurice, who did not recognise Emile as an inhabitant of the village and took him for some old tramp.

'I was waiting,' said Emile.

'Get out quick,' said Maurice. Only then did he notice the gun lying across the old man's lap.

'To shoot thrushes, I suppose. Well you must make your ambush somewhere else,' said Maurice good-humouredly.

'To shoot a wolf,' said Emile and stood up and pointed the gun at Maurice who turned and ran.

The barrels of the gun wavered and it was some seconds before Emile fired, during which time Maurice had almost reached the shelter of the plum-trees. This saved him for the shot had spread. The thick cloth of his tunic stopped the greater part of the charge and Maurice escaped with three pellets in the nape of his neck and one through his unlucky ear.

Maurice did not boast of his encounter with Emile. When he went into the surgery he said:

'I've had a lucky escape, Major. I was nearly knocked off by an old fellow shooting thrushes on the other side of a hedge The old devil had a better aim than any of the Boche pilots I've run into.'

The ear was bandaged and the pellets extracted under a local anaesthetic, and the incident would have remained unknown if Emile had not told the story. Soon the village was apprised of the drama in all its details and with embellishments varying according to whether the narrator was a friend of the Turpin family and liked Emile, or was critical

133

of Sylvie and thought that the old fellow was a blot on the village.

Sylvie first heard of the incident from her great-grand-mother. Eglantine was amused and appeared gratified as though it were a compliment paid to her by proxy.

'Fighting a duel over you already! We Lanfrey women have always set the men by the ears! I thought that now you've lost Georges you would be leading a quiet life for a little while. Oh! It's no good pulling a solemn face. . . . I know all about your goings-on with Georges though I never said a word to you.'

'Nonsense,' said Sylvie blushing.

'So now it's off with the old love and on with the new. We have a rude proverb for it. Well he's a handsome young officer and I'm sure you are not to blame, even if old Emile tries to protect your virginity. . . .'

Sylvie ran out of the room. She was very much upset and spent the day alone in the fields. Finally she decided to write a letter. She bought a sheet of notepaper and an envelope in Pierre's shop and wrote in pencil:

Dear Maurice,

I am so ashamed of Emile Carré's atrocious behaviour. I have hidden Georges's gun so that he cannot find it. After this awful affair I feel I cannot live any longer in the village where everyone is so awful. Even my great-grandmother makes me feel awfully ashamed. Please advise me what to do.

Your little comrade,
Sylvie Turpin

She addressed the letter to:

Lieutenant Air Service,
M. Maurice de L'Espinasse,
Neuilly Aerodrome.

and gave it to Marie Durand to post in Blaye. Marie, who had a strict code of honour, told no one of having performed this commission. A week later the little Hispano drew up at the corner of the wood near Belmont, Sylvie carrying a bundle slipped out from behind some bushes, got in beside Maurice and the car drove off. Sylvie Turpin was not seen again in the village. Her disappearance caused less gossip than might have been expected. Her mother and her cronies blamed old Eglantine.

'How can one expect an old woman of ninety in her second childhood to exert the necessary authority over a silly young girl whose head is turned by an officer's uniform?' Madame Blanchard declared to Pierre and Jeanne when she went into the shop.

'She is only a child too. That famous airman ought to be punished. But then she has no father to look after her.'

'It's an atrocity,' said Jeanne. Pierre said nothing. He felt that he was partly to blame. He ought to have spoken to Sylvie. One or two of the women took a different view.

'Well, she's hooked an officer and a famous one. He'll set her up in luxury. She'll be a grand lady and won't remember the time when she was running about our ruins barefoot. A lucky little minx, if you ask me.'

CHAPTER EIGHT

Three weeks later Pierre Lanfrey was in the middle of a discussion with the traveller of a wholesale supplier of groceries – a discussion of some importance, since Pierre had to avoid having his shelves loaded with a stock of expensive brands which the villagers would never buy, without giving offence to the traveller whose goodwill was essential at a time of general shortage. Just when he had begun to explain the position, he caught sight, through the shop window, of Georges Roux getting out of an army car with half a dozen soldiers packed into it.

'Excuse me, my friend,' he said and ran out in time to catch Georges who was turning down the lane to the fountain.

'So they have given you leave – and what's this?' asked Pierre, catching sight of the riband of the croix de guerre on the pale blue tunic. Then, without waiting, he blurted out : 'I have some terrible news for you, Georges.'

'Sylvie?'

Pierre nodded.

'What?'

'She has disappeared.'

'Lieutenant de L'Espinasse?'

'I'm told he deserted her after a week. She is, I'm told, at Chalons – in a house.'

The commercial traveller, tired of waiting, had come out.

'Aha! The return of the young hero! Decorated too. Don't let me interrupt your rejoicing. Youth must be served. I am enchanted to have been present at such a moment.'

'Jeanne will give you a cup of coffee. I'll be free in half an hour,' said Pierre. Then, turning to the commercial traveller: 'You must excuse me. That young man is like a son to my wife and me.'

The traveller accepted the list which Pierre had given him and made none of the difficulties that he had foreseen. He was a good-hearted fellow and admired Pierre's enterprise and strength of character.

But he was astonished when after driving down to the bottom of the hill, the young soldier whom Pierre Lanfrey had spoken of as a son, stopped him and asked if he could give him a lift to Chalons.

'Have you got a pass?' he asked, for it struck him that in spite of the croix de guerre, Georges might be a deserter.

Georges held out the paper.

'O.K. Jump in. I'll drop you in Chalons though it's a bit out of my way. Something gone wrong, eh?'

Georges looked at him but did not reply and the commercial traveller asked no more questions.

In Chalons there was a queue of soldiers outside the house and Georges was told angrily to take his place at the end and wait his turn as he walked stolidly to the head of it.

When one fellow grabbed hold of him, he hit him with the edge of his hand under the nostrils and spat out: 'I'm not here for pleasure.' The man whose nose was bleeding let go and swore, muttering vengeance.

'Not here for pleasure?' inquired his neighbour.

'Going to see your sister or your mother?' suggested another.

'Maybe he's married to one of the tarts,' said a third.

Georges remained deaf to these remarks and told the man at the door that he had come to see Sylvie Turpin, a new recruit to the establishment. He had a message for her.

'Go round to the other door, mate. For the officers.'

There were catcalls from the whole queue.

At the officers' entrance an elderly woman came out and Georges was admitted.

'The child is ill and isn't working. Yes, you can see her.'

She was in bed in a tiny room. She was flushed and looked feverish. Sylvie looked up at Georges with an expression he had never seen before. The fear and defiance were obvious, but there was hatred also.

Georges did not go up to the bed where she was lying. Her expression forbade his kissing her or taking her hand in his. He lumbered across the room and sat down on a small flimsy chair which, except for a bidet, was all the furniture that there was in the room. He unstrapped and took off his steel helmet; his overcoat, a brighter blue from being soaked with the rain, bent stiffly under him and the scabbard of his bayonet caught in the back of the chair.

'What have you come for, Georges?' asked Sylvie.

He was silent. Now that he was in her presence he did not know why he had come.

She looked at him spitefully and said: 'If you've come for a fuck I'm under doctor's orders. But if you tell Madame that you are my boy friend, she'll let you have a girl for free. I think Hélène would be the best value.'

The brutality of Sylvie's words astonished Georges. He wanted to ask: 'What makes you speak like that?' But he said nothing. After a silence Sylvie said: 'It's the old story. I believed what Maurice said. He got tired of me quickly . . . and he gave me a dose. I would like to pay him out. He with all his decorations, he thinks he's the hero of the French people. He's a rotter. A heartless rotter. But life is like that. Old Emile knew better than I did.'

Georges sat on the little chair with knees apart, sometimes looking at her, sometimes looking at the well-scrubbed wooden floor between his legs.

'He took a room for me at Chalons. He left me without any money. I think he gave me this address as a sort of dirty joke. I didn't know what the place was. I was ill too

138

and no money. The Madame took me in and they have all been kind to me. I can never go back to Dorlotte.'

'All the same, it's what you had better do when the doctor has patched you up,' said Georges.

'Never. I'll never go back.'

Georges understood. It was no use arguing. However he said hesitatingly: 'They are good-hearted people. Everyone makes mistakes . . . and you belong there'

'I don't belong anywhere now . . .' then, after a pause, she added: 'or to anybody.'

Georges was silent. It was far from his thoughts to contradict her, or to say: 'You belong to me.' And yet, if he had not had some such feeling, why had he come at all? He was not free. There was nothing he could do. In two hours time he must report for duty. They sat for a little while silent, Sylvie looking at him with wonder and contempt. She knew that he could do nothing to help her.

Suddenly she said in clear tones: 'There's not much difference between a soldier and a whore. Both are scum. We can't help ourselves and we can't help each other.'

Georges looked up at her and seeing the expression on his face, she said angrily: 'You don't understand anything, Georges. You don't know what you are. But I'm telling you. You are just the same as the girls here. You have to kill anyone you are told to kill. A butcher's boy. You can't choose. We girls have to pretend to love and have to fuck anyone we are told to. You can't choose. We can't choose.'

Georges made a sudden movement of disgust and repudiation. He looked at her with horror, wanting to say: 'How can you talk such drivel? I am a soldier of my own free will. I obey orders because only by doing so can we drive the Boches out of France.'

But he said nothing. He hadn't come to have an absurd argument.

Sylvie went on: 'Butcher boy! Butcher boy! You would have to shoot Frenchmen if you were ordered to. You will,

I'm sure, when they mutiny. And they are going to. . . . Why don't you say something?'

Georges stared at her hopelessly and opened the palms of his hands. But all he could bring out was: 'Why . . .'

'When the workers strike, you'll shoot them down. Because you are a good little butcher boy. Why haven't Frenchmen got guts like the Russians?'

Georges went on staring at Sylvie who suddenly sat up in bed and waved her fists above her head.

'We girls are here to keep the *poilus* contented so they will be willing to go on being massacred. All a French soldier wants is cunt. So we do our war work! Splendid isn't it? We put off the day of the revolution. Aren't you proud of me, Georges?'

Sylvie put her tongue out at him and then said more quietly: 'So you see, soldiers and whores are just the same: human beings who have lost the right to choose for themselves. That is scum, scum, scum.'

She fell back on the bed exhausted. The vehemence of her attack had left Georges bewildered. He put his head between his hands and then pulled out a handkerchief to wipe his face. Two aluminium rings that he had filed out of the fuse pipes of German shells fell on the floor and rolled away. He had made them for Sylvie when he thought she was still waiting for him in the village. He watched them rolling but made no effort to recover them.

The old woman put her head round the door.

'I'm coming,' said Georges. He stood up, knocking the little chair backwards with the scabbard of his bayonet. He bent down stiffly and picked it up. Sylvie looked at him as he took one or two heavy steps in his hobnailed boots and then stopped to put on his steel helmet and strap it under his chin. She was feeling dazed by her outburst.

'Good-bye, Sylvie,' said Georges and walked out of the room and out of the house.

'He only came to look at me as though I were the tattooed

woman at a fair,' said Sylvie to the old woman. Georges had not kissed her or touched her. That she would never forgive.

He walked away from the brothel like a man made of wood. All he was aware of were the wet square stone sets of the paved street under his feet. He walked slowly through the falling sleet and men moved out of his way to let him go by. He passed several officers without saluting for he did not see them. Only one of them looked at him sharply and then passed on, saying nothing. His greatcoat was saturated and the heavy tails dragged at his shoulders. Georges turned into an archway, unbuttoned his flies and made water. Looking at the arching stream of piss, clear and silvery like the blade of a foil, falling into the gutter, he thought: 'Piss. That is all I shall ever do with my cock, anyway.' He did up his fly and walked on remembering the soldiers in the queue standing in the rain outside the brothel.

'My mother was the village whore and, if I live, I may take a whore out of the house as my wife. Sylvie's not so far wrong anyway about me. But that's not what she was trying to say. . . . Like a cat in a steel trap.'

Georges looked about him. He had taken the wrong street and was walking up the hill to the maternity hospital. He turned back and got to the bus station in time not to be late in camp.

What Sylvie had said to Georges about prostitutes and soldiers was not entirely original. Two years before she had overheard a conversation between the young Englishman, Bruce, and Pierre Lanfrey. It was Bruce's explanation of why he could never be a soldier and since she had been in the brothel in Chalons their words had come back to her.

'It's not really the killing: it is giving up my right of choice – my right to decide what is wrong and what is right.' And Pierre had said: 'You won't accept an authority greater than yourself?'

'No. On some subjects I won't.'

'So you could never be a Catholic?'

'No, I could not. I cannot believe what I am told to believe just because I am told it. I need evidence. And I will not obey an order if my conscience tells me that the order is wicked.'

A fortnight after Georges's visit Sylvie was cured. The young doctor told the Madame that he was pleased.

'She really is clean. We caught her in time – and before she had done any harm herself – all thanks to you, Madame,' he said smiling.

'Well, as soon as she told me that that nasty fellow had sent her to me, I guessed what the trouble was. I won't have him in here, you know. Now he seduces that child and infects her. Well, she owes me a pretty penny and she'll have a busy time before she has paid me off.'

Actually Sylvie only stayed three days in the brothel after her cure. For on the third day an older man, a reservist captain of fifty, came to her and before leaving, asked: 'How did a girl like you come to take up this trade?'

'I might ask why you took up the trade of killing other men?' replied Sylvie.

'What do you mean? Every man has to be a soldier when the country is in danger.'

'And a lot of the girls have to become whores.'

'You exaggerate. And you haven't answered my question.'

'No I haven't. There was a mistake on my part. But what I was saying is that there is little difference between being a soldier and a whore. You can't choose who you kill. I can't choose who I pretend to love. You and I are equals. We act without choice.'

The man gaped at her and went away.

Captain and Deputy Sylvain de Parnac had gone to the brothel because he was desperately lonely and unhappy. He thought he had failed at everything in life and Sylvie's words about having no freedom of choice struck deep. He could not sleep that night. At half past three in the morning he said to himself – untruly – that he had never done a good action in his life and that he would do at least one before he was killed. He would buy that girl out of the brothel. She might not turn out to be as intelligent as her words suggested, but it would be a good action to save such a lovely young creature. By the time he was shaved and dressed and had had his roll and coffee, he was more than half in love with her.

He was back at the brothel hours before the day's work started. The old woman pushed him into Sylvie's little room while she was still half asleep.

'You are a remarkable young woman. I've been thinking over what you said yesterday, and I have decided to buy you out and give you your freedom of choice. Of course I don't expect you to choose an old fellow like me, or to pretend to love me.'

He had to repeat what he was saying and then Sylvie looked at him with an expression that he never forgot and said:

'Who knows? I may not have to pretend.'

She did not have to, for her heart was bursting with gratitude and the more she saw of Captain and Deputy Sylvain de Parnac the more she came to love him. They spent a fortnight together in Paris where he set her up in a flat of her own. A month later he was killed in one of the last of Nivelle's disastrous assaults on the Chemin des Dames – the assaults which led to the widepread mutiny of the French Army which Sylvie had predicted and which Georges was to witness.

Meissonier, the rigger, watched while two men under him wheeled the Nieuport fighter that de L'Espinasse was about to fly, out of the hangar. He walked up to it and began testing the tensions of the wires. Then one of the men got into the cockpit and moved the stick backwards and forwards and side to side and Meissonier verified that the ailerons and rudder moved to their full extent. Lebas, the armourer, climbed up and fixed

143

a new belt of cartridges. By the time that de L'Espinasse walked out to the plane pulling on first his white silk gloves and over them his big fur gauntlets, the plane was waiting. Lebreil stood waiting to swing the propeller. Meissonier's two men were holding the strings of the chocks which hung slack. Maurice climbed in, tested the ailerons and rudder and gave the signal to start the engine. Lebreil swung the propeller and jumped back. The engine fired and Maurice slowly pushed the throttle open. The engine roared and the little plane vibrated as though it would shake itself to pieces, while Maurice watched the rev. counter. Then he throttled back, waved his gloved hand and the men pulled away the chocks. Maurice eased the throttle open, the plane moved forward. He gave full throttle and the plane fled down the field leaving a cloud of dust and bits of dry grass. The plane lifted and disappeared. Then reappeared high up. The rigger and his assistants walked back to the hangar; Lebas, the armourer, had preceded them.

Not until he had reached a thousand metres did Maurice feel comfortable. Then he turned back north towards the front. There were white clouds at the east – a range of snow mountains among whose crevasses it would be possible to hide. So far there was no enemy in sight. It was perfect peace and the sense of great loneliness : a loneliness which was the only security – the only real happiness – that he knew. Time disappeared and Maurice's consciousness seemed to become intermittent, or to consist of two parts. First, an acute awareness of the moment, during which the hammering of the engine sounded louder and he realised to the full that he was high above the earth, riding on air. Second : the moment of peace passed and he was once again the alert duellist of the sky, searching every corner, above, below, behind, and keeping an eye also on the rev. counter, the oil pressure, altimeter and petrol gauge.

Maurice had not flown for a week : not since his escapade with Sylvie. He had not been in action for a month. Now he would have to seek out the enemy and it would have to be over Verdun.

Those were the orders which he was reluctant to obey. He flew a zigzag course so as to leave no blind spots in which an enemy might be ensconced. Presently he saw a formation of five aircraft below him, flying north-east. They were almost certainly French. And then eight planes – Germans – perhaps led by Boelcke himself. They were flying out of the cloud at an angle. They had seen the five French planes and were trying to intercept them. Maurice flew after them, watching, and high up. But the French squadron had too long a start and the Fokkers suddenly turned back, probably to execute their mission over Verdun. Maurice followed, weaving his way in and out of the clouds. As he turned he saw a German plane quite close. No doubt it was a pilot who like himself preferred loneliness and perhaps had fallen out of formation using getting lost in cloud as his excuse. The German was flying steadily and Maurice climbed until he was behind him. Then he opened the throttle and dived, and getting the Fokker's fuselage in his sights, fired a burst from his machine gun. The Fokker rolled over and almost stalled and then, as Maurice shot past, there was a burst of fire which riddled the Nieuport. The engine was hit. Suddenly and silently, Maurice dived: the ailerons were undamaged but there was no control of the rudder. He reached a cloud below him and was almost stunned by the silence and the darkness. When at last he came out of the cloud he realised that he was only a few hundred metres over the Verdun battlefield. It was raining and he would have to force land in that scarred and shell-pitted desert; whether it was held by the enemy or not he could not tell. Flak exploded so close that his aeroplane shuddered but neither it nor he was hit. He planed lower and lower and then rifle bullets began tearing holes in the fabric of the wings. They reminded Maurice of the splashes of thrown pebbles in a pond. But in spite of the bullets he held off from the ground till the very last moment and actually touched down with a perfect three point landing on a fairly level stretch. Next moment the undercarriage caught in wire, the plane somersaulted and Maurice was catapulted clear and fell into a crater on something wet and squashy. He lay there on his back and could feel the heat of the burning plane and hear the crackle of the flames and then the belt of cartridges exploding, over the lip of the crater, only a few metres away. He became aware of an overpowering nauseating smell. But he lay there winded and almost fainting with a pain in his left leg. He would have vomited, but it required an effort, and when at last the spasm came he had not the strength to turn his head. After what seemed a long time he realised that his bones were unbroken and he put out his hand to push himself upright. It went into something soft. It was the rotting body of a dead man, and, disturbed in their feeding ground, three enormous rats ran out over his legs. He made another gigantic effort, this time with his left arm. His hand found something solid to press on – a shattered rifle buried in the mud. He sat up incautiously and a few seconds later was almost stunned by the force of a bullet hitting the metal frame of his goggles and tearing them off his nose which felt as though it had been broken. He fell back at once into the hole. The stench of the corpse beside him was too much and he vomited and watched his last half-digested meal of wine and stewed chicken dribbling down the front of his flying coat. He spat and swore and in reply heard a voice saying: 'Keep still, mate. Keep your head down.' Then: 'Are you a goner?'

'I'm not sure. I don't think I'm wounded, but my leg . . .'

'That's fine. We'll try and get you out after dark,' interrupted the voice.

'Where am I?' asked Maurice.

'I'm going down the trench as they may lob some stuff over now they know you are alive. Keep quiet now and if they haven't got you by night, we'll come back and see if we can get you out.'

Maurice lay still in an agony of fear and misery, feeling the liquid from the corpse he was jammed up against, slowly penetrating his trousers. After a time he disengaged his right arm and shoulder in a vain attempt to shift his body to the left. He tried to scoop up some mud to cover the ooze that ran from the dead man but his fingers encountered more flesh – a hand – but it was bloodless and clean compared with the deliquescent body which seemed held together by bits of cloth so caked with mud that it was impossible to tell whether they were parts of a French or a German uniform.

After that Maurice did not move. Every now and again a bullet hit the rim of the crater not more than 15 centimetres above his head. But not moving involved the closest contact with the crater's other occupant, who from his condition must have been there in sole possession for many months.

Stench, nausea, extreme fear combined to produce a state of inert agony and the almost continuous rattle of machine-gun fire, punctuated at intervals by ear-splitting shell-bursts, helped to dull his reactions.

Then, as he lay pressed closely against the rotten torso he became aware of movement – of life itself inside that mass of corruption. Where his ribs were jammed against the body he could feel it nudging him and then something passing down and nudging him in a different place. During a lull in the machine gun fire he heard a squeaking: the rotting corpse was full of rats living and breeding in defiance of the rain of German shells.

Suddenly a shell fell close enough to cover him with fragments which it had thrown up: earth, small stones, cartridge cases and the heel of a boot.

Maurice prayed. He begged God to forgive him his sins though he did not remember what they were. He promised that if it pleased the Virgin to save him from the charnel pit into which he had been hurled headlong, he would lead a chaste life. He vowed he would be a different man – but it did not occur to him to repent of having sent Georges to the trenches, or for having seduced and abandoned Sylvie. Like a dog crawling on its belly before its master he knew that he had offended and begged forgiveness.

Darkness was a long time coming and then it was intermittent, for flares went up, revealing every crater, every line of sagging wire in no-man's land. Maurice called out several times and despaired. He had almost fallen into unconsciousness when he heard men talking in French close to him. He called out in vain: the voices took no notice. At last, however, a voice said: 'I'm throwing you a rope, mate. If you can get hold of it, we'll put you out of there into our trench.'

The rope was thrown and missed, then pulled back and thrown again. At the sixth attempt it hit him in the face, almost blinding him. He grabbed it.

'Tie it round your body under your arms so it can't slip loose.' Maurice managed to sit up and fastened the rope, though his eyes were watering from the pain of the smack in his face. Then the rope tightened and he was pulled out of the shallow crater and paddling with his hands and pushing with his feet was dragged for a few yards through the mud and tumbled over the parapet of the French trench into friendly hands.

He was stiff with bruises, very hungry and disappointed to find that there was no food. He forced himself to ask questions but received few answers. In what sector of the front was he? How soon could he get back from the front line? But his rescuers looked at him with dull eyes and Maurice was profoundly shocked by their indifference to his plight. They had made a great effort in dragging him into their trench and now that they had got him they were bored by his sufferings and wanted him to stop talking.

'If the Boche hears you kicking up such a shindy, he'll be likely to lob something over.'

Maurice gathered at last that they might be relieved before dawn and if so he could go back to support trenches where there might be bread and wine and from where he would be taken back to advance base. He offered to go down the trench alone but was told he would not find his way and might attract the enemy's attention.

Except for a few bruises Maurice was unhurt, but after he had got back and had a hot bath, shaved and been given a shampoo and put on clean clothes, he still did not feel clean. However much he scrubbed, however clean his nails, teeth, underpants, shirt and uniform, he could not purge himself of the odour of death, of the proximity of rotten flesh held together by mudcaked cloth, of the nuzzling rats and the ear-splitting shell bursts, chattering machine-guns and hammer blows of artillery. When he went for a medical check-up, he burst into hysterical sobs and the old doctor saw before him a changed and broken man.

CHAPTER NINE

It was difficult to see grey figures in the mist of dawn: it was impossible to focus on anything precisely. Georges lay behind his machine-gun and looking through the binoculars could make out a movement behind the wire. The Boches were cutting holes in it. But when he put the glasses down he could not be sure of the exact spots. Then, suddenly they were racing towards him, spreading out from the holes that they had made. He opened fire and on all sides of him the trench crackled with rifle fire. The important thing was to plug the hole through which they were crowding. Georges had got it in his sights and sprayed it with bullets. No more of the grey figures were getting through – and then, suddenly, he was aware of three of them running at him from the side, two with bayonets and a third pausing and holding a hand grenade. Georges swivelled his gun to the right and fired a burst at the man with the grenade which a moment later exploded. Another of the men had gone down but before Georges could do anything, the third German jumped at him – and fell while he was jumping. His rifle and bayonet fell across Georges's shoulders. He flung it aside and pushed the German clear of the barrel of his machine-gun. Then fired another burst at the hole in the wire. About a dozen men had come through and the riflemen near him picked them off.

There was a lull. The wounded German had been shot through the lungs and blood was frothing out of his mouth. Georges reached out, got hold of the man's rifle and shot him with it through the forehead. Then he had to change the belt of cartridges in his machine-gun and was ready for the next rush. But the sun was rising, long shadows stretched across the bare space between the trenches – the shadows of iron pickets and tangled wire and of the lumps which were dead or wounded men. The attack was over.

Lying on his face at full length, clutching the ground with his fingers, pressing the side of the shallow trench with his knees and elbows, Georges was hit by a quake in the earth which seemed to bruise every muscle fibre, while his senses were stunned and deafened by the vast explosion. A long time afterwards things began falling from the air – chunks of metal, stones and earth, splinters of wood, lengths of wire and soft wet pieces of flesh. These things covered him. Then Georges shook himself free of earth and oddments like a dog coming out of the water and lay flat in that shallowest of trenches, gripping its sides, and waited, becoming all the time aware of new pains and bruises and that his ears were packed tight with earth and aware of the smell of T.N.T. and of fear. The stink of his own fear.

Once again the very earth to which he was clinging hit him and his body seemed dismembered by the blast of the explosion. This time the sides of the trench collapsed upon him and a long time later he was buried still deeper in a fine rain of falling earth. Some hard object seemed to crack his skull. After that he could not shake himself free. There was something heavy pressing on the small of his back and his left leg gave him such pain that he dared not move.

A rifle with a fixed bayonet lay buried under his arm. He managed to unfix the bayonet and push it up through the earth and gravel covering his head, and by working it about made a hole through which he could breathe more easily. He left the blade of the bayonet projecting up. It was perhaps this which stopped the Boches from treading on him when soon afterwards they attacked. Although he could see nothing, he was very much aware of the attack. Lying there, lightly buried, they did not notice him as they doubled past. Two of them halted close beside him, uncertain perhaps how to negotiate the huge craters left by the explosions.

He could not see or hear them – yet he knew that they were there, as a mole is aware of a man walking overhead by the vibration of the earth. Many hours later they must have come back during the night, unable to hold the ground that they had won. For when he awoke, more in possession of his faculties, and managed to widen the hole until he could get his head free, he saw that it was daylight and a Frenchman, digging in near by, as he was attempting to dig himself out, noticed that he was alive. Later on they got him out, and carried him back to the casualty station.

Georges was in hospital. In his delirium he knew that and that he could not move, and yet it seemed to him that he was high up – perched precariously on a treetop. In this helpless condition he was watching a crowd of men – soldiers – French soldiers – streaming past. Yet though he was perched and in danger of falling, he was close to the crowd and could see every feature.

Faces, faces, hundreds of men's faces. There were smiling blue-eyed, red-cheeked boys, laughing men, older more serious faces, the face of a man in pain, whose feet hurt him but who kept up pluckily with the others, dark-haired men from the South, mean faces, faces of steady older men, here and there a black face, all being swept past like leaves in a torrent, or like a flock of sheep pressing on each other, afraid of the dog behind. There was the noise of their feet – but only the faces were visible, like hurrying sheep, like leaves in the wind, like apples floating down a river.

They were all French soldiers, officers in képis, infantry in steel helmets, thousands of faces. And then Georges noticed that here and there was a bad one – as you see a rotten apple when a sackful is being emptied. Yes – here and there a dead man's face among the jostling crowd of the living. At first, perhaps, there was only one among a hundred, then more, discoloured faces, grey, pale, or brown like rotten apples. But the eyes of the living did not notice the dead, but were swept by, laughing and smiling, arguing saying bitter things, nodding agreement. And then more and more dead men's faces – until they outnumbered the living. Grey, ashen faces with unseeing eyes, heads putrefying, the nose sunken, the lips gone, the eyes holes, then a river of skulls and just here and there among them the healthy fresh face of a boy, gay and laughing and unaware of the crowd among whom he was being swept, like a young trout careless of the pebbles of the brook.

Georges slowly became aware of his body: it was as though after a long absence he had slipped back into it and that it fitted him very badly. It was very tight round his chest and one leg pinched him, below the knee. The discomfort of this grew rapidly into an abominable pain in the calf of his leg. He opened his eyes, half expecting to see the river of skulls hurrying past, but instead there was a bearded man in a white coat talking to a woman dressed like a nurse with a red cross on the bib of her apron. Seeing that he was conscious the surgeon spoke to him, but it was too great an effort for Georges to understand what he was saying, so he closed his eyes again.

The sun was shining: everything was familiar: Dorlotte – and yet as Georges walked towards the people in the street they crumbled under his eyes and disappeared. And then there was that awful smell. Suddenly he saw Sylvie; he ran towards her and she smiled. But before he reached her, her smile changed into a toothless grin, the rippling tresses were grey and thin, the chin pointed, the eyes sunken. She held out an arm and the skin was loose and papery and the fingers crooked and gnarled. Georges stood still in horror and a bubble of gas, the stench of rottenness and corruption, burst in his face and filled his nostrils. Sylvie had vanished.

Georges recoiled and turned away – and there was Pierre

Lanfrey looking at him with his grave smile, with that wonderful look of understanding and of sympathy.

'Oh Pierre,' he cried in an agony, appealing to that look in the older man's face. And then the face itself changed, the head dropped, and as Georges rushed forward, Pierre crumbled and disappeared. There on the ground was the steel hook with its long shaft: the hook at least was incorruptible. And the smell was not that of rottenness and death but sweet and sickly, yet somehow soothing, and as he watched the shining hook it changed its shape a little and became very close to him. He gazed at it, seeing it perfectly for a little while before he realised that it was one half of a doctor's stethoscope and heard the words: 'Really extraordinary. This fellow's heart is as sound as a bell: beating as though there were nothing the matter with him.'

Georges was luckier that most wounded soldiers – he interested the specialists and became a medical case. For it turned out that he reacted differently from ordinary cases. Though his nervous responses were abnormal after the experience of being wounded and buried alive, he appeared cheerful and unafraid as he recovered his strength. Then an oculist discovered that he had exceptionally good vision and recommended that some use be made of it.

And just as Georges had been an exceptional case medically he became exceptional administratively. Though he was unaware of it, he was the subject of a whole folder of papers about what should be done with him. He ought, of course, to rejoin his company and his regiment. But while he was in hospital they had been dispatched to Salonika. And it was urged that instead of sending an individual soldier to Greece, some employment might be found for him until such time as a batch of men were sent out to make up for wastage in his regiment, or until it was ordered back to France. An intelligent officer, reading of Georges's exceptional vision, transferred him to special duties in an observation post which had been erected in what remained of a small copse just behind the front line.

His duty there was to watch for any movement in the enemy lines and report by telephone. During his hours of duty he scanned the enemy lines, sometimes using fieldglasses, sometimes a powerful telescope. At that point the front line was separated from the German by three hundred metres of no-man's land. It was a dull monotonous landscape of chalk fields sloping uphill, with the Craonne plateau on the right to the north-east and the Chemin des Dames in front and stretching on the left to the north-west.

In the foreground were picket stakes and wire, then an expanse of slippery chalk and clay and half-frozen ground with a few dry stalks of last year's thistles and mulleins before more iron stakes and rolls of barbed wire partially hid the chalky parapet of the German front line trenches beyond.

It was spring when Georges took up his new job, but it felt like winter. Nothing except the lengthening hours of daylight indicated that summer was on its way. Snow showers were frequent and blinded the observation post.

At that point there was very little exchange of fire between the two front lines. Hostilities were left largely to the artillery and as they were both shelled regularly, the trenches were often left nearly empty with only a few sentries ready to call the men from their deep dug-outs in the event of an attack. If Georges saw any movement in the German lines, a head poked up, the top of a coil of wire being carried along a support trench, he would ring up and report and if the movement were thought to be important, the message would be passed to the battery which had that section of the German line as an objective and a shell or two might be fired.

But after Georges had been at his new job for a fortnight it became clear that a big offensive was in preparation. The Colonial Corps of Senegalese suddenly filled the rear rest areas. Vast quantities of shells and munitions of all kinds were piled behind sandbags and camouflaged. And then the guns opened fire in a bombardment designed to pin down all enemy movement and destroy his wire.

Then came the great day, Monday 16 April, when General Nivelle's offensive was to break through the enemy lines and roll back the German army. It had not been put off because of the weather. There was a bitter wind, driving snow and sleet and seas of half-frozen mud.

Before dawn Georges was joined in his observation post by a major who was to play an important part in the later stages of the disastrous battle. At dawn the Senegalese attacked in three waves in quick succession. Through their fieldglasses Georges and Major Ybarnegaray could see them carry the first German line easily, then reach and carry the second line and in one or two places surge beyond to the third. Then the Germans opened up with massed machine-gun fire. A veil of sleet fell and hid the attack, then it cleared and Georges could see knots of the Senegalese clustering to get through holes in the wire. Suddenly a whole group of men would be swept away as the machine-guns chattered; soon there were only a few soldiers beyond the second line. A new wave of men leapt out of the second line trench and a barrage of the French seventy-fives opened. But the shells were falling short among the attacking troops. Georges shouted into the mouthpiece of his telephone, but the line was dead – a German shell must have cut the wire.

Together with the major he watched the Senegalese turn and run. Through his powerful glasses he could see their black faces and the open mouths of the nearest. They were running madly but one after another fell forward on his face and the ground was soon sprinkled with the bodies of dead and wounded men. Above the roar of the guns was a peal of thunder and a deluge of hail and sleet which left the ground covered with white lumps. One of the nearer lumps was moving and Georges focused his glasses on it. It was a big Senegalese whose legs were paralysed, probably by a wound in the spine, making desperate efforts to drag himself with his hands over the melting hail and mud. He stopped and raised his head and Georges could see his face. Then more and more slowly he began to drag himself a metre or two nearer to safety. But he was dying and Georges saw his head fall forward into the half-frozen mud.

The wounded men, who lay far out and could not be brought in, were lucky in their weather. In the height of summer many might have lived for days, even a week. But in that bitter April their agonies were soon numbed by the cold and all would be dead of exposure before the next day. Nevertheless, before the offensive was brought to a halt 96,000 wounded men had been evacuated to hospitals all over France. Provision had been made for 15,000 men.

And when the need for it was over, the French artillery barrage lifted and they could see the shells bursting in the German third line of trenches.

By the time Georges was relieved, the telephone wire was mended. The Senegalese first waves had been wiped out and a new attack was in preparation. Georges did not dally, but hurried away among the stretcher bearers carrying badly wounded men – the lucky ones who had been hit early in the attack and had fallen within a few metres of their starting point.

The slopes below the Craonne plateau were honeycombed with concrete machine-gun bunkers and with deep dug-outs where the Germans could wait safely until the bombardment was over and from which they could emerge to mow down the attacking infantry. These had scarcely been touched by the French bombardment which had not even cut gaps in the wire. Because of this the battle had been lost within an hour of its being begun.

It was renewed next day and the day after that, but once again with inadequate artillery bombardment. Supplies of ammunition were running short and the huge numbers of wounded who were waiting for attention helped to impede communications. The morale of troops and their officers was bad : the officers angry and despairing, the troops critical and sullen. The mutiny that Sylvie had spoken of and which had seemed so absurd to Georges at the time, might not be far away if the generals went on sending the troops to be massacred. Georges had heard Major Ybarnegaray exclaim : 'This has got to be stopped!' And that was within an hour of the offensive having started. It was still going on.

There were, however, lulls in the attack and during one of them, when Georges was on duty in the observation post, and was about to ring base and report, he realised that it was unnecessary to ring. His opposite number, the man to whom he reported but whom he had never seen, was speaking in a low voice, hardly more than a whisper, and the words were :

> The rain has steamed and washed us clean,
> The sun has dried and dyed us black;
> Magpies and crows have had our eyes
> And plucked our beards and our eyebrows.
> At no time have we been at rest,
> This way and that way with the wind,
> Ceaselessly we twist and twirl.
> No thimbles have ever been so pricked
> As we by the needling bills of birds.
> Man, do not mock us as we swing,
> But pray to God who would forgive all of us.

There was a silence. At last Georges said:
'Excuse me, but I was listening. Did you write that?'
'I beg your pardon.'
'What you were reciting just now – did you write it?'
'Do you like it?'
'I don't know what to say . . . . But it makes me see them,' said Georges confused.
'Have you ever heard of François Villon?'
'I'm not sure. Was he a poet?'

'He was almost the first great French poet. He was condemned to be hanged more than three hundred years ago. He wrote those lines in anticipation – but actually the King pardoned him and he wasn't hanged.'

'Thank you very much,' said Georges.

Next day Georges was told to report at 'the office' when he came off duty. 'The office' was situated in a big wine cellar, brilliantly lit by electricity. In it there was a captain seated at a desk, two lieutenants and half a dozen telephonists in uniform.

Georges went up to the captain and saluted.

Only then did the officer look up.

'Are you the observer from Heutebise O.P. who was ordered to report?'

'Yes, sir.'

'It has been suggested that your knowledge of the locality will make you a useful listener who can interpret reports quickly and without making mistakes.'

'Thank you, sir.'

'Report for duty in two hours time. Go and get something to eat now.'

Georges saluted and was leaving 'the office' when a tall dark artilleryman put his papers in a drawer and followed him up the stairs. Georges had not been at the base before and looked about wondering where he was to find a meal. His companion said: 'Come and have a drink. The mess hut is over there. We shall be working in the office together. You are the chap who liked those lines of Villon's, aren't you?'

Georges followed his new friend. He said that he would like a Pernod and his companion ordered a Verveine for himself. Then, noting Georges's surprise, he said: 'I don't drink alcohol.'

'Like some of the English I used to work with.'

'What English? Their troops live on rum and their officers on whisky. The name of their Commander in Chief is on the bottles: Haig is Haig and Haig's whisky.'

Georges explained about the English who had come out to rebuild the village he belonged to and that he had been employed to work for them.

'Everyone said that they were shirkers. But they were pleasant chaps. They had come out to help before there was compulsory military service in England. They had not volunteered because they thought it wrong to be a soldier – some religious sect. They built nearly fifty huts in our village and I worked with them. After they left I was fool enough to volunteer before I was due to be called up – when I was only sixteen.'

They discussed the English. The artilleryman did not like them. They had no capacity for logical thought, but when Georges told him his friend Bruce refused to be a soldier because it involved abdicating his freedom of choice, he exclaimed with delight.

'Yes, I agree with that. We soldiers are made to kill the wrong people.'

After a pause, during which Georges wondered what people his companion thought they ought to be killing – no doubt General Nivelle and his staff, but where would one stop? he was asked:

'Was there much destruction in your village, then?'

'The Boches burned all the houses and committed atrocities. Most of the people went away that winter, but others stuck it out, living in cellars.'

'I went through a place like that once, ages ago, at the beginning of the war. It made an impresion on me. There was a boy building a hut out of the stones of the ruins. It seemed to me so wonderful. The indomitable spirit of man. Quite a young boy too. I wrote a poem about him – making him symbolise France which could never be conquered. I was a patriotic Frenchman in those days.'

Georges looked at his companion oddly and grinned.

'I think I was that boy. You are the fellow who asked me if I ever read books and when I told him they had all got burned in the houses, gave me a volume of poetry.'

'I don't remember that. Haven't you got me mixed up with someone else?'

'Well, I've got the book in my pack though I haven't looked at it for a long while. There's a name on the flyleaf: Julien d'Aubrac.'

'That's me. So you must be right. Incredible.'

They smiled at each other, astonished, nodding their heads over the chance that had brought them together and the miracle that they should both have survived. From that moment they became inseparable friends. They slept in the same hut, ate at the same table, had conversation with no one else. Julien talked about his own life, but Georges never mentioned Maurice de L'Espinasse or Sylvie. Julien read Georges his poems and began educating him by continual discussions, anecdotes, descriptions of men and of their ideas, of places and the movements of peoples and growth of civilisations throughout the world. They seldom spoke during working hours but occasionally exchanged a glance. Georges was astonished to learn that his new friend, who knew so much more than himself, was an anarchist who wanted to destroy all governments, the French as much as the German, and that he thought that the war might accomplish this destruction.

Every day brought rumours – though little was definitely known, even among the officers. But the atmosphere was heavily charged, as before a thunderstorm. The officers kept apart from their men – and the men gathered in fierce and bitter groups. Their sullen looks did not so much threaten disobedience as defy their officers to give any orders at all. Although no one, neither Captain Mauritain nor any of his subordinates, knew it, the first crack came in the higher ranks of the command which led to the intervention of the politicians, the Minister for War and the President of the Republic.

General Hirschauer sent a message to the President, M. Poincaré, by his staff officer Major Ybarnegaray, to say that

the resumed attack, ordered by General Nivelle, must somehow be called off as the artillery preparation had been totally
inadequate and that supplies of ammunition were running
short.

None of this was known among the serving officers or
their troops, yet a sense of trouble in the highest ranks was
guessed at and hoped for. They could not know that Poincaré
had telephoned to Nivelle and that the latter, lying, had
replied that the date of the attack had not been fixed and the
ammunition not yet allocated. But the rumours of dissension
in the high command spread quickly and contributed to a
state of anger and despair among the officers. Then came an
incident the news of which did spread rapidly.

When Nivelle attacked General Micheler for mismanage-
ment of the offensive, that General had interrupted him to
open the door so that his words should be overheard and
said: 'You are about to commit an infamous action. You
wish to make me responsible for this mistake. In fact I never
ceased to warn you what the results would be. Do you know
what such an action is called? It's called cowardice.'

Nivelle had no reply to make and hurried away.

This scene was overheard, as intended, by Micheler's staff
and the story spread quickly through the French armies. Confidence in Nivelle and his staff had been destroyed by the
time the exhausted troops mutinied – or in most cases said:
'We will hold the line. But we will not attack massed
machine-guns behind unbroken wire.' But by then the politicians had interfered, Nivelle had been dismissed and General
Pétain appointed in his place. But many generals, even those
who thought Nivelle's offensive disastrous, thought it was
infamous to allow politicians to interfere in military matters.

Julien was jubilant as the trouble spread, though he was
careful not to let the officers guess at his opinions. But to
Georges he preached anarchism. All that any country needed
in the way of a government were local councils managing the
necessary affairs of the regions – areas nowhere bigger than

the departments. He realised that the day when central governments would be done away with might be far off. First there would be a revolution following a general refusal in the army to go on fighting.

'But the Germans will come through again,' objected Georges.

'Perhaps for a little while. But the revolution starting in France and Russia will sweep across Europe. The Germans have even more to gain from it than we have, for their government is even worse than ours.'

'I would choose anything rather than that the Germans should come back. We held them at Verdun and are still holding them there and at all costs we must continue to hold them here.'

'For how long?'

'Until the Americans come.'

'It may be too late then for the revolution. The Americans are more likely to bolster up our capitalist government than the Germans.'

'You can have your revolution after we have won the war. I'm a socialist, but we must save France first.'

'I abominate your socialist leaders. They are the lackeys of the capitalists and of the military. And if they had powers they would set up a slave state with a terrifically strong central government – all equality and no liberty – and the equality only on paper. Man's first need is freedom. As long as you have central governments you will have armies and professional soldiers and you will have war: one war after another.'

Georges was impressed and puzzled, but he did not agree.

In the office among the network of telephones the work went on, with uniformly depressing reports coming in day after day from the observation posts. The listeners would scribble them down:

'Enemy appears to be relieving trench in square 4567' or 'Wire has definitely been repaired in sections 692, 693 and

695. Wire in 138 either uncut or repaired.' At intervals the messages would be passed to the staff-captain who was correlating the reports from all sources and marking all the changes on a large scale map of the section of the line in front of Craonne and the Chemin des Dames On 20 May news came that the men in General Duchêsne's 10th Army had refused to return to the line and were running wild in the rest camp at Prouilly which was already full up with troops when they arrived there, so that they had to lie on the open ground. They had been ten days in trenches captured from the Germans without adequate supplies, and they were expecting to go on leave, when they were ordered back to the trenches. Men of the 5th Army near at hand also refused to return to the line. There were hundreds of them, drinking, shouting and singing the *Internationale*.

Julien and Georges went out and were soon swallowed up in the crowd. They kept together, watching and listening as an officer was shouted down. But the troops were good-tempered and they heard shouts of: 'We are due to go on leave. You know that as well as we do, chum. It's not your fault. But we are not going back to the line.' After a time they saw that a party armed with a couple of machine-guns was forming up. There were shouts of: 'Come on, mates. We're off to Paris. We'll help to make those bastards' minds up for them. Peace – or we'll know the reason why.' About two hundred men fell in and Georges and Julien followed out of curiosity. When they reached the town there was a halt. Then came a short chatter from the machine-gun. There was a barricade holding them up, but it was not manned. The soldiers cleared a way through it and went on. The two friends thought they had seen enough and were just about to turn back when there was a sudden rush of military police and dismounted cavalry from the side-street. Julien ran one way and Georges the other, and though shots were fired at them they got away unharmed. Georges took refuge in a barber's shop. To his surprise it was open, with half a dozen customers waiting their turn, and the barber, an old fellow with a red bulbous nose, was working. Soon there was a seat empty and Georges picked up a newspaper and sat down.

To his disgust he found that his hands were shaking uncontrollably and that he could not hold the newspaper steady enough to read it. There was a sudden burst of firing close by. The barber's customers spoke only in whispers to each other. Barbers are usually loquacious, but the old fellow in his soiled white coat only asked his customer in the chair how he wanted his hair cut and, later, whether he was satisfied. He was clearly afraid of committing himself one way or the other. Soon after Georges had come in, he had locked the door of his shop: as each man was ready to leave, he unlocked it, let him out and locked it again. Finally it was Georges's turn to sit in the barber's chair. He was afraid, although he would not have admitted it. The form that his fear took was to have everything done that was possible, so as to put off the moment when he would have to leave the shop.

His hair was cut, then shampooed, then oiled. He was shaved and then he had a face massage which meant that the powder given after the shave had to be given again.

The old barber seemed to understand and for the first time opened his mouth.

'You boys are going to let the Boches come back, aren't you? Well, I don't blame you. I would rather have Boche soldiers back in these chairs than have the slaughter going on. You know, it's a funny thing. There's a regimental barber for all soldiers, but they would always rather come and have it done properly though it means paying for it. And that's what's wrong with socialism. A barber paid by the state would snip your ears off. Well, good luck, and thank you, sir.'

The old man went to the door of his shop and unlocked and opened it and Georges unwillingly went out into the street. It was empty and everything seemed safe enough. But Georges was still afraid. He was feeling a strange childish terror such as he had never known facing the enemy. Then he had not the leisure necessary for such emotions. Georges knew that the military police could not tackle the main body of mutineers. But they would be rounding up and taking their revenge on stragglers. It was already nearly twilight and when Georges saw a narrow dark street on the other side of the road, he darted down it, hoping to avoid the main square. He didn't want to expose himself.

He walked slowly, stopping to listen. There was the noise of the engines of a German bomber circling about somewhere up in the sky. Otherwise only far away gunfire.

He went on and then, in the failing light, he saw the body of a soldier lying in the middle of the road. He was dead and had fallen on his face. Whoever had shot him had been down there at the end of the street towards which Georges was slowly making his way. Then twenty metres further on there was a pool of blood, and looking about him, Georges saw blood on the doorstep of a shop – a butcher's shop. It was wide open and there were carcases hanging on hooks, and a solid wooden counter. And then he saw suddenly that the carcases hanging from the steel hooks were men. There was blood running down on one side of the step. Georges stepped up on the other, careful not to bloody his boots. The men hanging there were military policemen. There were five of them. The nearest man had the hook stuck under his chin, and the head tilted back – he was hanging by his lower jaw : blood had run from the side of his mouth and his uniform was soaked with it. Georges would have stepped into the shop but he saw it was awash with blood, and he stood poised on the clean half of the doorstep. The next man had had the hook stuck into the back of his neck, under the skull. His head was tilted forward and he was staring, with dead eyes, at his toes which just touched the ground. There was a cavalry trooper. The hook had been thrust into his mouth and his helmet with its horsetail was pushed back revealing that he had been a red-haired man. Then Georges saw scrawled on a slate the notice: *Pigmeat for Sale.*

There was a terrific explosion. The German bomber had laid its egg not more than a hundred metres away and the corpses on the hooks were gently swinging. Their hands had not been tied and from that Georges concluded that they had not been put on the hooks until after they were dead.

He stepped back into the street and walked on in a stupor. As he came to the corner, where the alley ran into the boulevard, he was pounced on by a posse of military police. He was no longer afraid.

'What's up, mates?' he asked. Then: 'I work in the artillery liaison office. I went into town to have my hair cut.'

'Lucky for you that you smell of bay rum. Let him go, boys,' said the corporal.

Georges walked off stolidly.

Julien did not come into the hut until very late that night after Georges was asleep. Next morning the news of the corpses hanging in the butcher's shop and the notice *Pigmeat for Sale* was all over the camp. Julien told Georges the story with glee as they were having lunch.

'That's the kind of savage humour I adore. It's like a sword thrust,' he declared. Georges listened in silence. At last he said: 'You are no better than Maurice.'

'What Maurice?'

'A friend who persuaded me to enlist, saying he could get me into the Air Service working as a rigger. Really he wanted to get me out of the way, so that he could seduce my girl.'

'He sounds a nice sort of friend. Well, did he succeed?'

'He took her off to Chalons, gave her the clap and left her stranded without any money. But for a joke he gave her the address of a brothel. They took her in, patched her up and she's there now.'

Julien looked at his friend without saying anything. Then he asked: 'Why did you say that I am as bad as that fellow?'

'You see he thought it a joke to betray an innocent young girl who was taken in by his smart uniform and handsome face, to make promises and then to leave her without any money and send her to a whorehouse, a place she didn't know existed. He thought it was a joke but it was blasphemy.'

In this Georges was crediting Maurice with a sublimity in evil which would greatly have surprised that individual. He had advised Georges to volunteer because it was what he would have done himself at his age. He had given Sylvie the address of the brothel because it was the only place he knew in Chalons where a girl could live without his having to pay for her board and lodging. He did not think that he had done anything outside the ordinary accepted standards of behaviour, unless it were in befriending the two peasant children in the first place.

Georges continued: 'The joke of hanging men on hooks as though they were pigs is blasphemy too. Military police are human beings like you and me.'

Georges had expected Julien to flare up in anger, but he sat silent and finally said uncomfortably: 'Military policemen are not innocent young girls of sixteen – but I suppose you are right in principle.'

'Man, do not mock us as we swing,
     But pray to God who would forgive all of us.'
said Georges. 'I have been thinking of that poem all the morning. You see I saw them hanging in that butcher's shop.' And he described to Julien how he had taken refuge in the barber's and how the smell of bay rum had saved him from arrest or worse at the hands of the military police. That evening when they came off duty, Julien asked Georges,

'But who was this treacherous friend of yours? He sounds like an officer.'

'You may have heard of him: Lieutenant de L'Espinasse, the fighter pilot. Not quite an ace but getting on. He has shot down I don't exactly know how many Germans – but several.'

'What an extraordinary fellow you are, Georges. Was he

quartered close to your village or how on earth did you, a young peasant lad, get to know him?'

'It was an accident that brought us together,' said Georges uncomfortably. But Julien was not satisfied and smelt a drama behind Georges's reserve.

'Come on, out with it. Tell me the whole story.'

'Well, as I say, it was an accident. It was in the first weeks of the war and I happened to be carting clover in the field where the plane he was in crashed. I got him out with my pitchfork. He never forgave me, because I stuck one of the prongs through his ear.'

'What then?'

'The Germans were just coming in to the village. His ankle was broken, so I hid him in the crypt of the church. That's how I got to know the bastard.'

'And how old were you then?'

'Just fifteen.'

'My God. And how did you get your croix de guerre?'

'Oh, shut up. You know how they dish them out.'

That evening when Julien was alone with Georges he said:

'We are wasting our time here and every moment is precious.'

Georges laughed. 'Agreed that we are wasting our time. Agreed that every moment out of the line is something gained.'

'The mutiny here is no good to us; the soldiers only trust comrades who have been in the line with them. I'm disqualified as one of their leaders because I'm in the artillery and they tend to regard artillerymen as their natural enemies. You are disqualified because you have been working for the artillery.'

'That's lucky for both of us. We can't join in, even if we wanted to.'

Julien brushed this on one side, and said: 'It will be entirely different in Paris. And that's where the revolution will take place. So I am going to jump a train to Paris. And I hope you will come with me.'

'Why should I?' asked Georges.

'We shall probably be stood up against a wall and shot. But there is a chance that we might help to clean up some of the mess first. And I believe in you, Georges. You are a sort of mascot. Extraordinary things happen to you. You might end up as a new Danton.'

Georges shook his head. 'No, I don't want your revolution now. We have got to hold the Boches until the Americans come and finish them off. After that the survivors will have their hands full. They'll be too busy to make revolutions and cut each other's heads off.'

'The first thing must be to establish a society based on perfect freedom for the individual and justice between the nations,' said Julien.

'No, the first job will be to plough over the bones,' replied Georges.

'I should like battlefields left as they are, scattered with skeletons as a warning to mankind,' said Julien.

'But most of it is good wheat-growing land. It would be a sin to let it go to waste,' said Georges, genuinely shocked.

'So if you survive you look forward to a life of rolling up rusty wire and burying bones. I can't believe it. You will take part in the revolution. You must!'

Georges shook his head.

'Once the war is over I shan't kill anyone ever again,' he said decidedly. Then as Julien was silent he went on: 'If I live I shall go back to Dorlotte and become a stone mason. Pierre pointed out that there would be plenty of work for masons for a long while what with a war memorial in every village.'

'So you want to spend your life making memorials?' exclaimed Julien in tones of horror.

'No, I don't. I want to help to get back to the life we used to have. I would rather build houses. But the first duty is to plough over the bones and get the land back into cultivation. Whatever your revolution does, it won't produce food. You will never get justice between nations if you let them go hungry.' He looked at his friend and saw that he was terribly disappointed. 'I guess we'll see each other again,' he muttered.

'What makes you doubtful about the need for a revolution and for it now? You know that the war must be brought to an end; you know that under the capitalist system the workers are exploited and cheated and that most men's lives are made miserable; you know that we have the most corrupt government in Europe. You know that all this must be changed. How else can we change it? France is bleeding to death and you talk of waiting for the Americans who will bolster up the existing state of things, even if they do not defeat the Boches.'

Georges took a deep breath. It was difficult for him to explain. Julien could always put things so clearly. But he made an effort and said : 'You always think about humanity, about mankind. You talk always of France, Russia, Germany, England. But I only know individuals. My duty is not to mankind, or to France. It is to the people in Dorlotte. That is why I am fighting and will go on fighting. I am fighting for Pierre Lanfrey and his wife Jeanne, for old Eglantine, for poor old Emile, for Marcelle Duvernois wherever she is. They are the people who were good to me. They are the people who matter to me – not the proletariat, or France or any political party. I know them and they are real. I can be sure of them. And Julien, you are perhaps the most important of them all, though of course you are fighting yourself. All the fine things you talk about are abstractions : heroism, patriotism, revolution, the proletariat, socialism, anarchism . . . I don't know them. Some of them are just poppycock. Your revolution and anarchism may be just poppycock also for all I can tell. It's bound anyhow to be a mixture of good and bad and how do you know that it won't be more bad than good?'

'I can't live without faith in the future of mankind,' exclaimed Julien.

171

'Mankind will get along somehow as it always has done. And perhaps if the Germans lose this war they may not try again for a little while,' said Georges.

'Why should I be so fond of a peasant without any ideals — and a natural conservative too?' said Julien almost plaintively. Then he laughed and said: 'Perhaps our luck will last and we shall meet again. Anyhow I shall know where to look for you — in your blasted village.'

'That's right,' said Georges. 'I'll give you a map and you will know how to find me if I am alive.' After he had drawn it out on a sheet of paper and given it to Julien, the two friends stood up and kissed each other on each cheek and Julien went out into the night.

Next day he did not report for duty and Georges was questioned by the staff captain. In reply he said that his friend had not come in that night, his bed had not been slept in and that he was afraid that he must have come to some harm. No, Julien had never suggested deserting. He had been interested in his work. Yes, he had spoken critically of General Nivelle's offensive because of the terrible casualties and he believed things would be better under General Pétain who had done so well at Verdun. He had never advocated mutiny but he had expressed pity for the men who had suffered so much. He was a loyal Frenchman and soldier.

'Otherwise I would not have made him my best friend,' added Georges rather pompously.

At this the captain turned on Georges and said savagely:

'Admit that you tell lies.'

'Everyone tells lies sometimes. But I am not lying now,' replied Georges.

'I tell you that you are lying and that you are shielding this deserter.'

'No, sir. I am not lying and I do not believe he is a deserter. I think my friend has been killed and robbed. That is what I fear. His body can have been thrown into a hole or a bombed house and might not be found for weeks.'

'You have been observed having long and heated discussions with this man. What were they about?'

'About poetry. About literature. About the history of France.'

'Poetry?' asked the captain incredulously.

'Yes. My friend was a poet himself.'

'If you know any poems by heart, now's your chance. Repeat one. And not something that you learned at school, mind you.'

Georges was silent, thinking. Then just as the officer had begun to say jubilantly:

'You see I've caught you . . .' he held up his hand and said:

'This poem was written by a boy of seventeen in May 1871 after the siege of Paris and the defeat of the Communards.'

Then he began to recite in loud fierce tones that made all the men in the office look round.

'Paris Fills up Again

Disgorged by all the trains, you crowd of cowards
    Behold the sainted City of the West,
The burning sun has cleansed with his hot breath
    Boulevards where Barbarian hordes had pressed.
Forward! Forestall the tides of fire!
    There are the quays, the boulevards shining bright
There the pale blue streets of houses
    That reflected bursting bombs the other night.
What! Ruined palaces? So board them up.
    After the appalling days – with what eager joy you
      gazed!
Ah, there's a troop of bum-waggling girls
    They're madly comic, being half-crazed.'

The captain wanted to order Georges to stop. If he had been able to catch his eye, he would have done so with a gesture. But being a good officer, he was aware of his men. They were all listening to Georges and if he barked out an order, they might not only think him a fool who had made a mistake, but a martinet. And the captain prided himself on the notion that in the office they were all good comrades. Since he had let him start reciting he had better let the fellow finish. But he didn't want a poet in the office; he would have to send him back to the observation post.

'Drink until the mad light of morning
On all your luxury shines and dances.
Stiff and speechless how you dribble,
Into the future not one of you glances.'

The fellow's fierce and angry words went on – anybody would say that he was being insubordinate. But to be fair he was only obeying an order by repeating this stuff. The captain knew he had brought it on himself.

'Syphilitics, kings, madmen, ventriloquists, puppets,
What do you matter to Paris – that old whore?
She'll shake you off, you rotten vicious growlers
And know your poison'd bodies and your rags no more'

Captain Mauritain stopped listening while he watched the faces of his men : astonished, eager, excited. Anything that made men stop work and look like that was dangerous stuff. But it was clear that the fellow was coming to an end.

'Society and everything is re-established
The old vices rain death in their old haunts
Street lighting is back. On the reddened walls
Against the wan sky, a gas jet flickers and flaunts.'

There was a silence. Then the captain said:

'Paris in 1871 you say, written after the Germans had left. Emotional stuff but that's understandable enough. Subversive too. Whot wrote it?'

'Arthur Rimbaud, when he was younger than I am now.'

'Haven't heard of him. Did he go on writing when he was older?'

'No, sir. He gave up poetry and went into the arms trade.'

'Stout feller. Are you a poet too?'

'No, sir.'

'You volunteered, didn't you? Well, get back to your work. Your character is cleared all right, but I suspect your friend

174

has been leading you up the garden path. However, I'll circulate a description to the police in case they find his corpse.'

Georges's delivery of Rimbaud's poem had upset the safe and boring routine. Captain Mauritain was dismayed not only by discovering that there had been a poet in his office but in actually hearing a poem declaimed. He felt that it was a disturbing, irreconcilable intrusion. It made him uneasy to know that behind Georges's ugly peasant features there was a secret life which had nothing to do with the war, or the lives of his fellow workers. And the same uneasiness was felt by all. They could none of them dismiss the poem. It remained in their minds and worried them. It was all right for the men to have hobbies – that was to be encouraged. Laplace, over there, collected stamps. But poetry for some reason was different.

That night Captain Mauritain could not get to sleep. For though he had dined modestly, smoked a pipe and written a letter to his daughter, the unusual experience of having heard a poem recited (and it was at his own request – he had certainly stuck his neck out – that is what comes of being too clever) had unsettled him.

'I'll send that fellow back to the O.P. I only took him into the office on the suggestion of Major Ybarnegaray. And the major has rather cooked his goose among the higher ranks – though I wouldn't say he wasn't right as far as Nivelle and that damned death's-head d'Alençon were concerned. But to get back to my muttons: the fellow has been useful. He's actually a first-class soldier and I should never forgive myself if I victimised him. But he's a disturbing influence owing to his attachment to the other chap. Of course poetry has its place. . . . One of the glories of France – Corneille, Racine, Hugo. But he'll have to go.'

Having made this decision and swallowed a last *fine de champagne* Captain Mauritain fell asleep.

But next morning he felt embarrassed at the prospect of ordering Georges back to the O.P. Everyone in the office would know why. And then – to his dismay – Georges asked to speak to him.

'What is it now?' he asked sharply.

'If you'll excuse me saying so, sir, I'm not suited for an office job.'

'Like to go back to the observation post? Where I must say you were first rate.'

'Yes, sir.'

'That's settled then.'

'Thank you, sir.'

Captain Mauritain was a very decent fellow – what his opposite numbers in the British regular army would have spoken of as 'a white man,' and he said to himself: 'I'll put his name forward for sergeant and I won't mention this poetry business. They might think it was a blot on his copy-book; really he's a stout feller.'

Next day Georges was doing his regular shifts in the obser-vation post and Captain Mauritain, to do him justice, had taken the trouble to write a letter recommending him for promotion.

During the six weeks that Georges had spent working in the office a late spring had blossomed into an early summer and from the observation post he now looked out over fields of flowers. All the wild flowers which man destroys in his cultivation, had come back to the sloping chalky hillside. There were the clovers, white and red, vetches and wild pea, rest-harrow in solid patches, the frail blue harebells, the last of the white starry stitchworts, the first of the white cam-pions, ragged robin in profusion, the pale lilac cuckoo flower where it was damp and a whole variety of orchids.

Where the meadow grass was shorter, or the earth was broken, the little flowers found a place: blue rampaging speedwell, red pimpernel and pheasant's-eye and yellow bird's-foot trefoil, blue milkwort, tiny mouse-ear. Thus the eye looked out on a tapestry of beauty, a tapestry that changed through the weeks – for other flowers would follow: the scarlet wave of poppies and the sheaves of big white ox-eye daisies were to come.

But the flowering field between the observation post and the German lines was not sweet-scented. When the wind blew from the north or north-east the stench of rotting bodies was almost insupportable. They were at least invisible, for the Germans had removed the corpses from their wire for hygienic, rather than aesthetic reasons, and the grass now hid all those who were beyond the reach of the burial parties. When the wind was from the south the stench of death was carried to the enemy who suffered thus from the fruits of victory.

Georges had expected to discover the signs of a big German offensive in preparation. It was obvious to any thinking French soldier that it would be coming and coming soon. It was impossible that the Germans should not know of the widespread mutinies which had crippled and disorganised the French armies. They must know that the lines facing them were thinly held by bitter resentful men with no faith in their officers, or the conduct of the war – a body of men torn by rumours, internal suspicions and hatreds.

The Germans had only to attack and it would be a miracle if they did not sweep all before them and find all France between Verdun in the east and the British armies on the Somme wide open. But they did not. The Allies had no monopoly of wooden-headed generals. All remained quiet on this most vulnerable front.

Georges had time to reflect, and, unexpectedly, he saw himself, perched in his hiding place, with the eyes of the soldiers in the front line trenches. They saw him – and rightly – as part of the staff directing the campaign. It was true that a direct hit on the observation post would kill him, but the chance was slight and the danger very different from that of the men ordered over the top, attacking the enemy wire and exposed to massed machine-gun fire.

Since the mutinies had begun, a growing disgust, a growing indignation had taken possession of Georges and he hated being classed apart from the fighting soldiers. Whatever he might be doing, on duty or off, and particularly when he lay down to sleep and sleep eluded him, he repeated the following indictment to himself:

'Owing to their incapacity, incapacity to learn during the three years the war has lasted, incapacity to have the army equipped with artillery as good as that of the enemy, incapacity to provide the artillery that they have got with sufficient shells, incapacity to choose the right time and the right place for attack, incapacity to husband the lives of their men, our high command organised the massacre of our troops by sending them in appalling conditions against unbroken wire and massed machine guns. Thus they have driven their men to mutiny – and now these incapable officers, who ought themselves to have been court-martialled, are picking out the bravest of their men – for that is what the leaders of the mutineers are – are picking them out to shoot them. The whole thing stinks.

France owes the mutineers – the men who are being shot as traitors – an immense debt. Without them, Pétain, the first reasonable general we have had, would not have replaced Nivelle.

The tragedy is that the mutiny did not come earlier. For tens of thousands of men have been slaughtered in useless attacks, and the lives of Frenchmen are worth more than the lives of Germans and we lose more in these attacks than they do.'

That is how Georges would have argued if Julien had been there and that is how, in his absence, he formulated what he would have liked to declare in public. And he would have added:

'We do not want a revolution with still more bloodshed, civil war and confusion. We do not want "Peace at any Price". We want a set of generals who understand modern

178

war and do not imitate the tactics of Napoleon.'

After making up his mind, Georges walked into the 'office', went up to Captain Mauritain and saluted.

'Hullo. Has anything extraordinary brought you here?' asked the captain, giving him a close look.

'No, sir. Nothing exceptional to report,' said Georges.

'Why are you here then, without orders?'

'I would like to rejoin my regiment, sir. I had meant to ask . . .'

Captain Mauritain looked at him very hard. 'Is it some incident that makes you want to leave this relatively safe job?' he asked.

'Incident? No, sir, what incident? To be quite frank, sir, it stinks up there terribly. And I don't really belong to your unit.'

Better let him go.

'You're a stout feller and have done well both at the observation post and in the office. Of course you can rejoin your regiment and I shall recommend you for a commission. But you must carry on in the observation post until the papers come through.'

Ten days later Georges was ordered to rejoin his regiment as a lieutenant. He had the ribands of the croix de guerre and the médaille militaire on his chest and two wound stripes on his sleeve.

His company was part of the Allied force at Salonika commanded by General Sarrail and he spent the remainder of the war in Greece. He was occupied in routine duties: was never in action and never saw a Turk.

CHAPTER TEN

By the autumn of 1918 the population of Dorlotte had greatly increased. Some families had come back and several widows had sold their properties to newcomers who were attracted now the Allies seemed certain of winning the war, by the large sums which were anticipated as compensation for war damage. There was money too to be made from the American Army. With the advent of these newcomers, the character of the village changed.

When the war ended there were municipal elections all over France and a Mayor was to be elected. None of the older inhabitants put himself forward and the contest was between M. Courcel, a speculator in property and house agent (peculiar in a village where there were scarcely any houses) and M. Lenoir who was in the timber and building materials trade. He was a cousin of M. Muller, which probably lost him the election, as M. Muller was disliked by many of the older inhabitants. M. Courcel was moreover better spoken and better dressed. In some ways the choice was a good one. M. Courcel was determined to make Dorlotte into a show village – a model of reconstruction for the whole of the devastated areas of France. He had, because of this, won the approval and good will of the prefect of the department and set about the task of reconstruction in a grand way, actually having a survey carried out and a large-scale map drawn and painted in patches of pink, blue and green.

This was followed by a decision that the village must be tidied up. In other words that the heaps of stone and rubble must be carted away. M. Lenoir and the mayor made up the breach between them which had occurred during the election, and in the matter of tidying up worked hand in hand. M. Lenoir, with great public spirit, declared that he would clear away the heaps of rubble and stone free of charge. He did not explain that this would be preparatory to selling them back to their former owners when they started to rebuild in concrete, mixing the rubble with sand and cement which M. Lenoir would also be able to provide.

This excellently dovetailed scheme ran into opposition, for Pierre Lanfrey called on M. Courcel and asked him what compensation he was proposing for these acts of confiscation of private property. And Pierre pointed out that after their return many Dorlotte men serving in the army would wish to rebuild their homes themselves out of the materials from which they had been originally constructed.

M. Courcel was a small man with a flat face and pale little eyes. Pierre's demand for compensation and his use of the word 'confiscation' alarmed him and he took refuge in asking Pierre for a statement in writing.

'Certainly. And I shall forward a copy to the sous-préfet for information,' replied Pierre.

'Of course you realise that new houses have to be built to modern standards of safe construction and of hygiene. The use of concrete is strongly recommended by the ministry.'

'All that can be discussed by the individuals concerned – when they are demobilised,' said Pierre.

During the week following, the mayor issued a circular instructing the owners of heaps of stone and rubble to register their ownership if they did not wish them to be removed.

Few of the older inhabitants bothered to read papers pushed under their doors, even if they had spectacles, so that when M. Lenoir's lorry came along and started shovelling up a heap of rubble and putting blocks of stone into it, Madame Chevrillon, whose sons were in Germany in the occupying forces, ran out and began screaming at them. A crowd gathered and in the face of indignant comment, the men were made to unload the lorry and drove it off empty. Another attempt was made – on this occasion to cart away the debris from the Roux house.

Pierre was warned, a crowd again collected and Pierre told M. Lenoir, who on this occasion was present in person, that the confiscation of property belonging to soldiers not yet demobilised would be followed by legal action. It was a curious scene: Lenoir furious and ordering his men to load the lorry, while Pierre remained calm but repeating that he would sue anyone for theft who removed the stones, acting on behalf of Georges Roux who had left his property in his charge when he enlisted. He was sending to Blaye for gendarmes. At midday all adjourned for lunch and M. Lenoir and the lorry did not return.

Some supporters of the mayor's tidying-up campaign declared that the piles of stone and rubble harboured rats; which was certainly true. M. Courcel, however, abandoned his project, as the accusation of stealing property belonging to serving soldiers was one that nobody was ready to face.

The affair did however split Dorlotte into two hostile camps: that of the older inhabitants and that of the new-comers. They shared the same baker and pork butcher because there was only one of each in the village, but the natives all went to Pierre's shop although there was a more restricted choice. The newcomers went to the new combined grocer's and dry goods store on the Ste Menehould road belonging to M. Truffaut. The men of the newcomers drank at Muller's café while the natives gathered at Mother Zins's bistro where the spirits were better and the atmosphere more cosy. Joseph d'Oex went to Muller's. Emile had changed to Mother Zins after he came back to the village.

Brigitte still served in her father's shop though she had been married for more than a year to a young schoolteacher, serving in the infantry, whom she had met at Bar. She had a baby boy called Raoul, born at the time of the German offensive in

March 1918. Maternity suited her. She was more beautiful than ever, tall, fair-haired with rosy cheeks and complexion, the delicacy of which was revealed by the blue veins very noticeable in her temples and on her forearms and wrists. She laughed a great deal, joking with her customers, but in reality she was unhappy. Her husband was a communist: he had survived the mutiny in May and June 1917 because he was on leave with a poisoned hand. It was then he had married Brigitte. But he was a marked man and was sent to a dangerous section of the front. There was besides a secret question which had tormented her: she was not sure how much she loved him. He was the father of her son and his death would be appalling – but how well would they get on together when he came back after the war?

Then a few weeks before the armistice, the news came that he had been killed.

Brigitte went on serving in the shop, but she took to drinking spirits. Twice Pierre found her very drunk. After the second time he reasoned with her. 'It's not good for Raoul.'

'It's no good talking, Papa. If I didn't drink I should hang myself.'

Pierre drew his daughter to him, held her very close for a full minute and said: 'It will pass, darling.'

'I know that. It's what is so terrible about life. One loses all feeling about what is important and becomes a mechanical doll. Look at our neighbours in the village who have lost their sons or their husbands.'

'Not many mechanical dolls, really. They have the strength to live. And you have that strength, darling.'

'I can't think that a good crop of onions is the most important thing in the world, as Madame Blanchard seems to,' said Brigitte.

'You may come to it,' said Pierre, laughing and kissed her again before he let her go.

She was still drinking secretly when Georges Roux returned to Dorlotte after demobilisation in the spring of 1919. And perhaps it was a good thing that she had had a few nips that afternoon. Georges came back wearing a lieutenant's uniform and riding a motorbicycle with all his possessions strapped on the back of it.

He dismounted and leaned it up against the front of Pierre's shop and went in. There was Brigitte as he had feared. But her face lit up in welcome and she said: 'I want to apologise. I've always been unfair to you, Georges. I was jealous of Papa's affection for you and so I persuaded myself that you were exploiting him.'

'Getting my matches at three centimes a box.' They both laughed.

'Well, that's over – forgiven and forgotten, is it?' asked Brigitte.

'I shall still want a discount on the matches, but as long as I get that . . . ' said Georges.

'Yes, you are welcome. So let's kiss and be friends,' said Brigitte. Georges went to kiss her but was surprised to be kissed full on the lips and to feel a tiny touch of her tongue.

'I could do with some more like that,' he said.

'Do you expect to get them wholesale?' asked Brigitte.

'Yes, I do. There was something due to me on the books when I enlisted and it ought to have been mounting up by compound interest so that I am owed quite a lot . . . '

'In that case we must come to a special arrangement,' said Brigitte, laughing.

A woman whom Georges had never seen before came into the shop.

'Now I'll go and find Pierre,' he said and went out.

Georges was still talking to her father when Brigitte went home. He was standing on the doorstep saying goodbye for the third or fourth time. Brigitte smiled at him and said:

'I'll come round to your shed after supper and let you know about that business.'

'What's all this?' asked Pierre.

'Secrets and none of your business,' said Brigitte.

'Please explain, Georges.'

'I know nothing about it,' said Georges and waving his hand went away without even saying: 'I'll be seeing you.'

Brigitte and Georges surprised each other. She had not drunk any more and went to Georges's little shed more out of bravado mixed with despair than because she was looking for adventure, or from lust. She was sick of loneliness and anything was worth trying. Georges had grown into a strong healthy muscular man and she thought he looked interesting. At the best she expected the solace of human contact and the even greater solace of being able to give something. Also she had committed herself. But she would certainly regret her action if it involved further awkward relations which would upset her father. She had always been an unfair bitch as far as Georges was concerned. It was not his fault that he was ugly and that her father had an exaggerated regard for him. But who knows? Perhaps her instinct had been right.

When she went into Georges's shed, she was surprised because he held out his hand and did not kiss, or embrace her, but busied himself making coffee on a spirit lamp.

'I've come, you see, as I promised.'

'It's very sweet of you. I should have hated spending my first evening alone.' That was nonsense of course. If Brigitte had not told him she would visit his shed, Pierre would have insisted that he spend the evening with them all.

'But I am afraid that you are only being kind to a returning soldier,' he added.

'You know well enough, Georges, that I'm not kind. I have always been selfish and I am being now.'

He did not ask her to explain and they drank the coffee, strong, black and sweet with the flavour of real coffee beans and not chicory – a taste that Georges had acquired in Greece.

'Well, I hope you will go on being selfish if it leads you to come and see me. I don't want you to be kind because you were unfair in the past. I was unfair too. You know I loathed you.'

There was a silence while they looked at each other and burst out laughing.

'Will you make love to me?' asked Brigitte. Georges hesitated.

'Will it upset Pierre? I should not like that,' he said.

'He'll be delighted if you do want me . . . love me . . . If it turns out a mistake and you don't want me again, I will never tell him.'

'That is what I wanted to ask,' said Georges. They did not speak after that as they unbuttoned their clothes and lay down together on the narrow bunk.

'Is that right?' Brigitte whispered and then, unexpectedly, she was swept away by a flood of furious, passionate pleasure. She was no longer herself. Wave after wave engulfed her. She was drowning, and gave such wild cries that Georges, frightened, would have stopped and left her if she had not been clinging desperately to him, digging her nails into his shoulders, holding him round the waist with her heels.

And then it seemed as though she had actually been unconscious, for when she had recovered enough to be aware of anything, Georges was begging forgiveness. Had he hurt her? Was she all right?

'Don't be such an imbecile, darling. It has never been like that before. You are the most wonderful man in the world.'

Later he came back into her and she lay floating more at peace than she had ever felt in her life, although a slat of the bench on which she was lying was cutting into the small of her back. She was stroking Georges's hair. It was soft as a cat's fur. Then for a little while Georges was gasping and sobbing and then he also was at peace.

Lying there, feeling the weight of his body, Brigitte knew that this was for ever. That this fellow whom she had despised as an ugly little peasant boy was the man who would fill the rest of her life.

At first Georges was not in love with Brigitte. But he was astonished, whenever he looked at her, by her beauty. Her body was like a blanched almond. The pride and delight that such a lovely woman should seek him out, the realisation that she loved him with a passion that he had never guessed at, kindled in him a love and a sense of proprietorship. Soon it was transformed from an acceptance into the certainty that she belonged to him, and, therefore, he to her. After a week was over he had asked her to marry him and Pierre Lanfrey had embraced him and given him his blessing. 'I have always felt that you were my son and now you will be.'

Brigitte's little boy, Raoul, was just over a year old when Georges came back to Dorlotte. The child could not talk but walked precariously, rising to stand upright, tottering a few steps, and falling again. His father had been a red-haired man, but Raoul took after his mother, having inherited her very white skin, rosy complexion and deep blue eyes. His hair was the palest gold but would probably turn light brown later. But although he looked like a cherub, the little boy already had masculine interests: he was fascinated by Georges's carpenter's tools and whenever he had the chance crawled towards the basket in which they were kept. Once Brigitte found him sitting up surrounded by chisels and gouges that he had taken out of it and scattered round. In a few years he would be following Georges everywhere and constituting himself his infant apprentice.

Georges had always intended to build himself a new house on the site of the old one if he survived the war, and to build it with his own hands. Now, with the prospect of marriage it became urgent and the obvious thing to do. Fortunately there was no difficulty about money. He would receive generous compensation for the value of the old house and its contents under the reparation clauses of the peace treaty, and he could borrow in expectation of this payment. There was therefore nothing to prevent his devoting several months to building his own home before he had to start earning his own living as a mason.

It was typical of M. Courcel, the mayor, that he should have first become aware of Captain Maurice de L'Espinasse's connection with Dorlotte by happening to read a write-up of French Pilots in *Paris-Match*. In it was the bald statement that at the outset of his career, de L'Espinasse had crashed in the village of Dorlotte and that his life had been saved by a village lad who had pulled him out of the burning plane and that he had been hidden in the crypt of the church during the German occupation.

On reading this, M. Courcel rushed round to Pierre's shop, which he seldom entered as he dealt with M. Truffaut's store on the Ste Menehould road. He always felt a little awkward with Pierre Lanfrey and since the trouble over the heaps of stone, doubly so.

'Ah, my dear friend – I have come to you for information. Can you tell me the full story of the famous air pilot Captain de L'Espinasse being rescued from a burning plane somewhere in this village?'

'The man who can tell you the whole story – because he was present when the plane crashed, is M. d'Oex, Joseph. I didn't hear anything about it until the Germans retreated. But Joseph was in the field when the plane crashed.'

'A thousand thanks, my dear M. Lanfrey. We must have an evening together soon.'

'Always delighted to be any use,' said Pierre and M. Courcel went in search of Joseph – a man whom he wanted to run out of the village. He could not find him: he was away at work somewhere, and his wife had no idea where he was, or who he was working for. M. Courcel left a message that Joseph was to come to his office, but two days passed and Joseph did not come. On hearing that the mayor wished to interview him, Joseph had decided on flight, but his wife prevented his departure by hiding his boots and screaming at him:

'Don't go! He hasn't the right.'

In this she was correct and, as Joseph ignored his summons, M. Courcel realised that his message might have been misunderstood, or have seemed too peremptory. He asked the advice of his wife who asked Madame Labourer, their cook.

'That idiot won't come when my husband sent for him. I suppose he's frightened. We just want to ask him some friendly questions about the village. Joseph is likely to gain something by it.'

'I'll pop into Muller's. That's where he buys his bottle, and I'll let out that Joseph is missing a wonderful chance. The men there will make a fool of him tonight and he'll come round tomorrow.'

Next morning a bewildered Joseph presented himself. His scanty locks of sandy-grey hair were still wet and plastered down round a face soaped and shaved. He looked round the room carefully before entering it, as though he half expected – he wasn't sure what – perhaps the police hidden in a corner. Then he found himself shaking hands with the mayor.

'Sit down here. I'm told you were in the field when Captain de L'Espinasse crashed'. . . . It took a lot of repetitions before Joseph understood what the mayor was talking about. And when he did understand, he didn't know what to say. They might want to punish him for having run away. All he could remember was the shock of seeing the aeroplane hit the ground and burst into flames and then all the bullets and explosions. All hell had broken loose and he was lucky to have got clear.

'Well, tell me all about it.'

'Come down all on fire.'

'The boy with you pulled out the pilot, didn't he?'

'He stuck him in the earhole with his prong.'

'Who was the boy?'

'Idle young tell-tale.'

'He saved the pilot's life, didn't he?'

'I reckon it was La Fouine who saved him. She hid him in the church. But she's dead now.'

'But what happened while you were in the field?'

'We helped him to the ox cart. He'd hurt his foot. Then I ran off to get help – but I runs straight into the Boches. And I reckon while I held 'em in talk, he got into the church.'

'What was the boy's name?'

'I can't rightly remember which of them little bastards it was with me that morning. He did nothing. Only lead the ox cart. Cutting clover we were.'

M. Courcel saw that Joseph was lying but he realised that he could not get more out of him and dismissed him. Joseph went away to complain to anyone who would listen that *M. Le Maire* never gave him nothing. Thus, when Lieutenant Georges Roux returned to Dorlotte the mayor was far from suspecting that he was the boy who had saved the life of one of France's famous fighter pilots.

But though M. Courcel realised that his material was incomplete, he decided not to let the grass grow under his feet. He drove off to see the sous-préfet next morning, showed him the article in the *Paris-Match* and asked him if he would approve putting up a memorial linking the village of Dorlotte with the famous fighter pilot.

'And commemorating this heroic youngster. Who is he, by the way?' asked the sous-préfet.

'I thought the best thing is to get the real facts from Captain de L'Espinasse himself – you know how legends grow in small villages,' said M. Courcel.

'Very sensible of you. If the captain approves this scheme of ours, I'll be very happy to back it and see if we can get a grant for it.'

Thus encouraged, M. Courcel wrote a long and tactful letter to the minister for air, asking for permission to approach Captain de L'Espinasse. It was some weeks before he got a reply.

During the years of war, few of the inhabitants of Dorlotte possessed shotguns or were able to buy cartridges and the use of sporting guns was restricted to organised shoots, such as those of the wild swine. Rabbits, hares and even roedeer could be snared and thus were kept down to some extent, but the birds of the air were free from molestation except by boys and cats, and they had increased greatly. The singing birds, blackbirds and thrushes and, in their season, nightingales and all the warblers had come back into the village gardens and orchards where before the invasion, their lives had been in hazard, particularly on Sundays when every peasant slings his gun on his shoulder and is glad to return with thrush or robin.

Thus, when Georges woke in his little shed, it was to be greeted by a chorus of bird song and when he looked out through the doorway it was to see a blackbird perched on the nearest apple branch with its orange bill wide open, in full song.

Having lived all his life in the years of safety, when men only shot each other and not birds, he was bold and paid no attention to Georges when he came out and lifted water in his cupped hands from the bucket under the tree to wash his face. The blackbird, perching on its rim, had wetted his whistle there an hour earlier. Georges dried his face and put on his working clothes. The sun shone and every blade of grass sparkled. By the time Georges had made his coffee, drunk a bowl of it and eaten two crusts which he dipped into it, the dew had gone.

Soon the sun was so warm that Georges took off his jacket. He was collecting and sorting the square blocks of stone from which he would later build the outer walls of his house and he was arranging them in rows according to size. As he worked a feeling of intense happiness came over him and he stopped work, straightened his back, and looked around with joy.

The moments of such awareness are rare. Usually happiness steals over man when he is preoccupied with work, with play, with love. But when the moment of conscious awareness of happiness comes unexpectedly it is often almost overwhelming. So it was then with Georges, who would have liked to have shouted with joy like the blackbird which was singing again in the apple tree after hopping round the scene of Georges's breakfast. Everything about him was magical. The rough surface of the block of stone, the warm sun on his shoulders, the touch of the clothes on his skin, were all a delight. The love-making of the night before seemed to have changed his body and made it more sensitively aware of itself.

Every stick and stone, every plum blossom, every blade of grass was the subject for irrational joy. He looked at the world and, like the God of Genesis, he saw that it was good. But he had no touch of the vanity which Jehovah was surely entitled to feel on that occasion. For unlike Him, Georges was part of nature himself and identified himself with the sun and the air, the plum blossom and the blackbird and the sticks and stones about his feet.

He grinned and laughed and bending down grabbed a big block of stone, lifted it and set it down in its place tenderly, for he loved it. He loved its roughness, its weight which made him strain his muscles, the touch of red on one side where the flames of destruction had given it colour but had not split it.

A succession of showers, falling when the village was lit by brilliant sunshine, brought with each a rainbow. During the moments of violent rain Georges was driven to drop work and take refuge in his hut. He was alone and worked unseen, for the bridal whiteness of the plum trees veiled his little property from the eyes of passers-by. At midday, when the shop was closed for a couple of hours, Brigitte appeared with a basket on her arm. Georges in his old torn shirt and a pair of faded blue army trousers was heaving on a crowbar with which he was levering out a big block of stone from the calcined wall of the burnt house.

Seeing her, he stopped work, wiped the sweat off his forehead with his freckled forearm, rubbed his hands on the seat of his trousers and, when Brigitte had put down her basket, embraced her. After that Georges pulled out his knife and cut half a dozen rounds off the long loaf, while Brigitte poured out two glasses of wine, and put butter, pâté and cheese upon the bench. They ate without much talking. Later she said:

'You haven't started building yet. But you know you must finish your house – our house – before the autumn. This shed is all right if you only want a love affair. But if you want a wife you must build a house with a kitchen and a wash-house and two bedrooms upstairs – one for us and one for Raoul.'

'I shall have to engage a labourer if I'm to finish by September,' said Georges.

'I'll come and give you a hand – throwing up tiles,' said Brigitte.

She cleared away the food while she was talking and then took him by the wrist and drew him into the shed. Georges hung a blanket over the door.

When he took it down it was five minutes to two, the hour Brigitte had to open the shop. A shower had swept over Dorlotte without their noticing and the young leaves and branches of plum blossom were dripping and the grass was sparkling in the sun.

'What time is it?'

'Four minutes to two.'

'You are a cold-blooded devil. You look at your wrist watch while you are making love. You never lose control, but time it exactly, and send me off to work on the dot.'

'If I made you late I should never hear the last of it – or you might never come again. Now you attack me for doing what you insist on! Being punctual! You think the shop more important than me.'

'Never mind, I shall pay you out one of these days. You wait till we're married. I shall have you howling for mercy.

I shall cripple you,' and Brigitte ran off laughing while Georges shouted after her,

'I shall give as good as I get.' Then he went back to his crowbar.

While he was working Georges was served with two notices from the *mairie*. The first ordered him to have his piles of rubble and masonry removed as they were unsightly and harboured vermin. The second informed him that he was not allowed to rebuild until his plans had been approved. Georges folded the notices up carefully and put them inside his béret for safety and went on excavating the stones from the foundations of his old home. In the evening he discussed the papers with Pierre.

'Well, you needn't bother about the first one. It's out of date and anyhow you can appeal and you will have built your house out of the stone a year before the appeal is heard. But if he wanted to, the mayor could make himself a nuisance about approving the plans. Only I can't make him out. He was round here only a month ago wanting to find out all about that aeroplane crash when you pulled de L'Espinasse out and hid him in the church. I've heard since he wants to put up a plaque commemorating your heroic action. So what is he after? Persecuting you doesn't make sense. Better draw out some sort of plan, put on your lieutenant's uniform and go round and tell him to approve it – otherwise you object to the plaque.'

'But I can't stop him putting up a plaque.'

'No you can't. And he can't really stop you rebuilding your house. But it's a bluff against his bluff.'

Pierre was older. He looked tired and he spoke slowly. But he was happy, relaxing now that the war was over, that the Boches were not after all coming back, as he had always secretly expected, and that Georges was alive and well and Brigitte was in love with him and had stopped drinking as soon as he had appeared.

He cleared the table and together they drew out the plans for Georges's house. Georges did the actual drawing but

194

Pierre made suggestions advising about the height of the rooms and the dimensions of windows and doors.

It was already light though an hour before dawn, when Georges woke suddenly, all his faculties on the alert. Someone was moving outside his shed. He lay still, listening and watching the pale oblong of the open door. His gun was unloaded, his knife in his trouser pocket hanging at the end of the bed, his axe outside, out of reach. But he was not afraid – only puzzled. Brigitte could not come in the early morning and he had nothing any thief would want to steal. A head partly filled the oblong of the doorway.

'Hullo!' said Georges.

'Is it you, Georges?'

'Yes, Julien. I'll get up. How did you get here?'

'I bicycled. If you don't want me, I'll go on somewhere else.' Julien's voice was trembling with exhaustion and when Georges had got out of bed and pulled on his trousers, he found his friend sitting on the bench with his head hanging almost between his knees.

'You look done in,' Julien nodded.

'Get into bed while I make some coffee.'

'I must explain. I'm on the run. I've come to ask you to hide me. If I am caught you'll be sent to prison too.'

'You explain later. Get into bed now.'

'And remember because it's important: my name is not Julien d'Aubrac but Etienne Besse.'

'All right, Etienne. Have a drop of *prune?*'

Julien swallowed the spirit and said: 'Take this and hide it,' and handed Georges three large brown envelopes. Then he lay down on the narrow board bed and fell fast asleep. Georges looked at him and hung the rug over the doorway.

He finished dressing, found the bicycle and hid it under some sacks. If Julien were on the run there seemed to be no pursuers close on his track. The birds were singing. The sun rose in a clear sky. The dew sparkled There were already

195

circles of fallen plum petals lying under each of the trees. Georges looked at the envelopes. The flap on one had been torn open roughly; the other two were sealed.

Georges made his coffee and poured out a bowl of it. Then he pulled out the contents of the torn envelope. It contained packets of hundred-franc notes each held by a white paper band. A fortune. Georges put them back and sat thinking for a little while. His coffee was cold and he warmed it up before he opened the other two envelopes. Their contents were the same.

Georges took each packet of notes and rolled it lengthways into a sort of sausage which he wrapped in newspaper and tied with string. Then he put them in his wheelbarrow, covered them with a sack and wheeled the barrow to the quarry. He would soon be needing a load of sand. When he got there he pushed through to the old pit and waited for a minute or two so as to be sure that he had not been followed. In the face of the quarry were a lot of sandmartins' holes. He pushed his sausage rolls of notes into one after another of them, and blocked each one with stones so that the birds could not pull the notes out. Then he went back to his barrow, filled it with sand and returned to work. Etienne Besse, if that was his name, was still asleep.

He was still asleep when Georges looked up and saw Brigitte coming with the basket on her arm. Georges went to meet her and explained that his old army chum, Etienne Besse, had turned up and was asleep in the shed. He did not know how long he intended to stay, but he would be useful in helping him to build the house. With two men the work would go more than twice as fast.

'You never told me about him. I'm certain you never mentioned his name,' complained Brigitte. 'You said something about a man called Julien.'

'I've not had time to tell you about anything, even if I had wanted to. But I try to forget the past entirely: the present is good enough for me,' said Georges kissing her.

'He's going to be horribly in the way,' said Brigitte.

'We'll arrange things somehow. I'm hungry, let's eat.'

But the glasses were in the shed and in fetching them Georges woke his friend. Etienne came out and joined them and in a minute he and Brigitte were laughing and at ease together. It was only Georges who was uneasy. He had not heard Julien's story. He did not know how he had come by the banknotes, or whether police might not at any moment appear and arrest all three of them. But he had to wait and, with all the talk and Julien present, there would be no chance of lovemaking, or a private talk with Brigitte.

It was she however who arranged matters so that Etienne's arrival should interfere as little as possible with them. She went off early and talked to Madame Blanchard who had a two-roomed hut and persuaded her to take in Etienne as her lodger, providing him with breakfast and an evening meal. Georges and Brigitte would have to do their lovemaking at night, like married people. After Etienne came she often brought her baby Raoul with her to their lunch. While Brigitte was finding him a lodging, Julien told his story, or a small part of it.

In Paris he had met Etienne, a Protestant from La Rochelle who had been a seaman. He had been torpedoed and picked up off a raft four days later in the Atlantic. When he came out of hospital he deserted. 'We were both about the same height and complexion. He suggested that we should exchange papers in order to complicate matters for the authorities if we were picked up. I had spent several months before I met him, working with the communists, trying to stir up trouble. But I came to the conclusion that as far as the ordinary man is concerned there is no difference between communism and capitalism. So I was confirmed in my anarchism. I was ready for anything.'

'Where do all those banknotes you gave me come from?' asked Georges.

'Oh, those. . . . We robbed an army paymaster's van. Besse

was shot dead. I don't know how long they'll take to discover that he is not me. If they don't identify him and bury him as me, I shall be in the clear. Though he probably has a criminal record. What have you done with the money? Not that I want it.'

'Put it where no one will find it. Tell me when you want it.'

'I don't suppose I shall.' Later he said that there was nothing he would like better than to stay in Dorlotte and help Georges build his house.

A casual remark of his wife's threw the mayor into consternation. It was at breakfast while he was drinking his second bowl of coffee that she said: 'After being promoted to be an officer and being decorated three times, I expect that young man will hope to better himself. I wonder what he means to do?'

'What young man are you talking about?'

'Georges Roux, the one who pulled Captain de L'Espinasse out of the burning plane.'

'Georges Roux! But I was going to order him to stop building his house! An officer? Nobody ever tells me anything.'

'He was the poorest boy in the village and now he's something of a war hero himself.'

A letter from the air ministry, enclosing one from Captain de L'Espinasse, confirmed what his wife had told him. The mayor was on the point of rushing round to see Georges, when the latter presented himself in his lieutenant's uniform wearing his medals. The interview which followed was baffling for M. Courcel.

'Enchanted to meet you, lieutenant,' he exclaimed, holding out his whole hand frankly and not three fingers as he would have done before his conversation with his wife. Georges saluted but did not shake the hand. M. Courcel looked at him enquiringly.

'I have three complaints to make, M. le Maire,' said Georges.

'Oh, you speak of your building materials. It was a misunderstanding. When that order was issued I did not know of your intention to rebuild. I regret the mistake. Don't let's speak of it again.'

'Nevertheless I register my protest. The stones are my property. Other citizens of Dorlotte may be treated in the same way, with the same injustice.'

'You are pleased to be severe. I was too precipitate perhaps. But the appearance of the village is important. The minister may visit us. . . . But what other crime have I inadvertently committed?'

'In the second place I understand that you are putting up a plaque.'

'I am delighted to tell you that the préfet of the department approves. Your heroic action in rescuing the man who became one of that little band who are among the most glorious soldiers of France will be recorded and be an inspiration to subsequent generations.'

'I would prefer it to be forgotten.'

'But Lieutenant Roux, you astonish me. I do not understand.'

'There were on that day and in the weeks that followed, innumerable actions more heroic than pulling an aviator out of his plane with a pitchfork. They are not recorded. And, to tell you the truth, they are all best forgotten.'

'But my dear sir!' M. Courcel laughed and then said with bonhomie as though he were humouring a child: 'But you are wearing medals which are the proof of your courage. Why do you object to the earlier instance of your valour being recorded?'

'Those medals were awarded without my consent. It is my duty to wear them when in uniform. But actually I think that all such honours are a mistake. And so I would prefer that my name should not appear on your plaque.'

'It is too late, Lieutenant Roux. The stone has been engraved. The wording has been approved by the minister. Do you understand? Not only by the préfet but by the minister! I cannot possibly change it. And while your scruples do you infinite honour, not only I, but the whole people of France would tell you that they are mistaken. That plaque is like one of your medals and you must accept the gift of your grateful country.'

Georges shrugged his shoulders and then asked: 'And the plans for my house?'

'Naturally they are approved. And I congratulate you upon them; charming, traditional, admirable! I wish you would build a dozen more like it.'

'Well, it seems there is no more to be said; but I regret the plaque.'

'Future generations will look at it with pride,' said the mayor. Georges saluted, turned on his heel and left the *mairie*.

M. Courcel was bewildered. He gave his wife a full description of the extraordinary interview at lunch.

'Can you imagine such puritanism? Medieval. . . .'

'Puritanism, yes. It is due to the influence of those Englishmen – Quakers. A puritan sect. He worked with them at a very formative period! Everything the older people tell me about those English makes me see that their influence might have precisely that effect.' As usual the mayor's wife was not far out in her judgment.

It was a lovely morning. The orchards were no longer expanses of white blossom but the delicate green of little unrolling leaves. Georges and Etienne were at work with pegs and string, marking out the level for the damp course, when there was a grunt and looking up Georges saw that it was Emile Carré, but an Emile much thinner and much cleaner than he had ever seen him before. Georges dropped his hammer and embraced the old man, kissing him on each cheek.

'They put me in the lunatic asylum, you know. It's not too bad, so I stayed there for the winter. Now the fine weather has come they have let me out. Queer company though.'

Emile sat and watched them while they worked and then stayed on and shared their midday meal after Brigitte came. Emile had never liked her. 'Stuck-up girl. Fancies she is better than any of the other girls in the village,' was what he was fond of saying during the war years, and there was some truth in it. Now he was sorry to see that she and Georges were lovers.

'She'll turn him into some kind of stinking bourgeois: a shopkeeper or a commercial traveller, I bet. Georges is too good for that kind of thing. Such were Emile's reflections as he ate the home-made pâté and the salad of dandelions and bits of bacon, followed by stewed rabbit and fried cauliflower and drank the rough wine which had been so woefully rationed in the asylum. But Brigitte left early and when an hour later he wandered down to his miserable shack, it was to find that it had been swept and dusted and that a bed had been made up with three army blankets over a new palliasse of straw. Only later did he discover that it was the work of the girl he disliked and, later still, that she preferred Georges not to be a tradesman.

The weather continued fine and as a result the house-building went well. After the concrete foundations had set, the outside walls rose quickly. Georges chose the stones, Etienne mixed the mortar, handed the stone to the mason, laid shovelfuls of mortar on the board and pushed it along within Georges's reach. He ran about carrying stone and dumping mortar where it would be needed, but talked incessantly while Georges worked in silence. Had there been a listener he might have heard:

'You don't believe in God, but you do believe – deny it if you dare – in Christ's message to mankind. Of course there must have been hundreds of other Christs who didn't get the same publicity: crucifixion, rising from the dead and all that pantomime. You believe that men ought to love their neighbours. I don't admit that word *ought*. Once you let someone tell you you have a duty, you become a slave. To a priest or a politician, or your neighbour, or his wife. You are told you *ought* to pay for a new church, or fight for your country, or give money to some cause, or saddle yourself with some bitch you never want to see except in the dark. I have no duties. I am a rogue elephant. I take what I want where I can find it. Life for me . . .'

'No, I want that big one. The corner stone on the left. And the little bucket of water. I must wet the stone. The mortar's a bit dry,' said Georges with a slight hint of impatience in his voice.

'Oh, I'm terribly sorry. Is this the one? – Well as I was saying: Let the hunters beware. I repudiate your society – not because it is rotten and you know it is – not because I want peace and universal brotherhood and justice, as I used to do. No, I *prefer it rotten*. Can you understand that, Georges? I prefer it rotten because it is a better hunting ground. That's where I've got to. Answer me that!'

Georges had not been attending, but realising that a comment was necessary he said: 'Haven't you ever loved anyone except yourself?' Etienne was obviously put out by this remark.

He thought for a little and replied: 'Possibly – in the remote past – but now – I don't love Julien – I mean Etienne – I have no alternative. You see I am Julien – I mean Etienne – I cannot repudiate him and jump into someone else's skin.'

'I thought that was just what you had done,' said Georges laughing.

'Fuck you. Can't you be serious? It's important what I am saying.'

'Can't you imagine loving someone so much that Julien-Etienne was of no importance?'

'No. As Blake, a great English poet said: 'To love another as oneself is impossible to thought''.'

'In that case how can he discuss the question? Oh, I want the long spirit level. It's back there somewhere.'

Etienne found it and there was a silence. Then he said:

'If it had not been for the war I should not be a killer. That is what I have learned: ruthlessness. But I should have been, or have become an individualist repudiating society which is organised by the coward hyenas who cannot hunt alone. They have to organise a pack: whether church or government, or army. They cling to each other in terror. My pride is to hunt alone.'

Georges made no comment and they worked in silence except for occasional directions, 'More mortar please,' or 'that stone with the patch of moss'.

However it appeared that he had been listening, for he said suddenly: 'You say you are a killer who hunts alone. But you had a pal with you who was shot when you robbed the paymaster's van.'

'Yes, unfortunately there were two of us,' said Etienne.

'But two is the beginning of a pack. Perhaps you would have preferred to be three? I should have done if I went in for that sort of thing.'

'What happened then taught me to be a lone wolf in future. I shall never undertake any job like that, except alone.'

'If you get away this time, you'll have made enough to last you for a good long time,' said Georges.

'Did you count it?' asked Etienne.

'No. But it is a big pile.'

'Let's leave it where it is and forget about it. I can wait without knowing what my fortune is.'

Georges reflected that this was quite true. Julien had never cared about money. So it was odd that he should have risked his life to steal it.

Another morning Etienne suddenly looked fierce and said: 'You forget that I am first and foremost a poet.'

'Do you ever write any poems?' asked Georges. Etienne nodded.

A little while later Georges said: 'I am a poet too. That is, I have made up one poem.'

Etienne gazed at him with astonishment and delight. 'You must show it me at once.'

'Listen and I will recite it.' Georges struck an attitude and began:

'My friend has seen the Gorgon's head.
    His heart is turned to stone
And since that fearful sight he lives
    But for himself alone.
He looked into Medusa's eyes and snakes
    Writhed thick about her head.
He's felt no fear or pity since,
    Because his heart is dead.'

'I'll murder you, you little monster. You'll find my heart is stone when I get hold of you,' Etienne threatened.

'So you really have been turned into a stone man, have you?' asked Georges with innocent seriousness.

'Yes, that is what the war has done to me. And it isn't something to joke about,' said Etienne.

'You'll come in handy when I get my first commission,' said Georges reflectively.

'What do you mean?'

'I'll put you up in the square as a war memorial,' and Georges burst out laughing.

Etienne rushed at him and Georges took to his heels and was dodging round the plum trees when Brigitte appeared with her basket.

'What's all this?' she asked.

'Save me, save me; that man's a killer and his heart has been turned to stone,' cried Georges.

'I'll pay you out another time. Come and have lunch now,' said Etienne.

CHAPTER ELEVEN

'No house building today. We must dig the garden and plant potatoes,' Georges announced one morning.

The vegetable patch had run wild for four years. It was matted with couch grass, buttercups and nettles. Georges dug and shook each spadeful, throwing the tangled octopuses of roots aside. Etienne dug the ground over again, picking out every scrap of root that his second digging revealed. There were many earthworms: big ones the colour of lean beef, but blueish and iridescent underneath. The sight of them overcame the timidity of the blackbird who had sung to them at dawn, and he alighted courageously, seized one in his beak and flew off.

'There goes my dinner,' said Etienne.

'You are jealous. His song this morning was better than anything you'll ever write,' said Georges.

'Don't discourage me,' replied Etienne. He bent down and picked up a particularly large worm and threw it on to the edge of the plot. 'Here's the rival poet,' he said as the blackbird returned, seized the worm and flew off.

When the patch had been dug, they gathered up the weeds, and after they had wilted Georges built a big weed fire.

A few days later Etienne dug shallow trenches and Georges set the seed potatoes he had bought from old Conduchet, putting them in one by one, about thirty-five centimetres apart, and pulling some loose soil over each tenderly so as not to break their shoots.

Old Rouault came to watch and to criticise. 'You keep all the shoots. That's not the right way. I keep only the two strongest and rub off the others. And that's the way to get big potatoes. The ones that are worth baking.'

'Maybe you are right, old man. But I like a lot of little potatoes better than five or six whoppers.'

'You get weakly plants with all those shoots,' said Rouault, unwilling to give up his point. Most of the patch went to potatoes, a fine cleaning crop, but Georges sowed turnips also and some rows of lettuces and carrots. He put in a screen of Jerusalem artichokes along the edge of the road, and later he sowed marrows and cucumbers on mounds, and put in a dozen suckers of globe artichokes. He would wait a year to get the ground clean before he ventured on peas and tomatoes.

Moreover, building the house was all important. They could buy their haricots, but the house had to be habitable by the autumn.

There was however a distraction a week or two later. It was while Brigitte, Georges and Etienne were finishing their alfresco lunch. It was a hot day and the humming of bees became more noticeable. Suddenly Brigitte cried out: 'It's a swarm.'

They all got up and there, not high above them round a plum branch was a circling haze of bees. 'They are going to settle,' she cried. For some time it seemed uncertain. Then a small dark brown patch became visible along the branch. While they watched, it grew until it engulfed twigs and leaves, hanging down.

'It's like a bunch of grapes,' said Etienne. But actually it was not much like a bunch of grapes. More like a dark brown wig, or a net full of coffee beans. But it hung in a point and at every moment a few bees would fly off it and alight upon the mass of their stationary fellows.

'It must belong to old Chuquet,' said Georges.

'Yes. But he is giving up bees,' said Brigitte.

'I'll go and see him.'

'If he doesn't want them why don't you take them from

him and buy one of his empty hives to put them in?'

Georges went off and returned wheeling the empty hive on a barrow. Old Chuquet came with him, carrying a veil and a smoker. He was a very small man, bent double with rheumatism but hobbling along and keeping up with Georges without difficulty. His face was like a withered red apple and he kept shaking his head from side to side, a habit he had developed in order to look up, for he was so bent that unless he twisted his head he could only see what was under his feet. He kept up a constant stream of talk and of advice. 'They'll most likely hang there till tomorrow morning. But take 'em as soon as you may. Let them run into the hive before sundown. Then you'll have them safe.'

Following the old man's continual instructions, Georges put his ladder up against the tree, put on the veil and tucked it under the collar of his buttoned army tunic, and carrying a small wooden box in his hand, climbed up the ladder. Then, taking hold of the branch with one hand and holding the box underneath the swarm with the other, he shook the branch violently. The bulk of the swarm fell with a roar of surprise into the box – a sound which turned almost at once into a loud good-tempered hum. Georges climbed down gently and turned the box over onto a board, propping one corner up with a stone so that the bees outside the box could draw within.

Old Chuquet made him climb the ladder again, shake those bees that still clung there, off the branch and wrap a wet cloth round it where the swarm had been hanging in order to discourage conservatives who wanted to remain there.

As the bees which had spilled over on to the board drew in to the box, the note of their humming changed; the pitch rose a little and it sounded contented.

Old Chuquet, unprotected by a veil, peered down at them. 'Aye. She's in there all right. You can tell by the sound.' The big wooden hive was set up under an apple tree where the bees could have an uninterrupted line of flight and it could be approached from behind. It was put facing east, so the bees would get the first rays of the rising sun. There was no more to be done until the late afternoon and old Chuquet departed, Georges and Etienne went back to work and Brigitte and Emile went off, slightly disappointed because taking the swarm had been so simple an affair.

In the evening Chuquet came back and told Georges exactly how to arrange a sloping board in front of the hive, leading to the entrance with no gap or crack down which the bees could find a way, except into the hive. Then, carrying the box full of clustering bees, Georges shook it with a violent jerk over the board and the whole cluster was flung onto it, in a heap. The mound of bees flattened itself out and, after a few seconds, they began to march uphill, into the hive. Chuquet peered down on them with his unprotected face not more than half a metre above them. He was silent for the first time, eagerly looking for the queen bee.

'There she goes,' he cried excitedly, pointing with a straw and Georges saw a bee with slightly longer, reddish legs and a longer abdomen disappear into a knot of marching bees who paid no attention to her. The whole mass of bees had spread out on the board. They seemed to be waiting. But by the entrance some were going in, others hesitating. Then suddenly the mass of bees near the entrance made up the collective mind, and marched briskly in; the spread-out army followed and soon the entrance was almost blocked as they scrambled over each other eager to get inside.

'Here she comes again,' cried Chuquet, wild with delight, and this time Georges got a good view of the queen who was moving about the alighting board, apparently waiting to get into the hive. But to Georges's astonishment none of her subjects made way for her, or indeed, as far as he could see, paid any attention to her existence. He remarked on this, but Chuquet told him he was wrong.

'If she wasn't there, or if she didn't go in, they would all come out again within a quarter of an hour. But she'll go in;

she can tell it's the home they need by the way the others are tumbling over to get in.'

And sure enough the skirts of the army had soon drawn up the board and only a few doorkeepers and bees fanning with their wings were left in the entrance after another ten minutes.

'You listen. When you hear that high-pitched hum you know they are happy and that all's well.'

Before he went to bed that night Georges went down to the hive and lay on the grass, putting his ear to the wooden wall in order to listen to the subdued hum of the bees busily cleaning out their home and drawing out the wax to make cells where the queen could lay the first eggs of the new colony. He could hear the noise of their feet too.

Georges felt happily excited: he would keep bees; he would succeed old Chuquet as the beekeeper of Dorlotte. It was another delightful tie binding him to the village. But this was something he would never be able to explain to Etienne.

They did however have many discussions, for Etienne talked a great deal and sometimes provoked Georges into an answer.

One day Etienne began: 'I am continually astonished by man's sentimentality about death. He wages wars, murdering millions; he deliberately starves whole populations as we are still doing, or trying to do, in Germany, a year after the war has ended; he drops bombs from aeroplanes, bombarding cities indiscriminately, yet such is his sentimentality that he will do all these things and let an epidemic go unchecked, in order to keep an idiot or malformed baby alive. That is what your Christianity amounts to in practice. And a curious jealousy shows itself: the man responsible for starving whole populations and for burning babies in their beds, is horrified by the loss of life caused by an earthquake and subscribes handsomely for the relief of the sufferers. He disapproves of what he calls "acts of God". He wants a monopoly of evil doing.'

'Surely that shows an inherent goodness in mankind? A fraternal feeling?' said Georges, interrupting.

'No. It does not. The Germans torpedoed ships at random, so that hundreds of men were scalded to death by steam from the boilers, or blown to bits by explosions – and the same Germans then risked their lives to pick up one or two floating in the sea. How can one have any respect for such imbeciles?'

'Everyone dies sooner or later – but some deaths are more disgusting than others,' said Georges.

'By God, you do come out with some wise discoveries, Georges!' said Etienne.

Georges ignored this comment and went on: 'After you deserted I was sent back to the O.P. And there I decided that I would not be anything but a fighting soldier. Actually it worked out the opposite of my intention. But my reason was that I felt such disgust that I could hardly sleep or digest my food.

'I saw the generals who had thrown away tens of thousands of precious French lives in idiotic, badly planned attacks, generals who ought themselves to have been court-martialled and shot – sitting in judgment on the bravest of the brave – the leaders of the mutiny – and condemning them to death. I might forgive the general who made miscalculations and mistakes. But that he should cover up his own crime – and execute French soldiers for the treason that he himself had brought about – that was too much. Such cowardice and such incompetence stinks.

'So I asked to be sent back to my regiment. It didn't work out as I had planned. I was made an officer myself and sent to Greece. At least I was spared being on hand when such abominations were being perpetrated.'

'What you are saying, Georges, is that it is not the suffering that matters, but the state of mind of the men causing it. I don't really think that. Christ said: "By their fruits shall ye know them." I agree. One must judge men by the results of their actions, not by their intentions.'

'Some things are disgusting in themselves,' said Georges.

'Most things, I suppose, in the modern world. But it is because I agree with Christ in judging by results that I condemn utterly the religion called after that unfortunate man. There have been as many wars over details in the Christian religion as over anything else.'

By the end of May the outer walls were high enough for Georges to start looking for the beams to support the ceiling. M. Lenoir could offer joists ten by fifteen centimetres, but these were not strong enough to suit Georges. At last he heard of an old outlying barn which belonged to a family which had moved to Belmont. They had sold the field to Conduchet, but the old man had refused to buy the barn. Georges sought out widow Fournier at Belmont and bought it. The ruined building provided just the materials he wanted: old beams about twenty by twenty-five centimetres in cross-section: roofing tiles, rafters, and enough floor tiles for the kitchen and scullery. He hired Marie Durand's bullock cart – she was Madame Meunier now – and a widow – and he and Etienne demolished the barn and carted the materials back to the village, much to the annoyance of M. Lenoir, who talked to anyone who would listen, about the spread of disease by the use of unhygienic building materials.

Georges had left slots on the outside walls a metre apart to take the ends of the beams. First they had to be sawn to the right lengths, then raised with a pulley hanging from a triangle of stout poles until one end could be dropped into the slot prepared for it, and then the other end raised at a slight angle and pushed along the wall until it also dropped into its slot.

Although he was in a hurry to finish the house, marry Brigitte and move in by the autumn, Georges was an ambitious architect and was building his house of two storeys with a stone staircase. On the ground floor was a scullery or wash-house, a big kitchen, which was the living-room, with a huge fireplace and open hearth with a cooking stove on the other side of the room and a range of three charcoal grates beside it. Facing the front door was the broad stone staircase which led up to two communicating bedrooms. The kitchen living-room was on the right of the doorway and a tiny room for books and papers on the left.

All this took time and Georges did not hesitate to make Etienne work long hours. Still it would not be finished before the winter, particularly as the windows which were being made by the carpenter at Blaye would not be ready. Then the bedrooms would have to be plastered and dry out. Georges decided to concentrate on the big living-room, the outside walls and the roof and to leave the bedrooms and the partitions between them until after they had moved in. Brigitte and he could sleep in the living-room, Raoul in the wash-house.

Once the tiles were laid on the floor of the living-room and the hearth and chimney stack built, it began to feel like a habitable house.

'I suppose we shall have to put up with the furniture from *Le Bon Gîte* – and think ourselves lucky to get it,' said Georges reflectively.

A day or two later he was dismayed by Etienne asking for a part of his roll of notes and saying mysteriously that he had some urgent business but hoped to be back within a week or two.

'But do you think it's safe for you? Suppose the police are on the look-out for Etienne Besse? You don't know what crimes he may not have committed before he met you?'

'That's a risk I shall have to take some time, Georges. I cannot live on your bounty for the rest of my life.'

'On my bounty! You know I ought to be paying you a builder's labourer's wages. I've been working out what I owe you . . .'

'Don't be a fool. What I am most grateful to you for is not sheltering me – but making me feel that I am of some use.'

Etienne took one of the rolls of notes and went off on his bicycle. Without him Georges had to give up building the staircase and devoted himself to carpentering. He made the front door out of oak planks from the old manger from the barn and found old hinges for it. But though it was delightful to have his lunch alone with Brigitte, he missed Etienne and when two weeks had gone by, he began to feel anxious.

'If the police are on the look-out for him, it's better that they should not have found him here,' said Brigitte, to whom he had confided his fears.

'And it's just as well he only took one roll of notes and not the lot. There'll be something waiting for him when he comes out of jug,' reflected Georges, though he did not speak his thought aloud, as Etienne's huge fortune was a secret he would not impart even to Brigitte.

Georges had managed to get the frames for the three windows in the living-room and he was puttying in the panes one afternoon a fortnight after Etienne had gone, when he heard a lorry stop in the road beyond his garden. Then he heard someone pushing through the bushes.

'Does Georges Roux live round here?' asked a working man. Georges told him he had come to the right place.

'My mate and I have got a load of furniture for you. Can we back the lorry in nearer the house?'

Georges went out in wonder and showed the driver where to back his big van, keeping the wheels on the hard stone track that led to the new wash-house.

When the driver's mate was satisfied that the van could be got no nearer, the driver climbed down and the two men began to undo the ropes that held the green canvas cover over the contents of the van.

'There's a lot of small stuff, first of all,' said the man. And the two men began unloading six upright kitchen chairs, then two chairs of walnut with arms, a plate rack, a washing basket, some smaller baskets, a kitchen scales and weights, a big fish kettle, two zinc baths, three small tables of deal, then the legs of a big table, a grandfather clock, two upholstered chairs, a big looking-glass with a gilt frame, wrapped in a blanket, then the top of the big table, finally beds. There were two small *lits-bateaux* of a pattern that Georges had never seen before of walnut, and then a big double bed with a gilded angel blowing a trumpet at the head and a shepherd sitting on a rock and a few sheep, at the foot.

'Oh, and the gentleman said we must be sure to give you this last of all,' and the driver and his mate burst out laughing as they produced a cradle made of mahogany with split cane woven sides and hood.

'He said you wouldn't need it for a few months yet.'

Georges gave the men a couple of glasses of white wine each. They had come all the way from Châtillon-sur-Seine, had attended an auction at a farmhouse and the gentleman who had bought the things, had hired them to deliver them to Georges. The gentleman was obviously Etienne, but where was he himself?

Georges worked in a daze, carting his new possessions into the living-room and the wash-house. Most of the things had to be leaned against the walls, but he put the big kitchen table together and the grandfather clock in the corner by the fireplace and set it ticking. Then he arranged some of the chairs. It would be a wonderful surprise for Brigitte. But, damn it all, where was Etienne?

The great day for the village of Dorlotte was fine. It was the fifth anniversary of the German retreat from the village – a lovely day in early September. There were a great many flags. It was a holiday and the women and children had got on their best clothes. In the morning a service of thanksgiving was held in the open air between the church and the *mairie*.

Part of a regimental band from Chalons arrived in two army transport lorries, then the sous préfet of the department and his wife, then Captain de L'Espinasse in a chauffeur-driven car. These honoured guests were invited into the *mairie* to drink a *vin d'honneur*. A crowd of village women assembled: the gendarmes from Blaye were there with polished boots and the five *pompiers* or voluntary firemen, a body recently organised by the mayor, were present; they represented the civil administration as opposed to the military and police. They wore their uniforms, but as they had not received either ladders or a fire-engine, they had to parade without either and were not so impressive as they might have been. Joseph d'Oex was prominent among them, as he had discovered that though a *pompier* is a volunteer, he receives a retaining fee. They were loudly applauded by their wives and children as they marched to the memorial and stationed themselves between the veiled figure on its pedestal and the steps of the *mairie*.

The band struck up and the distinguished party in the *mairie* came out onto the steps. Among them Captain Maurice de L'Espinasse looked the most striking, tall, handsome, perfectly turned out in his well-fitting uniform, his breast bright with ribbons arranged in two rows. Beside him the sous-préfet looked tubby, cheerful and undistinguished, but his wife was most elegant in a well-cut Parisian dress and an impudent little hat which fascinated all the younger women of the village.

Emile had come to the ceremony and on seeing him, Pierre Lanfrey went over and stood near him. It occurred to him that Emile might make a disturbance and it would be as well for him to be at hand if he did.

The sous-préfet came forward and delivered his usual oration on these occasions, but with modifications. Thus after speaking of the sufferings of France he added that nowhere in France had the people suffered so much, or borne their sufferings more stoically than in Dorlotte – a place which would always be remembered with loving pride by all Frenchmen. 'But today we commemorate not the stoicism

215

of all the inhabitants, but those of its sons who gave their lives for France and by their deaths added to the sorrows of the survivors, but also became an inspiration and added to their resolution.'

The sous-préfet waved his hand, the mayoress and one of the *pompiers* pulled cords and the sheets in which the memorial had been hidden fell apart revealing a statue of a French soldier lunging with his bayonet, and the band struck up the *Marseillaise*.

The unveiling of the plaque to Captain de L'Espinasse and his gallant rescuer, Georges Roux, was a miserable anti-climax. For a crowd of women and children had surged round the war memorial spelling out the names of the dead and their buzz of talk drowned the words of the sous-préfet's wife who was saying a few appropriate words before pulling off the strip of canvas covering the inscription. Then as Captain de L'Espinasse bowed over the lady's hand and kissed her glove and presented her with a bouquet of chrysanthemums, Emile bawled out: 'Kill him! Kill him!'

Pierre saw the police start running. But he got to Emile first, took him firmly by the arm and saying to the gendarmes, 'I'll look after him,' he led him away.

It was Emile's sudden shouts of 'Kill him!' apparently directed at the heroic figure of de L'Espinasse which prompted the young Parisian reporter to investigate what might prove to be an exciting scandal. For one thing, he asked himself, why was Georges Roux not present?

He left the crowd still gathered round the memorial and ran off in the direction in which Pierre had led Emile. They had disappeared, but he met Malame Blanchard coming out of Pierre's shop, and asked her if Georges Roux were anywhere in the village.

'Yes, sir. I think he's in his house now. If you listen you can hear the hammering.'

Anatole Schwob found his way to the building and the following interview took place.

'Excuse me, are you M. Roux?' Georges looked up, and seeing the breathless young man, asked him kindly:

'What's the trouble? What can I do for you?'

'Can you explain why you didn't attend the unveiling of the plaque in your honour?'

'I am busy building, as you can see.'

'But you were wanted at the ceremony.'

'I don't like ceremonies.'

'An old man called out: "Kill him" at Captain de L'Espinasse, the famous pilot whom you rescued. Can you explain why?'

'That would be Emile Carré. He spent last winter in the lunatic asylum,' said Georges.

'Oh, I see. That explains it. I thought that it might be some private drama,' said M. Schwob, disappointed. However he came away from Dorlotte much impressed by Georges, particularly after discovering from the mayor that he had risen to be a lieutenant 'promoted on the field of battle' as he put it – and been decorated and wounded twice. On his way back to Paris he wrote a column about the modest hero of Dorlotte which was highly coloured enough to be published by his editor, and appeared next morning, in the *Petit Parisien*.

CHAPTER TWELVE

Georges would have liked Etienne to be his best man, but he might never return and the wedding could not be put off. The living-room at least was finished, the walls had dried out, the furniture could be put in place and he and Brigitte and Raoul could move in.

The wedding was a civil one at the *mairie*, but after the simple ceremony and the signing of the register, there was a wedding feast. Old Conduchet had lent his barn and acted as host. Long planks set on trestles and covered with white linen sheets, made a tablet at which forty people could sit down. All the survivors from the past of five years before, were invited and accepted. Besides these, Georges had invited M. Lenoir and his wife and the rival shopkeeper M. Truffaut and his, as he wanted to make it an occasion to wipe out any bad feelings. For the same reason he had invited Joseph d'Oex and his elder daughter, as Madame d'Oex had died the winter before.

On the bride and bridegroom's arrival, they were greeted by old Conduchet in his best brown broadcloth suit with a whole bouquet of white roses in his buttonhole.

'Before you come into luncheon your presence is requested by my aunt Eglantine. She's not well enough to attend, but we'll send dishes into her room. She's still got a splendid appetite. But mind your ps and qs Georges, or she'll slap your face.'

Eglantine was sitting up in bed in a little room leading out of the kitchen. There was a cage of canaries hanging at the top of the window and a pot of red geraniums in flower on the sill. Eglantine herself was propped up, bright-eyed and cheerful and wearing a white shawl.

'Come and kiss me. Yes, you too Georges. You don't deserve it after abandoning my darling Sylvie. But you are marrying into the family and you have always loved Dorlotte. They tell me that you are an officer now. And here is a present for you, Brigitte. About all I've got left. I took them out of my ears this morning.' And Eglantine handed her a pair of gold earrings, old and beautifully chased.

'They belonged to my grandmother, Thérèse, who was your great-great-great-grandmother and married a Lanfrey – so keep them carefully.'

'What exactly is the relationship with you?' asked Georges.

'Pierre's grandfather, Jean-Jacques, was my first cousin. He was a Jacobin and in the days of the Bourbons, he was always in trouble. Well, now I give you my blessing, and go to your luncheon. I hear my nephew is providing a good spread.'

'Yes indeed. He is providing all the game and the vegetables and the sweets, Papa the wine and everything that has to be bought. Monsieur Conduchet has been most generous,' said Brigitte.

'Don't praise that hypocrite to me. He always has an eye to the main chance,' said Eglantine crossly. Then she smiled at them and they went to meet the guests.

The great event was that Marcelle Duvernois had returned for a few hours to the village. Old Conduchet sat at one end of the table, and Pierre Lanfrey at the other. The newly married couple sat in the middle on one side.

Soon after they had sat down and while everyone was rather constrained, Monsieur Conduchet cried out: 'Pass your plate, Joseph. Let me give you some of the hare pâté. Oh, pardon me, I mean *cat* pâté. That's your favourite dish, isn't it? I've had it prepared specially for you.'

Even Georges could not help joining in the roar of laughter which followed and Joseph's discomfiture and the doubting way in which he tasted the slice of hare pâté, added to the general amusement. The old man's sally had broken the ice and soon all present were indulging in reminiscence and telling tall stories.

'Monsieur Lorcey, tell us all how you killed the Uhlan captain with his own sabre,' asked Madame Zins's grandson who had come through the whole war without a scratch, as owing to a twisted foot he had served in an army bakery.

Old Lorcey glared angrily. 'He nearly killed me, not I him,' he growled.

'I'm sure I've heard you tell it the other way round,' declared young Zins.

'Damned impertinent young puppy,' complained Lorcey as a laugh went round the table. For old Lorcey had sometimes told the story in such a way that he sounded more like the victor than the vanquished. Monsieur Conduchet came to his rescue.

'Never mind, old friend. If the Uhlans beat us in 1870, young Zins never beat anything but dough.'

Ham, pâtés, brawn of every sort, sausage, chicken livers en croûte, eggs, were followed by roast *marcassin* or young wild pig, and a roasted lamb. Then came the vegetables: haricots, pommes frites, courgettes, young carrots fried in butter, mashed turnip and stuffed cabbage. The vegetables were followed by fowls, ducks, geese, saddle of hare and roast partridges. The cheeses had been gathered from far and near: Brie and Coulommier from the Marne, goat from the Vosges, a Gruyère from the Swiss border. Then open fruit tarts of apple and quince, wild strawberries, blue plums and mirabelles. With the arrival of these sweets came the popping of champagne corks, for they had been drinking red wine with the meat. Then honey cakes and sweetmeats were passed round and cups of black coffee with little glasses of *prune* or *marc*. And then suddenly old Conduchet was on his feet.

'My friends. I am the most successful farmer in Dorlotte and I'll tell you why. I have always picked the best animals and bred from them. My bulls are the best beef animals, my cows the richest in butterfat. That is why I hope to live long enough to get to know Georges Roux's son out of Brigitte who is by Pierre Lanfrey. Leaving myself out of account – I am *hors concours* – that's the best stock we have in the whole village. And if you ask me how I pick men and women, well I'll tell you – I pick men for courage and honesty and I pick women for courage and beauty. As for their honesty, I can never be quite sure about that.' The old farmer sat down amid great applause and laughter.

At the end of the wedding breakfast which had lasted for three hours, the company split up. Georges and Brigitte went off to their new house with Raoul perched on Georges's shoulders and were not seen again that day. For the rest of the company there was a pause, which was long enough for digestion to begin. Then some of the older men reassembled to play *quilles* and *boules*. Many retired to rest. Six of the younger men, or older boys, examined their pimples and creamed and brushed their hair for the third time that day. Meanwhile six girls sponged and powdered their flushed faces. When all were ready a bullock waggon drawn by four oxen, each animal having a wreath round its horns, drew up at the crossroads. The six girls and the young men mounted in the waggon. One of the young men had a flageolet, another a concertina, a third a cornet. They began playing and the ox waggon proceeded at a snail pace out of the village along the road to Belmont. All the party stood – there were no seats. The girls sang and held hands with the three boys not playing instruments. An hour later, when they had reached the forest, the bullocks were turned off down a rough track and in a few hundred metres came to an open glade in the midst of which stood a spreading oak near to which, enclosed on three sides and on the top by stones, was a spring of water – the wishing well of Belmont. The bullocks came to a halt and all jumped down. A large garland which had been brought for the purpose was tied to one of the branches of the oak, which had several older withered garlands already hanging on it. Then each of the girls in turn wandered off to the wishing well, looking back often to see that none of the boys was following her. At the well she went down on her knees, dropped in a pin and looked at her reflection in the water. If she saw a man's face beside her own, it meant that she would marry him, usually within the year.

One boy, Achille Rouillac, who had hidden behind the stone before Mathilde Brabant set out for the well, tiptoed round and looked over her shoulder. Mathilde gave a shriek and only just saved herself from falling into the well. All the other girls and boys had watched this drama and kept silent as Mathilde returned scarlet in the cheeks and breathless whenever she glanced at Achille. Presently Angèle Conduchet said innocently:

'Whatever you see in the well always comes true.'

'How do you know?' asked Achille.

'Well look what happened to Marthe – that fat girl, the daughter of the man who comes round with the still in the late autumn. . . . She looked in the well and she saw two men's faces. One was Onesime Brebner and the other face was a black man – a negro. She married Onesime and they emigrated to Algeria. He died there, leaving her without any money, and what she had seen in the well came true. She married a black man.'

'How many other wives had he?' asked Joseph Muller and there was scandalised laughter.

Before they started back to the village, they all held hands and danced round the big garlanded oak. Then they broke up into couples who wandered off into the forest. But it was getting dark, the trees were casting long shadows and they climbed once more into the ox wagon and came back. The clear young voices and the sounds of the flageolet and the concertina could be heard for a long time before the ox wagon reached the village. By then it was quite dark. The stars had come out and a moon would rise later on.

'I only had two words with Marcelle Duvernois,' said Georges regretfully as he walked back with Brigitte to his new home.

'It was nice of her to come; she brought us a coffee grinder,' said Brigitte.

'I didn't even thank her,' said Georges.

'She was all right. She was talking a lot to papa.'

'I don't suppose I shall ever see her again. Well, that's the way the world is,' brooded Georges.

Brigitte was a little annoyed that Georges should be talking about an older woman, and not of the marriage – for the ceremony which meant little to Georges meant a great deal to her.

Before long, however, Georges had blown up a big log fire on the open hearth and their new home looked delightful. Darkness was falling and Georges came in from the wood-pile with a big armful of logs. When Brigitte went to shut the door, she paused and called Georges. Standing on their threshold they could hear the young people singing as they returned from the forest and the wishing well. They stood listening for some minutes, then shut the heavy oak door and drew the curtains. Raoul was given a bowl of bread and milk and put to sleep in the cradle that Etienne had sent. He was already almost too big for it.

'And this is how it is going to be for ever,' Brigitte said to herself in a mood of intense happiness.

Next morning they had many callers. Pierre and his wife, old Conduchet, Madame Courcel, who explained that her husband had been called that morning to Vitry-le-François on urgent business. Then Madame Blanchard, worried about Etienne's return : she had washed two of his shirts and they were ironed and waiting for him, old Lorcey, Madame Zins, Michel Fournier, M. and Mme Truffaut from the new shop, the Curé from Blaye, one of the gendarmes, the new school-teacher and Suzanne Leblond, engaged but not married yet –

to an American sergeant who had promised to return directly he was demobilised. But would he?

The room was packed and Georges had set out bottles and glasses on a table under the apple tree. Most of the men stayed outside, where they felt less awkward, and all the women went in as they had come to see the furniture and all the household equipment. Georges took several men into the entrance hall and showed them the unfinished staircase and where he had left slots in the walls into which he would fit the ends of the wide stone treads. He explained that he had to buy the stone from two ruined houses in order to find enough unbroken stones of the right width.

'Durand will be wanting to employ you, Georges. He's had one of M. Lenoir's concrete boxes built for him. He flattened out a heap of rubble and planted the house on top. Now one side has subsided into the cellar below and his concrete wall has cracked in half.' Old Conduchet was clearly delighted at his labourer's misfortune. Fools deserve their fate.

Then the crops were discussed: how the wheat was threshing out, what the percentage of sugar was likely to be in the beet which was the only large crop not yet gathered in.

Meanwhile the women were being shown the furniture that Etienne had sent, admiring the big bed and the *lits-bateaux*, fingering the heavy linen sheets and the stuffed feather quilts on the big bed.

'Well your friend was lucky to find an auction with all those things that everyone is wanting to buy today. The new stuff in the shops is so shoddy it's not worth having.'

'My grandmother had twenty-six pairs of sheets – heavy linen sheets, for every one of the beds. She changed them every fortnight and had a great wash at the end of the year. She always had her big wash in June and it lasted the whole of the month.'

'Well, that was nothing exceptional. I can't get used to modern ways. There's nothing like cold running water in

224

the *lavoir* to wash clean.'

'In the old days, sugar came in sugarloaves. One had to cut it up oneself.'

'Get along with you. You can't remember those days, Lisette.'

'No, I'm telling you what my mother remembered. And there was no paraffin for the lamps: only colza oil, and tallow candles for us poor folks.'

'Well, we all went to bed nice and early – specially in winter time.'

'Well, that's coming on soon. Good-bye, Brigitte. I expect I'll be seeing you tomorrow.'

'Good-bye, my dear. I dare say you would be glad of a basket of lettuce? I'll send Marie round with them on her way to school.'

At last the lingering visitors had all said good-bye, leaving empty bottles, empty plates with cake crumbs and dirty glasses.

'Well done, Brigitte!'

'Well done, Georges. And now we are alone at last.'

But their solitude *à deux* was interrupted during the afternoon when Etienne appeared. He leant his bicycle against the wall of the house and peeped in through the open doors. Georges was overjoyed to see him and Brigitte went to embrace him and thank him for their furniture. But her words were interrupted by Georges asking: 'How much do I owe you?' For he did not want it to be taken for granted that it was all a gift.

'So, poor chap, you have been wondering whether you will have to pay for it all and if you can afford it! I thought you looked a bit glum when you saw me on the doorstep,' said Etienne, chaffing him, and Georges shook his fist at his friend.

'Well, there's lots of food for you two men. Conduchet's daughter brought over two basketfuls of brawns and pâtés, sausages, there's a cold roast duck, a big jar of sour cream, another of pickled cabbage and a mirabelle flan. Then lots of nuts and things and a bottle of Conduchet's special mira-belle liqueur.'

Etienne told them the story of the auction and how he had waited till the last and then made a bid for the big bed which was knocked down while the former contestants were staring at him in indignation. Brigitte had drawn the curtains and lit the lamps when there was the sound of a motorcar stopping in the road beyond the garden. A minute later there was a timid knock at the door. Georges went and opened it. His broad shoulders blocked the view. Brigitte heard a woman's voice, then a woman's rippling laugh and Georges exclaiming:

'How marvellous! Come in, come in.'

Then the woman laughed again and said: 'May I really? I wasn't at all sure that you would not slam the door in my face. And Brigitte?'

'Come in,' repeated Georges. His voice sounded a little dazed – and he had been dazed by the outlines of the smart little hat, the collar of the fur coat turned up and wrapping the neck, the eyes gleaming at him out of the darkness, the voice – Sylvie. Then he stood aside, making way for her and she stepped over the threshold and came into the living-room. Etienne was standing on one side of the fireplace, Brigitte in her cotton frock and apron on the other.

Sylvie made towards her and stopped suddenly. 'Brigitte, how beautiful you've become! I am something of a shock to you both, but I read about Georges building this house and your getting married in the *Petit Parisien* – and I could not resist coming. I drove down from Paris this afternoon. It's so extraordinary, everything is so much changed. So much smaller. Perhaps you'll forgive my coming when you hear my story.'

'Are you alone?' asked Georges. Sylvie rippled with laughter.

'How like a man to imagine that I could not exist without a companion!'

When Sylvie's fur coat had been taken off she was revealed as wearing a very smart severely cut coat and skirt of thick ribbed dark blue silk. She wore black gloves and a little straw cloche hat, from under which her dark curls hung round her ears. Georges was bringing her an armchair to sit on when Brigitte quite unexpectedly pounced on her, took her by the shoulders and kissed her on both cheeks.

'Oh, my dear, you do surprise me! That's the last greeting I was expecting. So it's all right then, my coming?' And once again there sounded that fascinating ripple of laughter.

'Sit down,' commanded Georges. She sat down. Then, turning to Etienne, she appealed to him.

'We haven't been introduced. No matter. But perhaps you will tell me – you are an impartial witness – is it *really* all right my bursting in like this?'

'I'm a witness, but not an impartial one,' said Etienne. They were introduced and he shook hands with Sylvie sitting in her chair.

Brigitte said she must lay the supper and Sylvie jumping up said: 'Show me where I can put my car, Georges?' They went out together. It was already night. Half way to the road Sylvie stopped suddenly, put her arms round Georges's neck and kissed him vigorously. 'I have forgiven you, you see.' Georges was not sure for what he was being forgiven. However he said nothing and they went to the car. When he had shown her where to drive it – off the road and nearly up to the wash-house, she got out and said: 'I've a wedding present for you. It's a picture.'

She opened the back of the car and Georges took the big square as she lifted it out and carried it in carefully while she held open the doors.

It was held up in the light of the living-room revealing a portrait of a young peasant sitting on a yellow wooden kitchen chair facing the painter.

'Oh, my God! It's a masterpiece!' exclaimed Etienne.

Sylvie turned to him. 'So you like it? It is by an Italian friend of mine. Do you think it suitable? And Sylvie gave him a conspiratorial smile. Etienne flashed back a twinkle of understanding. Then Brigitte came forward.

'But it's wonderful! Are you giving us that? To hang on our wall? On this wall. That's where it must go. But Georges, this is a most wonderful gift. It will change our lives. . . .'

Georges smiled gratefully but said nothing. He would have liked to have asked: 'Who is this stranger whom we are expected to hang on our wall? What has he got to do with us? He isn't one of the family.'

But Georges saw what the others felt and as he listened to Etienne's questions and Sylvie's answers about the Italian painter whom they both regarded as a master, he looked at the picture again and began to believe that Sylvie must have given him a great work of art. Brigitte seemed to think so. So did Pierre Lanfrey when he saw it. In less than a week Georges was repeating what he could remember of Etienne's comments and Sylvie's explanations and he genuinely believed that he had always known the picture was a masterpiece and entirely forgot that his first feeling had been one of resentment.

'By an Italian. What's his name, Brigitte?' he said, showing the picture a few weeks later to M. Courcel.

'It's written there in the corner – Modigliani.'

'Never heard of him,' said the mayor.

'You will, Monsieur, you will,' said Georges confidently.

'A work of real genius,' said Madame Courcel.

But to return to the evening of Sylvie's arrival. There is nothing more delicious than a meal made up of the left-overs of a feast – particularly of a French wedding feast. All Brigitte had to do was to unpack the baskets and put out knives, forks, plates and glasses. All Georges had to do was to pull the corks of a bottle of still champagne and of a bottle of Morgon. Then they could pick and choose between the *pâté de canard truffé*, the *terrine de bécasse*, the *salmis de sanglier* and the *bloc de foie gras truffé*, which was followed by the cold roast duck with cherries, a salad of lettuce and baby artichokes. Then cheese and mirabelle tart.

But before they began, Sylvie said, suddenly serious: 'I did not expect this welcome. I thought I should have to tell my story on the doorstep if I was to be let in. I see you are all shy of asking me questions because you think I am a successful prostitute – a *poule de luxe*. I am not. I haven't got the right temperament. Moreover there aren't *successful* prostitutes in war time. There were hundreds of girls in brothels behind the front and at the camps of course. But in Paris there was too much amateur competition from women who are in love and who think it is the last chance before their man is killed – or that it's patriotic to go to bed with a soldier. Sylvain de Parnac, who bought me out of the brothel at Chalons, left me 50,000 francs. A Russian I knew, a communist who had to get out of Paris quickly, sold me his flower shop. He thought he was cheating me, but he made me a rich woman. For in war time, when expensive prostitutes are at a discount, flowers are at a premium. Everyone buys them. To give the girl you have just met, to give to her again the morning after, and of course for funerals. Also it became smart to buy them from Sylvie Turpin. So now I am a rich woman. I hope I have not destroyed any romantic dreams, Monsieur?' she asked, turning to Etienne. 'Good, so pass me that *terrine de bécasse* . . .'

'A very moral story and I'm sure that Georges, who accepts conventional morality, feels much relieved,' said Etienne. 'I am an anarchist and a poet and I don't care.'

'Then I am sure that I shall shock you when I tell you that I have sold my shop for a fabulous sum, because the war is over and flowers will soon give way to professional ladies, and that I am rich enough never to do another stroke of work and to live on my investments.'

'Touché, Mademoiselle,' laughed Etienne. Then he looked

at Georges and said: 'Old friend, I must tell you that I am leaving tomorrow and that you will have to finish your staircase with someone else. When are you leaving, Mademoiselle Turpin?'

'Either tonight or tomorrow. I would like to go and see my great-grandmother tomorrow.'

'But of course you will stay. We have a little bed in Georges's little office. Etienne can sleep in the old shed.'

These practical affairs being settled Etienne said: 'The only interesting thing is the truth. So, as we shall be parting and may not see each other for a long time, I think that we should each lift a corner of the curtain that hides our inner selves. We should each tell what it is that hurts us most to remember.'

'A pleasant way to spend our evening together – particularly as it is a house-warming party,' grumbled Georges.

'Telling our private nightmares may exorcise them. That is why I suggested it. All I ask is that I shall tell my story last.'

'Now that M. Besse has suggested it, we shall have to agree, otherwise we shall each be haunted by the most horrible memory that we might have told,' said Sylvie.

'That's true,' said Brigitte.

'Well, Brigitte, will you begin? I will follow, then Georges and finally M. Besse who has asked to be last because he is sure his bit of truth will surpass in horror all our nightmares.'

Brigitte looked at each of them in turn with hostility.

'It is like your devilish cunning, Etienne, to suggest these stories. Mine can be told in a few words. The last time that my husband Ernest came on long leave, I realised that I no longer loved him. He was almost mad and his madness took the form of political speeches accusing me and papa of complacency and sloth. One would have thought that papa had brought the war about and that he was enjoying it. Ernest never stopped lecturing us and what he said had no reality and was terribly boring. All about Marx. As we were

230

all living in that three-roomed hut, you can imagine what it was like. When he made love to me I felt it impossible to respond. It is very difficult to pretend to an emotion you have not got – particularly when you feel the exact opposite. I was with child by Ernest and the feelings of a pregnant woman for the father if she feels contempt for him, are very fierce, both for him and for herself : a terrible fierce bitter view of life. At least that was how I felt. I knew also that I had failed him. And when he next returned on leave, or after the war, how was I to tell him that though he was the father of my child, I never wanted to see him again? And of course I often wondered whether it was he that I no longer loved, or whether the war had changed him and changed me too, so that we were no longer the people who had once loved and believed in each other. I don't know about others, but I have to have belief in a man before I can love him and belong to him. Then Ernest was killed and I felt shame and guilt and relief. I could not face myself and started drinking a lot. And then this fellow came into the shop. That is my story.'

'Why were you so instantly attracted by me? You used to dislike me?' asked Georges.

'It was papa. First I was jealous of his regard for you, then after Ernest's death, he said "If you had only married Georges you would feel so differently. If he were killed it would not matter in the same way because you would always feel love and pride and that your marriage had not been a mistake." So when you came into the shop I looked at you and at once I knew what he meant.'

'So you can now look forward to widowhood with the happiest anticipation,' said Georges.

'I think many women do,' said Sylvie laughing.

'No, Sylvie. All our feelings are mixed,' said Etienne rather severely. 'Well, it's your turn now.'

Sylvie took a handkerchief from her bag, wiped her lips and said : 'Georges, give me a large glass of *prune*.' She drank it off, wiped her forehead, threw back her curls and began.

'Unlike Brigitte whose agonies were involved with another person, my worst memory only involves myself. It was simply terror, fear such as I had never felt before. It was the morning after the doctor had said that I was cured of gonorrhoea. I looked out of the window of the brothel at Chalons in which I was a prisoner, and I saw a line of men, waiting until the doors opened. There were I don't know how many, and that queue would be there all day and late into the night, each man waiting to take his turn. And we were perhaps twenty-five girls for the soldiers, and a dozen for the officers. I looked at that queue of dull, heavy, tired and always brutalised faces and I was almost mad with terror. That was the worst moment of my life.'

There was a long silence.

'It's your turn, Georges,' said Etienne.

Georges put his hands together and looked down between his knees, and said: 'The war has been my education. I am not speaking of the delightful things I learned from you, Etienne. I could have learned them in time of peace. No, I mean the things that the war taught me and which I should much rather never have known. Just as when your cat is suffering from a broken leg, he will bite or claw you savagely, so man when he is suffering from an agony of fear, or recovering from it, will do the kind of things that the Germans did when they burned this village.'

Georges paused and presently Sylvie asked:

'What horrors are you concealing now?'

'I was thinking of how during an attack only two-thirds of the men go all the way forward to meet the enemy. About a third of them stumble into shellholes pretending they have sprained an ankle and only go forward after the enemy trench has been captured, or join in the retreat if it has failed.

And only about two-thirds of the prisoners taken get back safely into the cages. The men in the front line are only too happy to take prisoners. The men who murder prisoners are the cowards who have hidden in shellholes. In order to regain their self-respect they will murder a disarmed man holding his hands above his head and boast about it afterwards. That is the kind of thing I would rather not have learned about my fellow men.'

There was a silence. Then Etienne said:

'The strains of war . . . And if we can get rid of wars. . . .'

'The way you propose to do that is by revolution. But the strains of a revolution, as we know from history, produce the Terror – so much mutual fear and suspicion that endless senseless murders are committed in the name of your new religion.'

'What Georges is telling us is very horrible, but is it worse than all the other killing and suffering during war?' asked Sylvie.

'Yes, it is, and Monsieur Conduchet could tell you why,' said Brigitte quickly. She went on: 'At our wedding he told us how he bred his animals, picking out the best bulls and rams – and he said he would like to live long enough to know our children, because Georges and my father were the two finest men that Dorlotte has produced, so they were likely to be exceptional. But in a war the meanest men, the little rats without courage, honour or compassion are the ones who survive to become the fathers of the next generation. So the crime of a war vitiates the whole breed and nature of the people.'

'Darling, you exaggerate a little,' said Georges.

'Meanwhile you haven't told us what was the worst: you haven't added your contribution to our pleasant evening,' said Sylvie.

Georges looked up and smiled at her.

'There have been so many horrible things in my life. Going to see you in Chalons was almost the worst. And then the ever-present fear and the sights that met one's eyes: a German dragging himself through the mud with his intes-

233

tines trailing beside him. So it is difficult to choose. But the thing which marked me and changed me, happened when I was a child of seven. It was very hot weather. My father was a labourer working in the harvest and he came home exhausted and rather drunk. My mother for some reason had lit a bonfire in the garden and had burned one of my father's books. It had not burned well and the half-charred pages were blowing about. Seeing them made my father very angry. He went into the kitchen where my mother was sitting on the table drinking and singing. He swore at her and she said something and then he hit her. She was a big woman. They fought for a long time and she got him down and began kicking him. I think I tried to stop her and she gave me a bloody nose and promised to give me a thrashing. I ran away and spent the night hiding under the currant bushes. I don't know how it was, but something happened to me then. I learned that I was alone and that when things are really bad, one always is alone. One cannot turn to others. It is no good looking round for help because there is no help. It is never there at the right place and the right time. It was something like that. I learned it that night lying under the currant bushes. It was terrible to find out that truth so young. But once I had learned it, I was happier. Most people cling like ivy to some support: God or Jesus or their fellow men. But I learned that night when I was seven years old that they are never there when you need them. I learned that one must stand alone on one's own feet in every crisis, when things are really bad – just as one has to die alone.

'You, Julien, were saying that you prided yourself on being a lone wolf and the enemy of society. I don't think that you are either. Because you live in a world of words, of ideas, of books. You always feel that you have all the great men at your elbow. At one moment it is Villon, at the next Gérard de Nerval, then Shakespeare, Byron, etcetera. You are just like a catholic with the saints. You imagine

234

what they would say, how they would behave . . . But when you find yourself in an impasse they won't help and you may be shattered.'

There was a long silence. Georges filled all their glasses.

'What about love?' asked Brigitte.

'Love is giving. One mustn't expect support in return. If one gets it that's fine. But one mustn't get in the habit of demanding or expecting it.'

'I admit that I do expect it,' said Brigitte.

'It was because you were so young and because of your parents fighting, that you have developed in the way you have,' said Etienne.

'Maybe. It is something that marked me, knowing that I was alone in the world.' Georges suddenly looked at Sylvie. 'That was before I had my cat. You remember Hercule, Sylvie? You remember how you brought me his skin after Joseph had eaten him?'

To their astonishment Sylvie burst into tears. She jumped up, fetched a handkerchief from her bag and began apologising while she was still laughing and crying.

'Please, please forgive me. I'm being sentimental. Oh, Georges I am so glad that I came.'

Georges put a log on the fire and they all looked at Etienne. He took a sip from his glass of *prune* and began: 'I don't know if this is the most horrible thing that has happened to me, but it has changed my personality and my life and even my name. The effect has been to make all my feelings numb. However to get on with it: I was hiding in Paris, not just from the police, but from a bunch of political associates. I had left them and I knew too much: their treacheries, their relations with the Sûreté, their earlier relations with German agents. I did not feel safe and I was very hungry and had no money, no money at all. I did not know where to go or what to do. It was late winter: everything shining and gleaming in the sun, but a chilly wind. There

235

were widows trotting along with shopping baskets, well-dressed women in furs taking the dog for a walk. I should explain that I was sitting on a bench in the Luxembourg Gardens. Children's voices, a little girl bowling a large wooden hoop. But I was so hungry that sometimes everything wavered indistinctly. A tall man came along, walked by and then came back again. He had another look at me and then came back and sat down beside me. I thought perhaps he was a policeman though he did not look like one. Presently he asked me whether I were down on my luck. I said yes, I was. When I looked at him more closely I saw that he was rather like me: a long face, hooked nose, dark eyes, brown skin. In fact we might easily have been brothers. He took me to a bistro, gave me a meal and a drink and presently said that he was looking for a partner to drive a car. Of course I guessed at once it was some kind of robbery.

'He took me to a big empty room and asked me for my papers as a precaution against my running away. I had quite good papers in my real name, but with a forged sheet saying: 'Given an honourable discharge,' you know the thing. I lived with my *doppelgänger* in that large almost empty room for nearly three weeks and I never went out. I was writing a long poem – unfortunately I've lost it. Perhaps one day I may write it again but it seems unlikely. Etienne did the shopping. We ate out of paper bags, but often I was alone all day. Oh, I did go out once, because I had to have a bath – I went to that barge moored in the Seine where one has baths. Usually I was alone all day, often at night too. Etienne would come in looking a bit shop-soiled, would throw himself on the bed and sleep all day. One odd thing was that he got to look more like me. One day he told me that he had been followed by a man who, he thought, had mistaken him for me. We were good friends on the surface but didn't confide in each other. He was a bit upset when he found out that I was a poet. Then, one day, he told me that it was going to be next morning. We rode out of Paris on bicycles, about fifty kilometres to a little town on the Marne, timing to arrive at night. Etienne led me off the road down a cart track to a ruined farm. It had not been touched since the battle – there was a lot of rusted-away farm machinery buried in brambles, near the railway – one could hear the trains going past. Etienne explained in great detail that there would be an army van at the station being loaded with bags of money for the paymaster's office at the camp. The railway station was a kilometre from the town. When they laid the tracks they would not go out of their way to bring it closer.

'Well, my job was to walk down into the station yard, shoot the driver of the van, push him into the road, start the car and climb into the driving seat, and go off like the wind when Etienne jumped in beside me. He would take care of all the rest. He was taking on a lot. There were two armed sentries, an officer and two unarmed men loading the bags. I was to drive by field tracks back to the ruined farm, we should divide the money – I was to have a third – and ride off in different directions on our bicycles. Of course we could not take all the money – only the bigger notes. I had my Browning automatic, Etienne an American submachine-gun. Oddly enough I slept soundly.

'In the morning Etienne woke me. It was daylight. We each had a mouthful of *marc*. He gave me back my papers, then we climbed over the fence onto the railway tracks and walked along to the station. It was quite close. We were wearing dirty blue overalls and looked like any couple of workmen. Etienne had a toolbag with his gun in it.

'I found walking along the railway line difficult. The stones between the sleepers were large and rather sharp and spotted with oil and the sleepers set too close for one to stride over them, too far apart for one step and too close for two. So one first stepped on the stones and slipped back and then on a raised metal sleeper. A signalman looked out of his box and saw us coming. But he did nothing. Before we reached him, Etienne told me to get off the tracks and follow a path through an allotment up to the road. That would lead me to the station yard.

"If you don't kill the driver first shot, go on shooting until you are certain that he's dead. We don't want witnesses," were the last words Etienne said to me.

'I walked up the path through the allotment looking at the weeds growing beside it with interest: I don't mean botanical interest, but rather with a hail and farewell sentiment. I remember looking at a patch of blue speedwell flowers and reflecting that if I had been Wordsworth I should have written a poem about them – but that only English poets do that. God would have been mentioned, but there would have been no love interest. When I came out on the road and started walking down into the station yard, everything was just as Etienne had foretold. There was the car, the two loitering sentries, the officer smoking a cigarette. It all seemed a long way off. There were potholes in the yellow expanse of the station yard and I was walking in slow motion. There were a couple of pigeons, the male puffing out his breast cooing and circling round the hen. I can swear that I remember the skin round his eye and how red his feet were. It was quite late on that I realised that the driver wasn't in his seat. I had avoided looking at him.

Then I saw Etienne coming round the corner of the station building. He was walking slightly sideways, dragging one leg and buttoning up his flies. I saw the officer and the sentry look at him and look away. No doubt a man doing up his fly buttons doesn't look dangerous. That was what Etienne intended them to think and he was a good psychologist. If so, it must have been the last thought of the sentry, for the next second Etienne was shooting. I didn't watch but started running for the van keeping it between me and the shooting. Perhaps it was as well that I did. Etienne was a marvellous shot. None of his targets were more than fifteen metres away from him – all that is except the old woman. She was standing on the kerb at the other end of the station building. After the burst of firing in which Etienne got both sentries, the officer and the two unarmed men putting a bag of heavy coin into the back of the van there was a last burst and I saw her topple over. I started the car and got into the driver's seat. There were a few isolated shots afterwards. Etienne was making sure that everyone was really dead. Then he was beside me and I was driving off at full speed. The first thing he did was to reload his gun, then he started looking back. His submachine-gun was lying on his lap. As he turned, the muzzle poked me in the knee. I put my hand out and put on the safety catch. It's a habit of mine. I always put on the safety catch, but apparently Etienne never did. I don't like loaded weapons pointing at me.

'I drove that short way along the farm track – it was scarcely more than a field path, and in a few moments we were at the farm, jumping down and pulling out the contents of the van. There were bags of coin – of no value to us, and two bags of small notes and a portfolio with the large ones.

'I was squatting, pulling packets of five and ten-franc notes out of a sack, and I had an odd feeling. You know it, Georges. Etienne was facing me, sitting on an old hay rake and had opened the portfolio.

'I said something like : "Don't bother to count them. Just give me what looks like a third." '

'Etienne looked at me and smiled. "You've done well, Julien. I shan't bother to count them. Because you've served your turn." And he reached for his gun. But the safety catch was on and I just had time to pull out my Browning and shoot him. I think the bullet went through the heart. Etienne just fell back into the hay rake. Then I emptied the contents of the portfolio into my satchel, picked up my bicycle and made off. I had asked for my papers in the morning and he had given me them in their folder, but I hadn't looked at them. When I did, I saw the name Etienne Besse and a passport photograph which just might have been me.

'It was a clever plan. My body would have been identified as that of a wanted criminal and buried and he would have started a new life with a large fortune as Julien D'Aubrac. You can understand why he was upset when he discovered that I was a poet who had had his poetry published. But now the question is: Who am I? Can I become Etienne Besse and live the kind of life I should have done? The real harm however is that I can never trust anyone again.

'You see he must have decided that I might do well enough to impersonate his corpse when he first picked on me sitting on that seat in the Luxembourg Gardens. Then he spent three weeks studying my habits and mannerisms — sharing the same room, living with me like a brother. Then we risked our lives together, and after all that he would calmly have murdered me because "I had served my turn." I can't understand such a man.'

'You can't imagine doing the same thing yourself?' asked Georges. Etienne looked at him startled.

'Really, Georges. . . . .'

'Then why do you pretend to care nothing for your fellow men? and to be a cold-blooded killer?' There was a silence. At last Etienne said: 'I don't think that I do pretend. The hatred I feel for them is quite genuine. But I haven't translated it into practice. . . . . . And there are degrees of cold-bloodedness.'

'I think Etienne feels an aesthetic objection rather than a moral one,' said Sylvie.

'That's exactly it. Thank you, Mademoiselle. You understand me perfectly,' said Etienne, looking at her gratefully.

'What is an aesthetic objection?' asked Georges puzzled.

'It means that he finds some crimes too disgusting to undertake them,' explained Sylvie. Georges laughed.

'Just what I thought. Splitting hairs. . . . You are a great one for that, Julien. You say that you cannot trust anyone but you have trusted us three with a most dangerous story.

The real Etienne would shoot us, but I don't see you fingering your automatic.'

Etienne smiled cheerfully: 'You are a wise fellow, Georges. But I am not so rash as you think. Because I have almost decided to give myself up. Only in that way can I recover my name and personality.'

'You'll spend the rest of your life on Devil's Island!' exclaimed Sylvie.

'I don't think so. The only person I murdered was my accomplice and that was in self-defence. Then I solve a mystery. Etienne Besse was perhaps the name of a man he had framed as he intended to frame me. But whatever his name, the man I shot was a criminal with a record. When they exhume him and take his fingerprints they will prove I am right. Then I shall offer to give a portion of the money back if I am given a light sentence. And five years of prison will give me new subjects for my poems.'

'You are wrong to think Etienne Besse was a criminal: he was only a previous innocent accomplice drawn in. Otherwise – if Besse had been the real name – you would have been arrested weeks ago. I am quite sure that your identity was checked and that nothing was found,' said Georges.

'It would be idiotic to give yourself up. In any case I hope you will wait a reasonable time,' said Sylvie.

'What has happened to all the money?' asked Brigitte.

'I gave it to Georges to take care of. Hasn't he told you?' said Etienne, surprised.

Next morning Sylvie repeated that she must see her great-grandmother, and set off alone to the Conduchet farmhouse. Bette, Conduchet's daughter-in-law, opened the door and looked at the smart Parisian lady with surprise – then she showed her into Eglantine's little room. The old woman was in bed, and greeted her warmly. 'Ah, Sylvie, my darling. I heard you had arrived in the village last night and I wondered whether you had forgotten me. I would like you to have stayed with me, but you see what has happened. I'm told you are a rich woman – perhaps you can help to obtain justice for me. I didn't say anything to Georges, because it was his wedding day, and I expect Brigitte knows about it but doesn't care. That miserable man M. Courcel won't do anything and the Notaire, Maitre Surlot at Blaye, won't take the case up. They are all afraid of the tyrant who keeps me prisoner.'

It was not difficult for Sylvie to hear the story as it presented itself to Eglantine. After her last great-grandchild, Sylvie's sister Mathilde, had got married and had gone to live at Ste Menehould, old Conduchet had persuaded her to come to the farmhouse and had forcibly detained her and was keeping her a prisoner. He would not allow her to return to her hut.

'That man, my nephew, is an ogre!' she exclaimed. 'I tell him so, whenever I see him, but he only laughs at me.'

'But he has made you very comfortable in this little room and I see you have all your precious things about you. I don't suppose he starves you either,' said Sylvie.

'No indeed. I said to him: "As long as you keep me here a prisoner against my will, I demand minced chicken for dinner every day." The monster only laughed at me and said: "You shall have it, my aunt".'

'So he isn't treating you too badly.'

'What! It is abominable! He won't let me live in my own house! He expects to gain something, I suppose. But I won't let him have the key, and that girl Bette won't let me have my clothes. I can't go back there in my nightgown.'

After listening for an hour to Eglantine's complaints of her ill-treatment, Sylvie embraced her aunt, presented her with a bottle of eau de cologne and said goodbye. In the kitchen Bette, who had listened to the conversation, received her more cordially and coming out on to the doorstep, gave her version.

'I overheard what Madame Turpin was saying to you. She is very angry with Monsieur Conduchet and abuses him all the time. But what could we do? After Mathilde left and got married there was no one willing to live with the old lady. It was not right to leave her alone at night. Sometimes she falls down and can't get up without help. And I should have had to be running to and fro between the farmhouse and her hut all day long. Here she has everything she wants – if I leave the door open she can hear what is going on. Of course she wants to be in her own place, but what can we do?'

'She says she insists on minced chicken every day for dinner,' said Sylvie smiling.

Bette laughed. 'You should have heard the storm she made one day when I gave her rabbit! She threw the plate on the floor! But you know we are all very fond of her. She's a marvel at ninety-two. One must make allowances.'

Sylvie left feeling sure that Eglantine was in good hands. Etienne had packed his few possessions and was examining her little car doubtfully.

When she stopped beside him he said: 'I'm afraid I can't take advantage of the lift you promised me. I don't think one can tie my bicycle on to the back of your tiny two-seater.'

'Why take the bicycle at all?'

'I shall want it when you drop me off on your way to Paris.'

'I am not going to Paris. In fact I was just going to ask you where you want to go, because I'll take you there.'

'I thought that you lived in Paris.'

'There is a man there who bores me – in fact several men who bore me. I had an idea of going to Italy. I've never been there. Why don't you come in that direction? You can always buy yourself a new bicycle. . . .'

'Are you inviting me to come with you to Italy?'

'If you care to and we get on together. . . .'

'Well, yes. I'll come, Sylvie.'

'Better not mention it in front of Brigitte and Georges. It

sounds absurd, but it might conceivably upset him.'

Etienne nodded.

Half an hour later they had kissed their hosts and Raoul, said good-bye and had driven off. As they were getting into the car Sylvie said: 'I gathered from your story that you are a very good driver. Do you mind being driven by a woman?'

Etienne laughed. 'No, I'll be guided by you in all respects.'

'What about all that money?' asked Brigitte as Georges and she walked back from the road after watching the little car disappear.

'He has left most of it behind and says he doesn't want it. I shall leave it where it is until he turns up again. He may need it badly one day. But as he doesn't care about money, I think it will stay where it is for ever.'

'Are you happy, Georges, about having stolen money in your charge?'

'It's only government money. They can always print more when they run short.'

'I suppose that's true,' said Brigitte.

'But Georges, you would not touch that money, would you?' she asked.

'No. But I don't go in for robbery and that sort of thing.'

'Do you think he will give himself up?'

'I think that Sylvie will dissuade him.'

'There certainly is something on between those two,' said Brigitte.

'There is the evidence,' said Georges pointing to the abandoned bicycle.

It was already autumn. The leaves on the plum-trees, always the first to change, had turned golden. Some had fallen sprinkling the dark soil of the vegetable patch with oval sequins. Where the potatoes had been, Georges would rake the ground level and plant out winter lettuces and endives. Beside them he would sow rows of corn salad and a few spring onions and beyond these plant out spring cabbage. On the best bit of ground, manured with well-rotted dung, he would a few months later, make his onion bed. On a poor patch he would sow turnips at once to come in for spring greens. All this was in his mind as he stood in the sunshine with Brigitte, looking at the roughly turned up earth. He roused himself and said:

'I haven't done a stroke of work for days. I suppose it's what comes of getting married.'

Brigitte laughed and looked at him mischievously.

'Perhaps other things will come from getting married.'

'We can't look too far forward into the future. Anyway we must cultivate our garden,' said Georges.

'Papa is always saying that. You must often have heard him,' said Brigitte.

'Well, it's true.'

'He says it's the last sentence in a famous book by Voltaire.'

'Voltaire must have been a sensible man. We must cultivate our garden, or as I said to Julien: we must plough over the bones and grow fields of wheat where men were massacred. That is the work that lies before humanity: to plough over the bones of the dead.'

And leaving Brigitte to take Raoul indoors, Georges fetched his rake and his trowel from the toolshed and set to work

THE END

POSTSCRIPT

Fifty-eight years have elapsed since I received the impressions on which this book is founded. It is fiction not history, most of the incidents having been invented. Yet there is truth behind it. The destruction of the village and the behaviour of the invaders is that described to me by eye-witnesses. The spirit of the inhabitants who remained I saw for myself. Georges Roux, Pierre Lanfrey (hook and all), Eglantine, Madame Blanchard, Lorcey, Rouault, Conduchet and Emile are drawn from my memories of people I knew but they have been imaginatively projected into their future after I left the village. Bruce was my friend for twenty years.

The latter part of the novel is entirely invented, though incidents in the mutiny of 1917 are historically true. The characters of Joseph, de L'Espinasse, Julien, Brigitte and M. Courcel are entirely fictional.

D.G.